TROUBLE IN
TANGIERS

Islamic Incursions, Portuguese Perfidy? 1661

A LUKE TREMAYNE ADVENTURE

TROUBLE IN TANGIERS

Islamic Incursions, Portuguese Perfidy? 1661

GEOFF QUAIFE

ARPress
45 Dan Road Suite 5
Canton MA 02021

Hotline: 1(888) 821-0229
Fax: 1(508) 545-7580

Ordering Information:

Quantity sales. Special discounts are available on quantity purchases by corporations, associations, and others. For details, contact the publisher at the address above.

Printed in the United States of America.

ISBN-13:   Softcover   979-8-89389-323-6
                    eBook   979-8-89389-324-3
                    Hardback   979-8-89389-966-5

Library of Congress Control Number: 2024916231

The Luke Tremayne Adventures

(In chronological order of the events portrayed)

CHARACTERS

(Real historical characters indicated by italics)

ENGLISH

LUKE'S UNIT FOR THE TANGIERS MISSION

Sir Luke Tremayne (Colonel)	Special agent for Charles II
Jack Moon (Captain)	Deputy for Tangiers mission
George Harris	Sergeant
Thomas Smith	Silversmith and valet
Gregory Pickford (Lieutenant)	Naval surgeon, seconded from fleet

ENGLISH IN TANGIERS

John Lawson (Vice Admiral)	*Deputy commander of the English fleet*
Willie Street	A sailor

PORTUGUESE

ROYALTY

Luisa de Guzman	*Queen Regent of Portugal 1655-1662, mother of Afonso, Pedro and Catarina*

PORTUGUESE IN TANGIERS

Luis de Almeida	*Governor of Tangiers*
Antonio de Melo (Father)	Franciscan friar, Luke's interpreter, advisor to Queen Luisa
Mario de Silva (General)	Deputy Governor of Tangiers, military commandant.
Arturo Magellan (Ensign)	Head of Mario's bodyguard
Lidia de Silva	Mario's wife, Catarina's niece
Dona Catarina Sarmento	The most powerful woman in Tangiers
Gabriela Sarmento	Her niece
Dina, Fada, Rachel	Gabriela's servants
Aristotle da Gama	Catarina's steward, lawyer, and manager of her commercial interests
Carlos Pimento, (Colonel)	Cavalry commander, later military commandant and acting Governor
Micaela Pimento	His wife
Andrea Pimento	Their daughter
Miguel Lopez (Colonel)	Infantry commander
Catia Lopez	His sister
Dimas Vento (Major)	Miguel's deputy
Bruno Costa	An infantry master sergeant
Cornelio Rios alias Gigante	An infantry lance sergeant
Gil Serano, (Captain)	Police commandant, later deputy and acting governor
Leo Coval (Major)	Portuguese military intelligence, governor's aide
Roberto da Braga (Father)	Head of Franciscan friary
Diego de Cisneros (Father)	Head of Dominican friary, and agent of the Inquisition
Johan Barros	Husband to Miriam.

MOROCCAN

Khadir Ghailan	*Northern Moroccan Berber war lord*
Ibrahim Yedder	His vizier
Takama Khirri	Converted Berber, companion to Dona Catarina
Jamila Khirri	Her English born mother
Fadel Khirri	Takama's brother
Majid Khirri	local chief in alliance with Portuguese, Takama's father Anti-Ghailan
Omar Koubi	Representative of Al Rashid
Ibram Zammit (Colonel)	His deputy
Miriam Barros	Owns most of the souk and controls its operation

PERSONS REFERRED TO

Abram Falcone	Catarina's father, wealthy merchant and shipowner
Raphael Sarmento	One time governor, Catarina was his second wife
Dominic Elcano	Business rival of Catarina's
Juan Elcano	His son
Moulay Al Rashid	*Emerging Sultan, controls eastern and southern Morocco but moving north and west*
Mohamed Al Hajj	*Sufi leader controls Fez and north central Morocco*
Catarina de Braganza	*Infanta of Portugal, bride for Charles I Sister to Afonso VI*

*Edward Montague, Earl
of Sandwich*

*Commander English
Mediterranean and Atlantic fleet
(Admiral)*

In 1661 Charles II put an end to the diplomatic wrangle between European powers to provide him with a wife. He announced that he would marry the sister of the disabled King of Portugal, Catherine of Braganza. As part of their marriage treaty Portugal ceded the strategic North African port of Tangiers to England, and England in return was to provide three thousand troops to assist Portugal maintain its independence against Spanish aggression. The instability of both Portuguese and Moroccan politics, (Tangiers was surrounded by Morocco), and the alleged problems within the city itself, forced Charles to send his special agent, Colonel Luke Tremayne to investigate the general situation—and confront an emerging problem of a silver and emerald ring, the possession of which by Moroccan warlords could endanger England's future control of the city.

1

Whitehall, June1661

Luke waited in the King's antechamber.

He was about to leave on his second visit to Portugal. He had been sent by Oliver Cromwell and Cardinal Mazarin in 1658 to assess the Portuguese military situation and determine if continued English and French help against Spain was viable and justified.

His current mission at first appeared similar. Charles II's marriage treaty promised 3000 English troops to Portugal as soon as possible to assist in its ongoing fight for independence from Spain, but on this trip his priority was Tangiers which the Portuguese were to cede to England as part of the same marriage treaty.

The door of the antechamber opened, and a valet led Luke into the King's reception room. Standing beside the King was a man dressed in the habit of a Franciscan friar who looked vaguely familiar. Receiving a nod from Charles, the friar spoke in English, "I am Antonio de Melo, advisor to Queen Luisa, and brother of our ambassador here, whom I know you have met. My queen has suggested to His Majesty that I accompany you on your mission to Tangiers. I have her authority for any actions you might need to take in Portuguese territory—and I can act as your interpreter."

The King added. "Our large fleet leaves here in the morning under the Earl of Sandwich. It will pay a courtesy visit to Lisbon, drop you off at Tangiers and proceed further west where negotiations with various Islamic pirate states will be undertaken. After that, Sandwich returns to Lisbon with part of the fleet to eventually escort the Infanta to England. While located there he will assist the Portuguese sugar fleet from Brazil fend off its Spanish and Dutch enemies. It also positions him to more readily intercept the Spanish treasure fleets from the Americas should hostilities with Spain resume. The other part of the fleet under Lawson will remain in Tangiers to supervise the handover and await the arrival of a permanent garrison in the new year. Queen Luisa has warned us that problems within Tangiers may reach crisis point at any minute which refocusses your mission. Father Antonio will explain."

"Tangiers is in chaos. The governor, now sacked, said he would not hand over the city to the English, and appeared to encourage the Spaniards based at Ceuta, just along the coast to the east, to seize it. I have asked your King to allow three Portuguese officials to join you on the trip to Tangiers—myself, the new governor, Luis de Almeida and his aide. They will board at Lisbon."

"Father Antonio confirms the general chaos that I initially thought your mission would assess, and if possible, rectify, before we took over—but he also brings even more dangerous news, which does change the emphasis of your mission."

The friar continued, "We are alarmed by rumours heard by our agents throughout Morocco. There is a concerted attempt by various Moroccan factions to unify all of the peoples of the area to remove both Portugal and England from Tangiers."

"Is this possible?" asked Luke.

"Yes, if our enemies can unite under a leader who according to local tradition and Moslem legend has to possess at least a silver and emerald ring," Antonio replied.

The King intervened, "In simple terms, you must find this ring and prevent it falling into Islamic hands. Consequently, I have on advice of your former comrade, John Thurloe, put together a special team to help you deal with this refocused mission. You will have a platoon of experienced sharp shooting musketeers who have had experience in the

Ottoman Empire or North Africa led by Captain Jack Moon and his sergeant George Harris. Attached to this unit is an amazing specialist just freed from one of my prisons."

The King laughed at his own weak witticism and continued. "Tom Smith is a disgraced silversmith who learnt his trade as a slave captured by the North African corsairs and sold to a master Moroccan silversmith located in Fez. He regained his freedom as part of negotiations between the former English regime and the Sufi brotherhood who control Fez and the surrounding region. Smith knows the area well and is familiar with the legend of the Islamic rings and the proliferation of fake examples created over the years by various parties to confuse the situation. He is also fluent in Berber, Arabic and Portuguese. To the outside world, Smith will be your personal valet."

"Any further instructions, sire?" asked a slightly stunned Luke.

"When the fleet lands at Lisbon you will visit the Queen Regent for further updates on the general situation and the possible location of this troublesome ring. I wish you well."

A week later Luke and Father Antonio were received by the real ruler of Portugal, the Queen Regent, Luisa. She apologised, "I am sorry that our gift to England is compromised by the developing situation. Antonio will exercise my full authority in support of your endeavours to redeem the situation."

She then changed the topic. "This will be our last meeting, Tremayne. When you return to Portugal I shall be exiled to a distant convent. My son becomes of age in a few months and has been convinced by a conniving adviser that he is capable of ruling in his own right. This advisor will exert the real power—but his ascendancy will not change our relationship with England. Despite his faults, this emerging chief minister is a Portuguese nationalist who strongly supports the marriage treaty, and the need for English naval support to protect our sugar fleet, despite its unpopularity with the populace."

Antonio added, "Even among Her Majesty's advisers there are many who would have preferred that Tangiers and Bombay be leased to England, rather than ceded. You will find that both cities are difficult to defend, and expensive to maintain. Many would have preferred Catherine to have married the King of France, but the Spaniards successfully provided their Infanta for King Louis before Queen Luisa acted. Her alliance with England, while vital to our survival, is certainly not popular among the common people. Our court remains divided between pro-English and pro-French factions, but we need the support of both powers in the face of Spanish and more recently, Dutch aggression."

Next morning Luke, the incoming Portuguese Governor of Tangiers, Luis de Almeida and Father Antonio met in a cabin aboard the Earl of Sandwich's flagship as it headed for the North African coast. Antonio addressed the other two, "Gentlemen, I will update you on the emerging situation in Tangiers. The Saadi sultanate collapsed one or two years ago. Immediately the leader of a powerful Sufi brotherhood of Berber Islamic mystics out of Dila, Mohammed al-Hajj, proclaimed himself Sultan. He controls north central Morocco out of his capital at Fez and is pushing north towards Tangiers. The Alouite family who claim descent from the Prophet Mohammed dominate the south and east of Morocco and have begun their attack on Sufi strongholds as they move north and west. Their leader Moulay Mohammed al-Rashid is recognised by anti-Sufi tribes as the emerging Sultan. In the far north local pro-Spanish warlord, Khadir Ghailan is trying to unite the local Berber tribes against both al-Hajj and European occupation of Tangiers.

"Can Tangiers hold out against these various enemies?" asked Almeida.

"Against a united Moroccan attack, no! Against Ghailan alone, probably yes."

"Why these different responses?" asked Luke.

"Neglect! The defences of the city are poor, and its walls and forts would easily be destroyed by mining and explosives. You English will need to spend a fortune to strengthen these basic defences. Secondly the garrison is largely manned by local militia, not by royal troops. This militia keeps itself supplied with essentials by raiding the surrounding countryside. The English navy will be essential not only to the transfer of power, but as an immediate defence against Ghailan."

Luke turned to Almeida, "Given what we have just heard, how are you to effectively take charge? Initially after we disembark at Tangiers, both sections of the English fleet will be elsewhere. The English navy will not be able to assist us for several weeks, if not months."

"My task will not be easy. I have only a platoon of Royal troops with me, but I believe I can rely on the local cavalry. The Portuguese garrison at full strength has twenty-five hundred troops, but I have reason to distrust the loyalty of many of them."

"What are your immediate aims within the broad brief of preparing the city for transfer to us?" asked Luke.

"To ensure that the city does not fall to the Moors before English naval support returns, and an English garrison eventually arrives."

"How will you achieve this?" asked a concerned Luke.

"Negotiation—and division."

"In what sense?"

"The immediate threat to Tangiers is Khadir Ghailan. He can be bribed or can be convinced that dealing with us could enhance his strength to combat rival Islamic lords. The town has survived the last few years with such an arrangement. I hope to strengthen it. We must keep the Islamic forces divided. Now it is Ghailan against al-Hajj, both opposed by smaller warlords, some loyal to the deposed Saadi sultanate, others proclaiming heretical Islamic or ethnic Berber views. You must have the city ready to withstand a united Morocco which the Alouite dynasty moving up from the south will achieve within the next two or three years. The key to maintaining division among our enemies and forestalling any immediate united attack is to find the missing silver ring which both our monarchs have agreed is your priority," concluded Antonio.

The next morning the English fleet arrived off Tangiers and two of its flagship's longboats were launched. The first contained the new Portuguese governor and his personal aide, Father Antonio and some of the Governor's bodyguard. The second contained the English envoy, Sir Luke Tremayne and his small unit.

The city's defences had remained silent. There was neither welcoming, nor destructive cannonades. A small detachment of troops with a couple of senior officers were assembled on the harbor front to formally welcome the new governor.

Suddenly there was the sound of gunfire.

Jack Moon was struck a glancing blow. Several English sailors slumped over their oars.

The welcoming party on shore immediately sprang into action. A small group remained in position and prepared to welcome the governor. The second group divided. A few waded out to the partially disabled longboat and an officer enquired into the state of the wounded English sailors. The remainder fired round after round in direction of a small galley that was escaping the harbour.

Luke rejected the offer to take the wounded ashore. Instead, he and all his uninjured troops disembarked, but he accepted the offer of the Portuguese to replace the injured or dead oarsmen, and row the longboat back to the English flagship where the ship's surgeon could attend to the wounded.

The governor's boat had not been attacked. The English were clearly the target—not the reception that the crowns of England and Portugal had expected.

Next day Luke and Antonio met with the Governor who introduced three senior military officers—General Mario de Silva, commandant of the garrison and deputy governor; Colonel Carlos Pimento, commander of the cavalry; and Colonel Miguel Lopez, commander of the garrison's infantry.

"Gentlemen this is Colonel Tremayne, personal envoy of the English King, here to understand, and help remove any obstacles to a peaceful transfer of sovereignty from Portugal to England, and Father Antonio, personal secretary to our Queen Regent.

This meeting is for the local military authorities to update me on the current situation within the city, and on the investigation into yesterday's attack on the English longboat. Colonel Lopez, what is the strength and nature of the infantry under your control?"

"On paper the strength of the garrison is 3000 men, it is nearer 2000, of which 1500 are infantry. They are a diverse group. Only 200 are troops of the line—my own regiment that was enlisted in Portugal by the previous Governor. The remaining troops are local militia and Berber auxilaries. The city's tradesmen and traders are on call and rotate on a bi-monthly basis for active service. We make great use of those local tribesmen who are the traditional enemies of the Moroccan forces that oppose us—essentially anti-Ghalain and anti-Sufi Berbers."

"You allow armed Moslem recruits to enter the city?" asked the alarmed governor.

"No."

"Then how can they defend the city, yet not enter it?" asked a bemused Luke.

"They are restricted to the southern wall. They are excellent marksmen who live in the small forts attached to the outside of the southern wall," Lopez replied.

2

Almeida changed the subject, "Was my predecessor about to hand over the city to the Spaniards? Did he have much local support?"

"A vile rumour circulated by his Lisbon based enemies. While most of the city are concerned that it being handed over to a heretic nation, the vast majority are aware that Spain is our current enemy, and our successful fight for independence depends heavily on the English fleet," replied Colonel Pimento.

Luke turned to him, "I understand by the terms of the treaty your cavalry is to remain and be paid for by the English after the transfer takes place."

"That is the proposal, but I cannot guarantee that any of my men would wish to remain."

The governor continued, "How immediate is the external threat?"

Mario de Silva responded, "The city is under intermittent attack by raiding parties of Ghailan, the local warlord who is simultaneously fighting tribes loyal to the former Saadi Sultan, and those aligned with the Islamic brotherhood that currently control Fez but are steadily advancing in this direction. Ghailan is no real threat to us on his own as his men do not have the capability of mining our walls, but we should seek an alliance with the Alouite family who control the south and east of Morocco and are currently attacking Sufi held territory. Already many Berber and Arab tribes see the Alouite leader, al-Rashid, as the new

Sultan rejecting the claims of other warlords. Nevertheless, Ghailan remains an irritant. He intersperses each of his raids with truces to enable both the city's traders and his farmers to exchange their goods."

"Is he financed by Spain?" asked Luke.

"He has had some help from the Spaniards in Ceuta, but he is his own man. He has also been approached by the Ottoman Turks who want to extend their influence while Morocco is weak. If the Ottomans strike it will be from the sea. They would use their satellite privateers from Algiers and Tripoli. The Ottoman fleet itself would not sail so far west, and now with the English fleet in the area they will stay well away," continued Mario.

Father Antonio unexpectedly intervened, "The Queen had reports that part of the garrison here is out of control, and that its leader, Gil Serano is a law to himself."

Mario responded quickly—perhaps too quickly thought Luke.

"Her Majesty's informants are mistaken. Serano's infantry company was made semi-autonomous by the previous governor to perform a different function from the rest of us."

"And what was that? asked Luke in almost passable Portuguese.

"Our task is to defend the city from outside attack, Serano's is to maintain law and order within the city. His men police the city. However, if Tangiers is attacked his company comes back under Lopez's command," explained Mario.

"Do the law-and-order requirements of this police force conflict with your security concerns?" asked the astute governor.

Mario, Miguel and Carlos exchanged anxious glances.

Carlos responded, "There have been moments of tension between my requirements at times not to deal with the Islamic traders outside our borders, and Serano's need to keep the lines of trade open between the citizens of the town and essential external providers."

Apparently satisfied with the answer Almeida changed focus.

"And what has been discovered about the yesterday's attack on Tremayne?"

"External forces, not elements within the city! A small galley entered the edge of the harbor just as all of you were disembarking from the English flagship. Its marksmen opened fire but after the initial concentrated burst, the galley immediately escaped the harbor and sailed eastward along the coast. By the time our lookouts in the tower realized that it was source of the gunfire, it was out of range of our cannons," reported Mario.

"Did your lookouts in the tower identify the galley?" asked Luke.

"It was a common vessel used for rapid communication along the North African coast, but who directed it is uncertain. Most likely it was Ghailan or the Spaniards," Mario continued.

The governor suddenly brought the meeting to an end, but asked Antonio and Luke to remain. The local soldiers saluted the governor and withdrew. The governor left the room for a few minutes and returned with another Portuguese officer.

"Gentlemen, you met Major Leo Coval on the ship from Lisbon. He is overtly my logistics officer to help me plan the Portuguese withdrawal. But on reading my sealed instructions from the Queen, I discover that he was especially chosen because for most of his life, he was, like you Tremayne, a special agent, who spent much of his career behind Spanish lines. In recent times he was attached to Portuguese military intelligence. I was also informed that you, Father Antonio, would explain the precise reasons for his selection—and that you are not here simply to nursemaid Tremayne."

"Her Majesty was concerned regarding the unusual autonomy granted to Captain Serano by your predecessor. She assumed that his group may contain a faction determined to hinder the handover to the English. Major Coval is to investigate covertly the loyalty and aims of Serano and his men. The attack on Tremayne has given some immediacy to this covert role. The timing of the galley attack suggests that an internal source revealed the exact time of our arrival."

"Could the attack have come from some of their members fearing that I might revoke their autonomy, or at least change the conditions under which they operate?" interrupted the governor.

"It is possible. The one body that would normally investigate such an attack could be the guilty party. Let it be known that you have asked Major Coval and myself to investigate the incident, acting under the direct authority of the Queen. Unofficially I will ask Colonel Tremayne to assist. On his last visit to Portugal, he helped unravel a number of political problems and solve several homicides," commented Antonio.

Luke smiled to himself. The Queen had not sent her top adviser simply to assist the English envoy. Surely, he was here to root out opponents of the Queen and her policies.

Antonio then informed those present, "I have arranged for Tremayne, his captain, sergeant and myself to reside in the local Franciscan friary. This will create the picture that I am independent of you. Given his overt role, Major Coval will nevertheless remain here."

"The rest of my men will be located where?" asked Luke.

"Next to the friary. The house is empty as the owner left Tangiers with the previous governor. The soldiers will eat in the friary's refectory."

Residence in the local Franciscan friary was a pleasant surprise to Luke. While accommodation was a small cell, food was plentiful, varied and delicious. He was led into the refectory by Antonio who introduced him to the prior, Father Roberto who indicated that Luke sit next to him at the head of the table.

The prior said a long grace during which the delectable smells from the kitchen had reached the hungry Luke. If he had expected a European meal, he was disappointed. Steaming dishes of a variety of slowly cooked, heavily spiced stews were placed on the table by several novices, who then took their place at the far end of the long table.

The prior who had formally welcomed them in Portuguese, took his coat and surprised Luke with an individual welcome in English with a marked west country accent. Father Roberto was English.

"How does a west country lad finish up in a Franciscan house in a Portuguese enclave in North Africa?" Luke asked.

"Father was a Plymouth merchant who traded with Portugal. I often travelled with him to Oporto. When our civil war began father suggested that as a Catholic, I should stay in Portugal and train as a priest. After graduating I joined the Franciscan order and was sent here fifteen years ago. Enough talk, you must be hungry!"

"Everything smells very inviting," replied Luke.

"This friary has for centuries adopted the local Berber cuisine. The four nearest dishes to us are traditional tajines—the nearest is a turkey and potato stew; the second, lamb and caramelized plum; the third, legumes and endives; and the fourth heavily spiced tuna. To your English taste they are all heavily enhanced with dozens of spices. You spoon the stews onto the wooden platter in front of you. There is no personal cutlery. Use your hands—and the bread provided to mop up the meal."

"Your order's culinary needs must take your people into the local community both within and without the city. It must provide a good source of information."

"Yes, in addition to their pastoral activities, they roam the souk and other markets within the city looking for the ingredients they need. Bazaar gossip is a real thermometer of how locals feel. Outside the city they travel widely seeking lemons from Fez, and various spices from all over Morocco. We raise money for the order by having a stall in the souk where we sell the spices obtained from outside the city. Our external suppliers do provide vital information on what is happening in the world outside the city."

Antonio joined the conversation. "Roberto then passes relevant information on to me. I inform the queen."

Luke wondered whether Roberto and his friars were the source of the rumor that someone in the city was planning to sell or give an emerald ring to Ghailan.

He suddenly turned to Antonio, "Why are you really here, father? As English envoy I am not of the status to need the Queen's leading advisor and confidant as my interpreter in a city about to leave Portuguese jurisdiction."

Antonio smiled, "I am here to prevent the Queen's decisions being thwarted. Roberto had isolated various groups within the city who might seek to prevent the transfer—Portuguese nationalists who wish to retain it for Portugal, Catholic extremists, perhaps financed by Spain, who do not want to see it transferred to a Protestant power, locals who desire an independent city that could play off both European and Islamic powers, and others who see independence in the form of a Tangerine-Islamic Berber alliance. There was even a suggestion that the Ottoman Empire has agents in the city who might create a situation where the Ottoman fleet could arrive unchallenged and take over the city but your fleet puts an end to that possibility."

"Only when it is here in Tangerine waters. Its arrival could be months off. I would not discount Algerian raids during this period but you can ignore these problems. Handing the city over to us, removes you from the scene. You need do nothing."

"Not true, Tremayne! We must stay involved to achieve the transfer. If certain elements have their way the city will not be transferred to you, and you need to be aware of the real issues you will face. My immediate task is to discover who tried to kill you and why? That may open the broader issues which you are here to unravel—and even throw some light on the specific problem of the ring," concluded Antonio.

Next morning Leo, Antonio, Luke, and Jack arrived at the headquarters of police commandant, Captain Gil Serano. Leo was frank. "Captain, Father Antonio and I have direct orders from the Queen to investigate slightly different aspects of the situation here. Our English friends are with us for obvious reasons. Primarily, I am here to smooth the path of transition to English control. In this regard what role will your men play in that transition, and then after English rule is established?"

"The answer to the second question is in the lap of the English. I doubt that they would want to continue with a Portuguese police force," Gil replied.

Luke agreed, "Captain Serano, is correct. We will not retain a Portuguese police force as it is, but that would not prevent individual members of the force joining whatever we create to maintain internal law enforcement. Most of your members are militia who have families and other occupations here. Would many stay on into the English occupation?"

"The news of the transfer is very recent. Many of my men were born here and have followed their fathers and in some cases grandfathers into military service while developing enterprises of their own and marrying into local families, both Portuguese and Moroccan. They have had little time to consider the advantages and disadvantages of moving out or staying here under a foreign power. At the moment their dominant reaction is anger."

"And that brings me to my real concern—are you out to hinder me preparing a smooth handover, or can I count on your assistance?" demanded Leo. "Put more bluntly, are you a loyal servant of the Queen willing to implement her policies, or a subversive plotting to undermine those decisions?"

3

Gil smiled, "You have been listening to the past governor's enemies who claimed we were helping him to hand over the city to Spain. Nothing could be further from the truth. Our previous Governor was a Spanish-hating Portuguese nationalist who simply did not believe that the city should leave Portuguese hands—the view of most of my men—but we are in no position to stop it. The King will soon take over from his mother, and my sources tell me he and his advisers are even more dedicated to the English alliance than she."

"For one reason, Captain, Portugal depends on the arrival of its sugar fleet which in turn depends on the English navy protecting it from Dutch and Spanish attack. Having an English fleet in the area is in Portugal's interest. Without it, Portugal will not survive."

"You cannot guarantee that your men will accept the transfer, but will they actively oppose it?" asked Antonio.

"Discipline will prevail with most of them, but there are unruly and troublesome individuals in every unit. Overall, my men are better disciplined than the rogue elements in the infantry. Lopez has a very serious problem," replied Gil.

"This brings us to a specific matter that needs investigation. You are the relevant authority. Who tried to kill Colonel Tremayne?" asked Leo.

"What elements in the community would you suspect to adopt such an approach to the English envoy," added the more diplomatic Antonio.

"I have no relevant information. I was barred from the investigation. Mario declared the attackers to be an external force which placed any enquiry in his hands not mine."

"Mario specifically ordered you not to investigate the attack on me?" probed a suspicious Luke.

"Yes."

"Over the time that you have been police chief, you must have isolated possible internal suspects that could have organized such an attack?" Antonio continued.

"Yes, but there are countless possibilities. There is no doubt that although the attackers were external to the city, elements within it must have provided the information necessary for it to occur. The timing was perfect," Gil explained. "But the probe is now closed."

"What do you mean?" asked Luke.

"You survived. There are multiple groups who may have organized the attempt. There is no way we can discover those culprits now, unless someone confesses—and no one will brag about a failure. Case closed! In that I agree with Mario. I see no point in continuing the investigation of the incident," concluded Gil.

Antonio reacted. "Thank you, captain, for such frank views but Major Coval and myself, acting under the Queen's direct authority, must continue to investigate the attempted murder of a foreign envoy. If you can give us the names of the those who have anti-English views, it will give us a start—as will the massive reward I will make available to anyone whose information leads to the arrest of the would-be assassins."

As Antonio rose to leave, Gil commented, "I am surprised Father that you have not asked me about the real power in Tangiers."

"And who is that?" asked a surprised Leo.

"Dona Catarina Sarmento."

Antonio did not comment and quickly guided his two companions out of the room.

Leo was furious. "Why bring the discussion to an end just when Serano raised what might be a crucial issue?"

Luke had a similar reaction. "What are you hiding from us, Father? What does the government know about Dona Catarina that we cannot discuss with Serano?"

"The possible role of Dona Catarina in past and future events is a very delicate matter—not something to be discussed with a suspected subversive police chief," replied a recalcitrant Antonio.

"What does the government know of this woman?" repeated an insistent Leo.

"Catarina is the daughter of Tangier's former wealthiest man— the converso merchant Abram Falcone. Falcone controlled the imports into the city, and the merchant vessels that traded these goods with the rest of Europe. A decade ago, the wife of Raphael Sarmento, the then Governor, died. The widower was quickly remarried to the beautiful, wealthy and talented Catarina. Through the quirks of different hereditary laws when both her husband and her father died, Catarina inherited most of their wealth and property. The Queen Regent has been aware for years of Catarina's dominant role in the city and for some time has maintained a regular personal connection with her through letter writing and regular annual visits of Catarina and her close companion, the converted Moroccan woman, Takama Khirri, to the court at Lisbon.

"For years Catarina was the Queen's source of information and influence in the city but given your comment that the matter is delicate, Her Majesty now has some doubts?" asked the perceptive Leo.

"Precisely," replied Antonio.

"And what has created this doubt?" asked Luke.

"Some years ago, when it was proposed to give Tangiers to the French in return for their continued military operations against Spain, Catarina came to Lisbon and in an impassioned discussion with the Queen argued very strongly against the proposition. Similarly, since Catarina became aware twelve months ago that Tangiers might be given to the English as part of a marriage treaty, the queen detected a cooling in Catarina's approach to her. The Queen recalled that on that previous occasion Catarina had been in favor of Tangiers as an independent city state, guaranteed by Portugal or another European power, or by an Islamic state, either the Ottoman Empire or the sultanate of Morocco. Given her mercantile background, Catarina could see the advantages of Tangiers as an independent free city. Italy provides many successful examples. Venice has shown some support for this solution, as has its ally Spain," was Antonio's long response.

"What do you know about Takama Khirri?" asked Leo changing the subject.

"The Portuguese garrison over the centuries have raided the local countryside seizing cattle and women. Some of these women became the unwilling sexual playthings of their captors, but most were sold as slaves and purchased by locals across the social spectrum. Our rival order the Dominicans devoted much of their energy in the city in converting these women to Christianity and encouraging locals then to marry them. Takama is the daughter of a powerful local Berber chieftain who is a major opponent of Ghailan."

"How does an enslaved woman become the trusted companion to the powerful Dona Catarina?" asked Luke.

"That is both a mystery and a worry," answered Antonio.

"I can understand the mystery, but what is the specific worry?" asked Luke.

"On the surface Catarina is companion to a converted Berber who is now allegedly more Portuguese Catholic than those born as such. But what if Catarina has secretly been converted to Islam and ready to follow Takama's lead? A Moslem agent in such an influential position is indeed a security risk," continued a somewhat obsessed Antonio.

"A bit far-fetched!" mumbled Gil.

"It appears that a major priority is to question both these women to clarify what precise influence Dona Catarina exerts in present day Tangiers—and what part is played in this by Takama Khirri?" asserted Luke.

"And you may be the very man to question Takama?" Antonio remarked. "Her mother was an English slave. She taught her daughter English. When we talk to Catarina, Takama can translate for you."

On returning to the friary Antonio was handed a note. It was an invitation from the deputy governor, General Mario de Silva for Colonel Tremayne, Captain Moon and himself for dinner that evening. The reception was held on the roof top of the deputy's governor's residence from which one had a magnificent view of the harbor below. Luke noted his fellow guests—the governor, Colonel Carlos Pimento and his wife Micaela, Colonel Miguel Lopez and his sister Catia, Father Antonio, Father Roberto, Dona Catarina and Takama Khirri who was referred to with the honorific status of Dona. Father Roberto's presence surprised him—as did the absence of Leo Coval and Gil Serano.

"Can we read anything into such a guest list?" Luke whispered to his deputy, Jack Moon.

Mario welcomed them, and they were immediately plied with Portuguese white wine and an array of cold meats. These preliminaries were well under way before Dona Catarina and Takama made their grand entrance. Luke was impressed. Catarina in her mid- thirties was still a woman of great beauty and dressed in the French fashion of revealing considerable flesh, rather than the conservative Hispanic fashions. Dona Takama was also most striking. Her tanned complexion, considerable height and sparkling brown eyes combined with an azure blue tight-fitting bodice but with a very conservative neckline created a picture of a very confident woman.

Luke may have imagined it, but he was sure that Dona Catarina had pointed the alluring Takama in his direction. She approached him and in perfect English with a fetching West country accent, welcomed him. "And what do our new masters think of the city?" she purred.

Luke was in two minds. Should he engage in flirtatious chit-chat or begin a gentle interrogation?

Takama provided the answer, "Dona Catarina would like you to call on her at ten tomorrow."

"I will be delighted to accept. By your English, I assume your mother must have been taken from the same area in which I was born—Cornwall," commented Luke.

"I see you have already been briefed on my parents. Mother was taken from the Cornish coast by Algerian pirates who sold some of their prisoners here in Tangiers where father bought her. He immediately freed and married her—and in the reverse to my own history, she renounced Christianity and became a Moslem."

"I would like to chat about this further," continued a very interested Luke.

"But not here, colonel." she replied as she left Luke, and moved onto to Father Roberto.

"At least that is a simple ploy. The two Englishmen in the room are welcomed in their own tongue by Catarina's right-hand woman—but why? Are we to be key elements in whatever Catarina has planned?" pondered Luke.

Luke found that much of the Portuguese he had picked up on his earlier visit came back to him. As soon as Takama moved on, a petite, vibrant young woman approached him. and commented, "I see it has not taken that devious manipulating witch, Catarina, long to draw our future masters into her circle. You only arrived yesterday, and you are already ensnared by the unofficial queen of Tangiers. I am Catia Lopez, sister to Miguel."

"And clearly not one of Catarina's inner circles?" was Luke's accurate but unthinking reply.

"Exactly! My brother and I are both relative newcomers and seen of more lowly status by her self-defined elite group. We are only in this god forsaken city because of my brother's success in Brazil solving a problem which seems endemic here."

"Which is?"

"Lack of military discipline among sections of the local infantry."

Luke turned the topic to less controversial grounds. "Where are you and your brother from originally?"

"We were born in what was then part of the Spanish kingdom. Father joined the rebellion of the Braganzas, and my brother joined the Portuguese army and was sent to Brazil to fight the Dutch and protect our sugar plantations. Five years ago, he was ordered here, and to escape father's constant attempts to marry me off, I joined him."

"Why does Catarina wish to ensnare me?"

"She is in trouble and does not want to reveal her stupidity to those around her. She thinks you will have the authority to help her without engaging the withdrawing Portuguese authorities. And her former strong link with the Queen Regent is fractured. The witch is suddenly vulnerable to the dozens of people she has tried to destroy in the past."

Luke noted Catarina's alleged penchant for creating enemies and attempting to destroy them. This needed probing but for the moment he commented, "Surely her influence on the Deputy Governor who still has the ultimate authority in Tangiers can assist her. The new Governor is only concerned to organize the transfer of power to us. He has left the running of the city, until we take over, in the hands of Mario de Silva."

Catia was about to expand on the relationship between the deputy governor and Catarina when a servant announced that the meal was about to be served. The guests took their place around a large round table, with a missing section to allow the servants to deliver the food to its center.

4

The seating arrangements intrigued Luke. The host sat at a twelve o'clock position. Next to him, moving clockwise were Lidia his wife, then Miguel, Catia, Carlos, Micaela, Jack, Luke, Takama and Roberto. Luke noted that the four English speaking guests had been placed together. There was a gap between the two friars for the servant access. Next to Antonio was the Governor Luis de Almeida, Catarina and then back to Mario.

At first there was little conversation. Mario ignored his wife and concentrated on his military commanders and their partners. Catarina directed her attention to the two representatives of the Queen, the governor, and Antonio—and ignored everybody else. At Luke's section of the table, Takama and Roberto engaged in a conversation that indicated to him that they were much closer than he had expected.

Gaining confidence in his Portuguese, Luke asked his near neighbor Micaela Pimento, "The marriage treaty suggests that the Portuguese cavalry remain and become part of the English military establishment. Would you be happy to stay?"

"No, but I can see why the English want my husband's unit to remain. They are not only the most professional of the troops here, but they are also the most effective source of intelligence. Their constant patrols keep the authorities alert to any changes in the military situation beyond the city. An individual or two might stay, but most of the group will not."

"Why?"

"To a man they are Portuguese born veterans. They include no Tangerine militia nor local Berber auxiliaries. If they cannot serve Portugal here, they will return to Portugal to carry on the fight against Spain."

Her husband Carlos agreed. "I am surprised that our retention is part of the marriage treaty. You were a cavalry commander yourself. Under the previous regime English cavalry was renowned for its efficiency and discipline. It should be easy to replace us with your elite troops."

"Our King has disbanded most of those cavalry regiments. To our negotiators your knowledge of the surrounding countryside and of the competing Islamic factions was seen as an asset, which will take us years to obtain."

"Micaela is right. We serve Portugal and will return there to continue the fight for independence."

"Will any current inhabitants of Tangiers stay, and experience English rule?" asked a growingly pessimistic Luke.

"Not many! Some who are second or third generation Tangerines and those that have married locally might, as may the converso and hidden Jewish population. Although never admitted openly, some converso merchants harbor unconverted Jews. Between them they have developed a key trade link to transport North African goods to the Netherlands where many fleeing Portuguese Jews settled. They will try to maintain this network under English rule," suggested Micaela.

These comments prompted Takama to suddenly join the conversation. "The local conversos and Jews are not popular now because of these very links. Both Spain, that controls their part of the Netherlands; and the Dutch Republic that governs the rest, are our current enemies. Spain seeks to destroy our independence, and the Dutch our colonial empire."

"And what do you intend to do, Takama, when we takeover?" Luke unexpectedly asked.

"I have no answer for you now. After your talk with Catarina tomorrow, my future may be clearer," she whispered.

Luke asked the same question of Roberto who responded, "The Franciscans wish to remain, but your government will expel all things Catholic. We will move a short distance away under the protection of the emerging Sultan of Morocco. Takama has already opened negotiations with his officials on our behalf."

Luke felt rebuked.

Next morning Catarina welcomed Luke alone. There was no Takama, no servants. Catarina was direct. "Colonel, I need your help on two matters."

"My lady, I have no authority here. Seek help from the Portuguese authorities which you strongly influence, if not control!"

"They refuse to act on the grounds that they are about to withdraw, but I suspect their refusal is that some of them are involved, even if indirectly. And don't lie to me! You already exert considerable authority. The locals will co-operate with you, as they know you have the ear of our Queen, let alone the power of the English navy which within a few weeks will be back in our harbor with its guns trained on the city."

"I do not know when our fleet will return. It could be months away. England has many issues to negotiate with several Catholic and Islamic states in the area. In any case my authority is irrelevant. Surely you retain enough influence to have any of your problems investigated, even unofficially, by your friends and servants?"

"I thought so, but the universal refusal of any of them to help, with one exception, has increased my suspicions that something is seriously amiss. Yes, I used to get my way. Why has my influence suddenly evaporated? This is perhaps a greater worry than the two specific issues on which I need your help. I feel suddenly impotent."

"What are these troubling issues that the local authorities choose to ignore?"

"A week before your arrival my niece, Gabriela, disappeared."

"Tell me about her!"

"Gabriela is fifteen years younger than I. Her uncle, my late husband adopted her and her older sister after their upbringing in a northern Portuguese convent became unacceptable. She needed to be disciplined and learn the sense of responsibility expected of our class. That became my responsibility which I continued after my husband's death."

"And were you successful?" asked Luke cheekily.

"Initially I thought so, but over the last year or so she has come under the influence of a sluttish newcomer who has led her into all types of debauchery. I acted against this embodiment of evil. I asked for her to be removed from the city and dealt with by the Inquisition for heresy and witchcraft. During her stay in Brazil, she picked up the most obnoxious and hideous rituals from the African slaves. Mario claimed that if I had Catia Lopez charged, he would lose his infantry commander. Her brother Miguel refuses to believe the depth of her depravity. The Inquisitor proved useless. He said he would soon be gone from the city, and any process involving heresy or witchcraft would take months to get off the ground."

"Is this evil Catia involved in Gabriela's disappearance?"

"Possibly! Gabriela's disappearance, and the immediate refusal by the authorities to act, makes me wonder if some of these very officials are in some way involved."

"Why have they failed to investigate?"

"When I challenged Mario as to why he refused to probe Gabriela's disappearance he became angry and simply said any investigation would destroy my family, and the reputation of too many people. Therefore, my first request of you is to probe Gabriela's disappearance—or as I fear, her murder."

"Why do you think someone in authority may be involved?"

"I am a very wealthy woman. My father, anticipating the decline of Tangiers as a port transformed many of our assets into portable silver ingots. This wealth, on my death was to be shared between my nieces. Unlike you English who leave everything to the single nearest male, our laws permit women to inherit and for the inheritance to be divided."

"Who is Gabriela's older sister?"

"Lidia de Silva, the general's wife. I am now contemplating leaving a considerable legacy to Takama. Gabriela's disappearance maybe part of a plot to reduce the number of my heirs and leave only Lidia."

Luke feigned disbelief. "My lady, you are not suggesting that the deputy governor would kill off his sister-in- law so that his wife would inherit a greater fortune. If you are right Takama then could be the next to disappear."

"Will you help?"

"I will try but my Portuguese is not the best, and my Berber and Arabic non- existent."

"No worries! I have already asked a person to assist you who is fluent in all three languages."

'Takama?"

Catarina seemed surprised at the suggestion. "No, Father Roberto, who alone among my friends expressed concern at the lack of action."

"I am surprised that Takama is not with you this morning. I gained the impression that you were inseparable."

"True, but the second problem on which your help is required involves her. At this stage I do not want her to suspect I doubt her loyalty and confidentiality. There are rumors of lost items that affect our control of Tangiers resurfacing, which if true will certainly create problems for the English in the future. What do you know about Islam and precious gems?"

"Nothing much!" lied Luke.

"Centuries ago, a Sultan of Morocco created three silver rings which he claimed gave him his authority from God. Subsequently a legend developed that to exercise total power in this land, and to unite the various tribes under a central leadership, a person needed to possess all three rings. One ring contained an emerald—green representing the fertile lands, another an amethyst with the purple symbolizing the many mountain ranges, and the third contained a yellow citrine to represent the deserts. When Portugal took over Tangiers a local chieftain was captured and one the rings, that with a green emerald, was taken from him. At the time our people were unaware of its significance and made no attempt to search him further. It is possible that he had the other two rings with him. The inability of any local leaders since to display all three rings has helped keep the country divided—to the advantage of the Portuguese in Tangiers. Recently the local warlord, Ghailan, claimed that he would soon be in possession of all three rings, which would bring all the local tribes to his banner. If that happened neither the Portuguese nor the English could resist him."

"I understand something of this problem. Your queen informed my government of this development. It is why I have attached to my mission a silversmith, but how are you involved?"

"The ring was kept for centuries within the crypt of the local church. It was brought out annually and displayed to the congregation while prayers were said for the security of this Christian city. Twenty years ago, during a disturbance when the city declared for John of Portugal, and not Philip of Spain, it disappeared from the crypt. The Dominican friars who supported Spanish hegemony took it for safe-keeping."

"Why has the issue resurfaced?"

"If Ghailan expects to be in possession of all three rings, then the one that disappeared from our church has to be one of them. The former's governor's secretary just before he departed claimed that the authorities did not probe the disappearance of my niece too deeply because just prior to her disappearance, Gabriela had been wearing the missing silver and emerald ring. He claimed that the situation was not investigated to preserve my family's reputation."

"And Takama is not here because she may in some way be involved?"

"A precaution. She knows the legend of the rings and has obvious contacts with the Moslem chieftains of the interior."

"Investigating the disappearance of your niece will be difficult enough, tracing a missing ring almost impossible."

"Get help from those two devious, but astute Franciscans—Roberto and Antonio. One has the local knowledge and is to be trusted, and the other has the Queen's authority if you need it—but do not trust him. Why is he really here? What is his hidden agenda, and is it the Queen's?"

Later that day Luke was visited by Mario, the deputy Governor.

"My apologies, Colonel, for the behavior of Dona Catarina. She has not fully accepted the possible death of her niece and is convinced that the authorities refuse to investigate it to cover up the crimes of its officials."

"She was very convincing. She did not appear to me to a woman obsessed by conspiracy theories. Rather she impressed as a rational, logical and sensible woman with strong evidence for her opinions," countered Luke, who had intuitively taken a dislike to this pompous official.

Mario quickly modified his approach. "You—and she—are absolutely right. There was no investigation, but it was to protect Catarina."

5

"From what?"

"Involvement in the scandalous re-appearance and subsequent loss of an important Islamic ring. In the hands of a local chieftain this ring could end European rule in Tangiers—Portuguese or English. Keeping the local Moroccan tribes divided is our only guarantee of preserving the city from their successful assault."

"I am aware of the legend of the rings and the immense political repercussions of that emerald ring returning to Islamic hands—and the imminent possible possession of all three by a Moslem leader. Its recovery is a priority of the English government, but how does this issue relate to Catarina, and the failure to investigate the disappearance of Gabriela?"

"I persuaded my colleagues not to pursue Gabriela's disappearance and possible death, not only to protect Catarina from devastating news that would have destroyed her, but also given our imminent departure, it seemed a futile pursuit when there are so many other issues to be resolved."

"From what were you saving Catarina?"

"Gabriela disappeared after several days of entertaining various males of the city, during which she flaunted the emerald ring. Gabriela is no innocent. She had numerous affairs mainly with married men, some of whom I believe she tries to blackmail. As I said there are more important things that we must do in the last days of our administration than probe the disappearance of a promiscuous woman, who may have deserved whatever she got."

"Even though she is your sister-in-law?" asked a surprised Luke.

Mario grimaced but said nothing.

Luke continued, "Perhaps Gabriela disappeared of her own accord, rather than be murdered by parties alarmed at the resurfacing of the ring?"

"A possibility, but where is she? It is ten days since she was last seen."

"Has any ransom note been received?"

"If so, I have not been informed which suggests murder rather than abduction!"

"Yes, or as I optimistically hope, she may have vanished voluntarily. In the circumstances, how do you suggest I deal with Catarina's request?" asked the now more diplomatic Luke.

Mario smiled, "Pretend to carry out her request, but instead thoroughly investigate the loyalty of Takama to the Portuguese state. She must have assisted Gabriela to obtain the ring which by now will be with her Islamic Berber relations to the danger of the city."

Next morning Luke discussed the situation with the friars, Antonio and Roberto.

"How do you intend to handle this delicate situation?" asked Roberto.

"I have no authority here to act on Catarina's request. Father Antonio, you have the Queen's authority, and Roberto you have the local knowledge. Combined we may be able to achieve something. I certainly can act on the allegations regarding Takama as they could affect the security of Tangiers after we take over, but I need your assistance to interview those concerned."

"And we need your investigative skills in probing Gabriela's probable murder," added a blunt Antonio.

"Then all is clear, we three investigate both Gabriela's death and Takama's loyalty, while pretending to Mario that we are only paying lip service to Catarina's concerns," concluded Roberto.

"We must involve Gil Serano. He is technically the local officer responsible for such an investigation—and I sense he is out of favor with the ruling cabal," insisted Luke.

Luke's plans to begin these investigations were unexpectedly delayed. He overslept and was awakened by Roberto who suggested he view the harbor from the friary roof. Looking out to sea he could see a single English ship of the line heading for the harbor. He recognized it as the flagship of the vice admiral of the English fleet, John Lawson. Where was the rest of the fleet? Why had only a single ship returned? Had it suffered a monumental disaster?

Within the hour an English naval lieutenant found Luke and escorted him to the English warship where Luke was immediately taken to the commander. He was an old acquaintance—one of Cromwell's and the English republic's most loyal officers. Like Luke, John Lawson was not dismissed by the King, but promoted to Vice Admiral of his Atlantic Mediterranean fleet. The old comrades hugged each other, and the sailor commented, "Thanks for your speedy response. I have new orders for you from the King which arrived from England two days ago when we were off Algiers. You were to receive them immediately."

"Surely they could have been delivered by a less important officer?" said Luke.

"I command the fastest ship in the fleet and a personal set of orders from the King could scarcely have been trusted to junior officers, but I must rejoin the armada without delay. I trust the situation here is conducive to English control?"

"Difficult to assess!"

Luke explained to Lawson the complex situation in Tangiers. His assessment was that the Portuguese citizens would not oppose the English takeover, but they would do little to assist. "The greatest danger lies in the surrounding Moslem tribes. If they can unite before our garrison is in place, they could take the city," was his pessimistic conclusion.

"That may explain part of my new orders. Our garrison will not arrive until the beginning of next year, and the return of half of our fleet here could be months off. In the interim, I am to leave you fifty of my musketeers to help you enforce your decisions on the city, and ominously one of my naval surgeons."

"Fifty will hardly be effective against several thousand Portuguese troops should our current allies change sides," countered a depressed Luke.

"You of all people should know that our great strength is the ability of the fleet to demolish the city by its immense firepower. Our enemies don't know when the fleet will return. You must mislead them into thinking the return is imminent. That is your real power. Perhaps your only power!"

"That might have worked under our previous regime when Cromwell's fleet dominated the Western Mediterranean, but our enemies know that the King has decommissioned most of the fleet. In addition, they realize that we would not be stupid enough to demolish a city which is about to come under our control. What are my new orders?"

Lawson took from his desk a sealed letter bearing the royal crest. "You are asked to read the contents and then in my presence burn the letter."

Luke opened the letter. It simply reaffirmed that his priority was to recover the green ring, and if possible, the other two, to forestall any united Moslem attack on the city, and that the fleet would immediately provide him with an extra fifty men.

"I have hired some local boatmen to return you, your reinforcements and boxes of supplies to shore as I must leave immediately," announced Lawson.

By the time Luke and his new men reached the shore, Lawson had left the harbor and his ship a speck on the horizon.

Luke and his now slightly inflated company moved from the friary and were relocated in part of the Portuguese cavalry barracks. Luke spent the afternoon drinking with his new men.

Jack recalled that his path and that of several of these newcomers had crossed three years earlier when Luke commanded *The Cromwell* and was the ambassador to the North African Islamic states. "I commanded the troops aboard one of the ships that came to assist *The Cromwell* on one occasion. What are our new orders? They must be important for a vice admiral to leave the fleet and deliver them in person."

"I will brief you all in detail tomorrow, this afternoon we eat and drink."

Next day Luke explained their mission.

"Gentlemen, the King has re- emphasized that our major task is to find a silver and emerald ring. In the process we may discover the fate of a missing woman. The real purpose of the vice-admiral's quick visit was not the re-iteration that we must find the ring, but the provision of an additional fifty troops. My valet Thomas Smith is a silversmith and an expert on these rings. He will explain."

"Although for decades the three rings have been seen as emerald, amethyst and citrine, they are not. They are simply a purple, green and yellow variant of fluorite."

"Does that matter?" asked Jack.

"Crucial to our investigation," replied Thomas.

"I don't follow," admitted Luke.

"If possession of these rings can lead you to political dominance, given the unknown location of all of them at present, would you not be tempted to recreate three such rings? When I was in Fez decades ago my then master inspected dozens of false rings. I could easily replicate them. That wily Sultan centuries ago deliberately and falsely claimed the gems were emeralds, citrines and amethysts, concealing the nature and the source of the real element involved—a peculiar and localized range of fluorites. He also did his best to prevent future duplication of his rings."

"How do you know all this?" asked Luke.

"When the Portuguese possessed the green ring, it was examined by their experts who recognized it as a fluorite. It had flashes of darker and lighter green which would help to locate its actual source. Unfortunately, they never found it, or if they did, they did not reveal it to anybody."

"So, if Ghailan claims to have one or more of the rings, they could be fakes?" commented Jack.

"The only genuine ring that we know of is the one that was recently seen on the finger of Gabriela Sarmento," added Luke.

"No, sir! That was most likely also a fake," Thomas responded.

"Someone probably created a silver and green ring. We will not know for sure until an expert examines it. Those who reported the ring on the missing girl's finger were not experts."

Luke smiled, "If we cannot find the originals, we may achieve our ends by flooding the market with fake duplicates and distribute them to rival tribes which will destroy their currency and value."

"It would only be a short-term advantage," said Thomas.

"Why?" asked Jack   .

"Because according to the legend the senior Islamic scholar attached to the mosque at Fez must authenticate the rings. Through the centuries the details of the peculiar flashes of the different hues within each stone have been recorded."

"Does this mean should we discover any rings; we must take them to Fez for authentication?" Jack continued.

"Yes," replied Thomas "Someone might find similar, but not identical fluorite and fool everybody except the experts. I am able to reject most of the rings that we may be confronted with."

"Is there anything else I should know about these rings?" asked the bemused Luke

"Yes, the origin of the silver is also critical. The original silver was not from the mines of the western Mediterranean. The original silver used came from the Balkans."

"So, you are not able to successfully duplicate this aspect of the rings!" commented Jack.

"But I can. The ship that arrived yesterday brought me a trunk containing Balkan silver, and enough emeralds, citrines and amethysts to recreate as many fake duplicates as I need to make," replied an enthusiastic Thomas.

"That would be a lot of work for you for little lasting effect," muttered a cynical Jack.

Luke agreed and was slightly concerned. "The government in London seems to know more about the rings than they have confided in me."

Luke pruned his investigative team to Leo Coval representing Portuguese intelligence, Gil Serano the local police chief, Jack and himself.

Antonio objected, not to his own exclusion, but to the inclusion of Serano. "Serano is one of the town's high-profile bachelors who attended many of the functions at which Gabriela Sarmento disgraced herself. I have been told he was one of her lovers, and popular rumor in the souk is that her disappearance was not followed up because Serano was involved.|"

"You have kept that to yourself," commented an annoyed Luke.

"I only heard that piece of gossip this morning from one of the brothers who had been selling some of the friary's produce in the souk. Also, our commander of infantry, another bachelor, Miguel Lopez is definitely another admirer of young Gabriela. I suggest you start your investigation by questioning his sister Catia who apparently detests the girl, and then Takama, who depending on your sources manipulated Gabriela, or tried to destroy her. Dona Catarina has not revealed the full story. As far as Catarina and Takama are concerned, question Father Roberto again. I fear his support for them is grievously misplaced."

Whether Antonio's picture had been colored by information he received in the confessional which he could not relay, or from further information from Portuguese authorities, Luke was eager to follow up his allegations. Three women, Catia, Catarina and Takama, might prove the weak link in the alleged cover-up.

6

That afternoon Luke, Jack and Leo visited Catia Lopez. Luke was direct, "We have been asked to re-open the case of the missing Gabriela Sarmento. What can you tell us about her?"

"To be blunt, she is a nasty, immoral, ambitious slut."

"That response surprises me. I was led to believe you were very close friends and partners in many misdemeanors, if not crimes," said a surprised and undiplomatic Luke.

"Very true once—but not since she betrayed my brother."

"You express your views with some venom," commented a shocked Jack.

"That woman is evil."

"Evidence?" asked the skeptical Luke.

"She used her charms to incriminate males—and then black mail them, particularly the married men she seduced. Her murder was only a matter of time. Discarded and put-upon lovers, or their female associates give you dozens of suspects. Don't waste time on her. Her activities don't involve the security of the state."

"Your brother is an admirer and possible lover of Gabriela. As he is a single man, she would have less to blackmail him about? Why does their relationship anger you so much?" Leo asked.

"She has done far worse to Miguel than simple blackmail," Catia declared.

"Which is?" probed an aggressive Luke.

"She broke his heart. He is besotted with her and firmly believes she feels the same about him. He has already asked her aunt for Gabriela's hand in marriage. I know she remains close to several other men and lies constantly about it to my brother. He refuses to listen to me. At the reception held by the deputy governor to farewell the previous governor, he and Gabriela were to announce their engagement."

"This was the reception from which she disappeared?" ask Jack seeking clarification.

"Yes, just before the announcement was to be made she vanished. My brother was shattered."

Luke thanked Catia for her assistance and ended the interrogation. The trio moved to the infantry barracks to question Miguel.

As they walked together Leo expressed his suspicion of the evidence they had just heard. "Venomous and vindictive—hardly an unbiased portrayal."

"There is certainly a hidden agenda in the responses of that young woman," agreed Luke.

Miguel was delighted to have the issue re-opened. "The authorities were too quick to curtail the investigation, claiming that it was in all our interests."

"You did not accept that view?" asked Jack.

"No, the only one it helps is her abductor or murderer."

Luke exaggerated some of the evidence he possessed and asked, "Miguel, we have been given four options regarding Gabriela's disappearance—that she has been murdered, that she committed suicide, or that she has conveniently disappeared, either of her own volition or under pressure from others. What's your view?"

"You are all newcomers to the city and may not be aware that I was about to become engaged to Gabriela. I had already sought approval from her aunt and guardian, Dona Catarina, and from my own parents. Gabriela and I had discussed it at length, and we were to announce our engagement the evening she disappeared. She was so happy that you can rule out suicide."

"Your sister suggests her possible murder maybe the work of a jealous ex-lover, a disappointed current boyfriend or a furious female partner of such men. Could she have been murdered by a discarded lover?" probed Luke.

"Do not believe my sister! She has become obsessed with Gabriela, and insanely jealous of her effect on men. Catia and she were for a year or more rivals for every available young man in the city. In most cases they chose Gabriela over Catia which soured the relationship. The last straw for my disturbed sister was when I became besotted with Gabriela."

"What exactly happened at the reception from which she disappeared?" asked Leo.

"Four of us attended together. Gil took my sister Catia, and I went with Gabriela. We were immediately seated in a large banquet hall and plied with food and drink. After much eating and even more drink, Gabriela whispered that she was not feeling well and suggested I take her home. Our hostess, her sister Lidia, overheard the request and offered to lead her upstairs to a bedroom where she might recuperate. Lidia and she left the room."

"You did not immediately check on her?" asked Jack.

"No! Two hours later Lidia suggested I should, and as I did not know the house well, I asked her to take me to the bedroom. We entered the room together. It was empty."

Luke suddenly changed the direction of the questioning, "You are aware of the current tensions regarding the three rings of Islam?"

"That Ghailan claims he will soon be in possession of all three and enabled to unite all of northern Morocco and drive the European from Tangiers. Yes!"

"That would have been impossible twenty years ago because one of those rings, the emerald ring, was in the possession of the Tangiers authorities. Given Ghailan's boast, we can only assume that that ring has been found and someone is willing to return it to the Moroccans. Gabriela was the last to be seen with that ring and wore it to the reception from which she disappeared," continued Luke.

Miguel laughed. "That ring was a joke. It was a fake which she wore to worry our leaders. It was a childish prank which I tried to discourage."

"How did you know it was a fake?" asked Leo.

"Gabriela told me—and I already knew the real ring had flashes of darker and lighter green in it. This was uniformly the same hue of green."

"Did she tell you where she obtained this fake ring, and what she intended to do with it?" continued Leo.

"She was going to sell it to one of the lesser Berber tribes to make a bit of money. She was always complaining that Dona Catarina was very frugal with her allowance. This petty greed was combined with an intense nationalism. None of this was going to happen until the English had taken over. The united Islamic thrust would only develop after the Portuguese had left."

"Where did she get the fake?" Jack asked.

"She didn't say, but claimed that when the original went missing twenty years ago a number of duplicates were made by a mix of criminal and legitimate agencies within Tangiers."

It was Leo's turn to suddenly change the subject, "What was Gabriela's relationship with Dona Takama?"

"They both lived within Catarina's complex. Gabriela was frightened of Takama."

"Was this fear related to the rings?"

"Possibly, she sought Takama's advice on the sale of her ring to the anti-Ghailan Berbers. Takama was appalled by the plan."

"Your view on Takama?" probed Leo.

"Despite Dona Catarina telling us that Takama is a Christian, and more Portuguese than those born as such, I have my doubts."

"Any evidence?" asked Luke.

"She is the official go-between for the government of Tangiers and surrounding Arab and Berber tribes. On many of her missions she is unaccompanied by any other officials. Who knows what she gets up to?"

"But no evidence of actual treachery?" demanded Leo.

"Not so far, but how she is reacting to the handover should worry you Englishmen. She feels if Tangiers cannot be Catholic Portuguese, it is better served as part of Islamic Morocco than Protestant England, which is also the view of many Tangerines."

On leaving Miguel the interrogators with Luke's prompting, sought out Dona Takama.

"To what do I owe this visit?" she asked.

"The disappearance of Gabriela," answered Luke.

"What do you know about Gabriela and the emerald ring of Islam?" added Leo.

"Stupid little girl! She somehow came into possession of one the many duplicates and fake rings made after the genuine one disappeared. She asked me if I could find a buyer for her among the surrounding tribes."

"Which you refused to do?" said Luke.

"Yes, it was hardly worth anything, and such an offer would have been an insult to our allies—the anti-Ghailan tribes. They are not fools. Their leaders are aware of the fiery nature of the genuine green ring. Gabriela's was a poor-quality fake."

"How did she take your refusal to help?" continued Luke.

"She blamed my refusal on Catarina and told me she would continue to amuse herself by confronting everybody with her possession of such a powerful weapon. She thought you English might be tempted to buy it—if she threatened to give it to Ghailan."

"Surely she was aware that people who were interested in the real ring knew that hers was a fake."

"Gabriela is a child who needs to make herself appear important. Sadly, there are enough ignorant inhabitants of the city who would believe anything. Many who had not seen the ring thought it was the genuine article."

"Is Gabriela still alive?" asked Jack.

"I do not know. Her childish pranks and stupid activities may have spooked someone involved in the sale of the real ring to remove her. It is highly likely."

Luke expressed surprise.

"So, you think her disappearance or death is related to the ring and national security, rather than an array of disappointed or jealous lovers and their partners."

"Yes! Nobody took Gabriela seriously in affairs of the heart. They were all about her. I doubt that she showed any real affection towards anybody else."

"Not even Miguel?" continued Luke.

"A very recent affair but his influence did appear to be having some affect, but Gabriela probably started the affair simply to annoy Catia who had turned from closest friend to vindictive enemy."

"Would you suspect Miguel of being involved in her murder or disappearance?" asked Jack.

"No, but if she was murdered because of her personal relationships, my suspect would be his sister. Catia hates Gabriela with an unnatural ferocity."

"We were told that if any other woman was involved, it might, be you? probed a provocative Leo.

"And why would I want to remove Gabriela?"

Luke decided to lie once more. "For fear that she was usurping your place with Dona Catarina. With the trauma of the handover and the ultimate dispersal of Catarina's wealth, Gabriela was set to inherit at your expense."

Takama was shaken. Clearly such a thought had never entered her head and she was troubled by how Luke had come up with the idea. She responded simply, "But that is not how Catarina sees the future. I am taken well care of in her latest will. My future is secure."

Luke concerned at Takama's emotional response, changed the subject yet again, "I am interested in your suggestion that Gabriela was murdered by those anxious to deal in the real Islamic rings. Who in Tangiers is involved in such activity?"

"The obvious suspect is me, she admitted"

"That has been suggested to us," admitted Jack.

"It could be true. I was born into an Islamic Berber household but have spent most of my life as a Portuguese Catholic. I have no love of the Protestant English—despite my mother. I see them as fanatical heretics who will expel all supporters of the true church from this city. I must plan a future for myself. The real ring would be worth a fortune. Competing groups will be ruthless to gain possession—not only Ghailan and his local northern rivals, but the Sufi brotherhood who control central Morocco, and the emerging new sultanate in the south. Even the former sultanate dynasty believes it could reverse its misfortune, if it had the rings. Rumor is that Ghailan has the amethyst and is about to obtain the citrine or the emerald. If the latter, someone in the city is the source. I am surprised I have not been contacted by any potential bidders."

"So, the simple motive is greed?" commented Leo.

"Not necessarily! For some, it may be their objection to the transfer of the city into English hands. They may not be able to change the mind of the Queen, but they can make English accession and retention of the city almost impossible."

"Apart from someone with a pro-Islamic attitude whom else in Tangiers would hold such extreme views?" asked Jack.

"The more extreme of the Catholic religious orders," was the surprise response.

"They would surely have limited influence in such a cosmopolitan city," commented Luke.

"I don't include the Franciscans who are missionaries in the hinterland, and minister to the poor of the city. I would suspect the Dominicans, many of whom are Spaniards, and associated with the Inquisition and our cathedral church. Catarina claims they took the original ring at the time of our Portuguese uprising against the King of Spain."

"Thank you for your assistance," remarked Luke.

"All the plotting and deaths in the last weeks are part of the simple desire to prevent an English takeover of this city. The Queen Regent of Portugal by her decision to hand Tangiers over to the English, has lost much influence among the powerbrokers here. Be careful, colonel! Trust no one!"

As the trio left, Takama whispered to Luke, "Come back alone! There is more I need to tell you, but I do not trust that Portuguese major. Tonight—for a late supper."

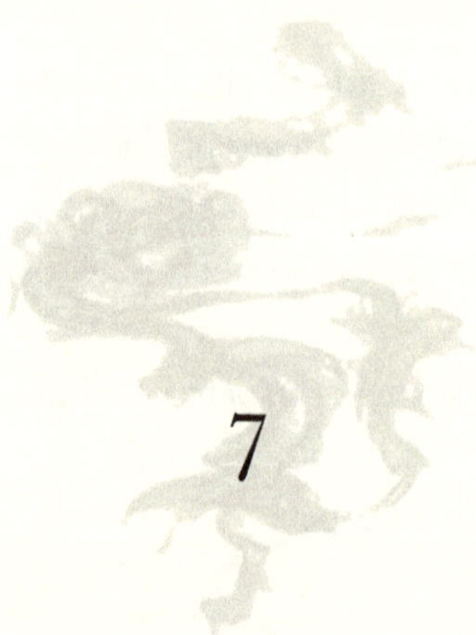

7

Luke arrived at Catarina's complex at dusk. He walked across a courtyard to Takama's villa where a female servant informed him that he was expected, but must wait in an antechamber, as his hostess had not finished dressing. Luke cooled his heels for almost half an hour when the servant re-appeared and expressed surprise that Takama had not emerged from her dressing room. She entered the room, and after a short delay returned.

She was shaken. Takama had disappeared.

Luke's examined the room. There had been a struggle. Takama appeared to have been abducted. He informed Catarina who was devastated.

An initial silence was replaced by a rhythmic sobbing. A servant administered some calming medication. When Luke made to leave, Catarina asked him to remain. After another awkward period of silence she dismissed her servants and told Luke. "I have two conflicting views as to why Takama is missing."

"Which are?"

"Some sections of the community are determined to make it difficult for the English to maintain control of this city. Takama with her contacts across Tangiers and within Morocco itself may have become aware of their plans. The plotters may have believed she was about to reveal all to you."

"Did she mention any names?"

"No."

"So, you cannot help me further on this matter?"

"I cannot, but there is someone who might—my niece Gabriela."

"But I assumed she is dead."

"So did I, but apparently not. An hour ago, I received a note demanding a ransom for her return. This note arrived at the same time as Takama disappeared. Although I am loathe to think it, did Takama deliver that note, and then disappear? Is she another victim of Gabriela's abductor or is she the perpetrator of the kidnapping?"

"May I see the ransom note?"

"It contains few details. The kidnappers require silver and gold coin—and fluorite. I will be informed of the delivery details later."

"Do not to pay, unless you have absolute proof that Gabriela is still alive. Suggest that your representative must verify this before you proceed. I will act for you, if you wish. Can you contact the kidnapper?"

"Yes, I am to leave any messages under a cushion outside the confessional in the Dominican chapel."

Luke informed Roberto of the latest development the friar seemed pre-occupied. "Forget the missing two women for the moment. I have issues which must take priority. Tomorrow you will meet the local warlord Ghailan. He sent a message through one of my brothers that he wished to talk with the English as a matter of urgency. He claimed any discussion would be mutually advantageous."

"And other issues?"

"Not good news at all! Do not trust Antonio or Leo Corval. They are on a secret mission from their queen, which may not be in England's interest."

"Surely they are not trying to reverse the decision to handover the city to us?"

"No, but they are working to remove most of the assets of the city so that by the time of the takeover, the English will be left with an empty shell, bereft of any meaningful trade."

"I half expected something like this. I could not see that the handover of the city and a visit by an English representative required the attendance of the queen's personal adviser and a senior intelligence officer," commented a growing disillusioned Luke.

The following day Luke led a unit of twenty men into the hills. Largely ship-board musketeers riding borrowed Portuguese cavalry horses they created for Luke the type of unit he had found most useful in England—the dragoon. Roberto acted as guide and interpreter. Luke informed the Portuguese authorities of his intended movements.

After the climb into the mountains entered its second hour, Roberto expressed some concern. "I had expected Ghailan's men to have met us by now."

"And this is perfect country for an ambush," noted an alarmed Luke.

As they entered a narrow upland valley a group of horsemen galloped towards them. "Thank goodness. Contact at last!" exclaimed Luke.

"No, these men are not Ghailan's. This is trouble. The approaching troops are strangers to the area. Their flowing burgundy robes reflect a loyalty not of this region. Disaster! Look behind us! An equally large body of men in similar dress have cut off our retreat. We are surrounded by strangers."

Luke gave the order to dismount and form a defensive square. Suddenly the advancing cohort stopped, and two of its officers dismounted. They approached the scrambling English with arms outstretched indicating that they were unarmed. Luke and Roberto moved towards him.

The taller stranger spoke, and Roberto translated. "Forgive this intrusion, we mean you no harm. I am Omar Koubi, commander of the palace guard of his Highness Moulay Mohammed al-Rashid, Sultan of Morocco. His Highness would like to contact the English envoy. He wishes to discuss relations with England and the future of Tangiers. This is my deputy, Colonel Ibram Zammit."

"You are a long way from your base. How did you know that the English envoy would be here?" asked a suspicious Roberto.

"We have been in the area for weeks, largely hidden by a local tribe who has already proclaimed its loyalty to Sultan al-Rashid. More than a month ago His Highness received two pieces of disturbing news and dispatched us north to investigate."

"And what news alarmed the Sultan?" asked Luke.

"That Tangiers was being transferred to the English, and that the traitor Ghailan was boasting that he would soon possess the three rings of Islam. In regard to the latter our agent in the city suggested that you may be taking the emerald ring to him on this expedition. Consequently, my men must conduct a search."

After further discussion the temporary English dragoons submitted to a search.

Suddenly there was a burst of gunfire. Zammit fell to the ground as did several of his men. Luke faced an immediate dilemma. Was this a rescue attempt by friendly tribesmen or an attack on both the Sultan's men and the English? The answer was immediate. He was struck on the arm and Roberto uttered a cry of pain as Luke's defensive square of musketeers became the target of concentrated fire.

With a mild flesh wound himself, Luke examined the friar. He had been nicked in the upper leg. Colonel Zammit was more seriously wounded. He was bleeding profusely from the chest. Having inspected that wound Luke declared, "He will bleed to death unless we get him to a surgeon as a soon as possible. Our naval surgeon is Zammit's only hope. Jack, lead Koubi and his men to the outskirts of Tangiers and then take Zammit to the surgeon. I will cover your retreat with the rest of our men."

Koubi united both sections of his cavalry. Jack with two other English soldiers led them back down the mountain. The remainder of the English square returned a constant stream of musket fire into the area from which the attack had come, as they too backed away down the mountain—and eventually beyond the range of the assailants.

"Who are our attackers?" Luke asked of Roberto.

"I cannot be sure, but the village that we were approaching is a Ghailan stronghold."

"But why would Ghailan attack us? He asked for a meeting."

"Unfortunately, that is Ghailan. He constantly keeps his enemies confused by announcing contradictory policies, going back on his word, and then claiming everybody else is lying. He probably couldn't resist the temptation of killing both the English and the Sultan's men in the one attack. He will of course claim that it was a rogue element that attacked us when he arranges another meeting, as he surely will."

Luke caught up with the Sultan's cavalry well before they reached Tangiers.

The sight of the approaching combined force, and aware of the identity of the burgundy robe wearing cavalry, the Portuguese authorities were momentarily alarmed. What was this combined English/ Moroccan force intending to do? The panic dissipated when only Luke, Jack, Roberto, Koubi and the stricken Zammit entered the city.

The rest of the combined group gathered on the beach outside the city's walls.

While the surgeon operated on Zammit, Luke in an adjacent room questioned Koubi. "Why exactly do you desire of me?"

"The sultan will within a few years reunite all of Morocco under his rule. The other contestants to power in central and northern Morocco do not have the capability of removing you from Tangiers—my master has. His experts have already mined and destroyed the walls off several cities. The walls of Tangiers will be one of the easiest to demolish."

"What then do you want of me?" Luke asked.

"The Portuguese have given you a useless possession. This harbor is poor and subject to the worst of Atlantic weather, and any trade through it from the hinterland is already being transferred by the Portuguese to their western ports along the Atlantic coastline, especially Casablanca. Most Portuguese traders have already transferred their assets and activities elsewhere. Consequently, the Sultan suggests that you sell Tangiers to him. It will save England the great cost of maintaining a garrison and fleet in the area. To negotiate on this matter, he asks that your King send a formal envoy to the Sultan and permit him to send an ambassador to England."

An hour later the surgeon emerged and drew Luke aside, "Colonel, the musket balls I removed from the patient are Iberian not Moroccan."

"Probably supplied by the Spaniards to Ghailan," commented Luke.

Koubi overheard the surgeon and added, "They must have supplied the muskets as well. Moroccans of all factions use a very long barreled weapon which produces a different sound to the those used by the Europeans. We were attacked by men using European weapons, if not by European assailants."

The surgeon offered a chilling alternative. "Your attackers were not necessarily pro-Spanish. You may have been attacked by your so-called allies—the Portuguese. They were the only group that knew exactly where you would have been at that time."

During the week following Zammit's life-saving operation the Sultan's men were admitted to the city on the condition that the English take responsibility for their conduct. Koubi's requests were immediately dispatched to England aboard a passing English merchantman, carried by Luke's sergeant, George Harris.

Luke immediately appointed the surgeon Gregory Pickford as George's replacement and Jack's deputy. Against Luke's advice Mario sent a company of troops to completely obliterate the two nearest pro-Ghailan villages. The inhabitants who did not flee were massacred, the village and surrounding crops burnt to the ground.

Luke's protest was met by a simple reply from Mario. "You may be the diplomat Tremayne, but my instructions are clear. Any attack on European nationals, their shipping or trade has to be met by ten times the original force."

Within a few days a message was received that Ghailan wished to negotiate with the English envoy. Luke, anxious to pursue his investigations within Tangiers would be in no hurry to reply. He turned his attention back to the missing women, Gabriela and Takama—and revisited Catarina.

He was surprised as he entered the complex to see Commander Koubi leaving the premises. Luke's initial astonishment turned to concern. "What do those two have in common?" he pondered.

After being greeted warmly by Catarina, Luke could not resist asking, somewhat bluntly, "Why was Koubi here?"

"He came to accept my offer. One of my coastal traders is about to depart for Casablanca and I suggested that he and his men may find the sea trip quicker and more convenient than the ten to fourteen days riding through enemy territory. As I already have interests in Casablanca for me to assist servants of the most powerful man in that area could do me no harm."

A plausible, direct answer, but Luke's intuition was convinced that Catarina's reply concealed the real reasons for their meeting. Was Catarina to implement her growing alliance with the Sultan by orchestrating his takeover of the city, either now or before the English garrison was in place. The English fleet must return soon or it may be too late.

8

Luke changed focus. "Regarding Gabriela, have you heard anything more from the kidnapper?"

"Yes, she is alive and Takama has also returned. She was kidnapped and taken to Gabriela and was given a further letter from the abductors. It demands that I deposit one thousand silver ducats under a flagstone on a particular grave in the cemetery. On placing the silver there, I should find a further note telling me where to find Gabriela."

Luke was pleased. "The speed of the reply suggests that the kidnapper and Gabriela are within the city. Will you pay?"

Catarina smiled, "Not really! I will fill a calico bag with a couple of layers of coins on the top of some base metal. It should weigh the same amount as a full bag of a thousand silver coins."

"Too risky!" replied an alarmed Luke.

"I am relying on you to apprehend the kidnapper before any harm befalls Gabriela. I have already informed him that my representative, that is you, will deliver the ransom one hour after sunset tomorrow night."

"No, I will not be party to such dangerous behavior. Fill the bag with the promised amount, or my role in this enterprise is at an end! If you trick the kidnapper, you can expect him to go back on his word and kill Gabriela."

Catarina grudgingly agreed, but at the same time decided to take out extra cover. Without informing Luke, another of her agents would monitor the handover.

Luke asked to see Takama who eagerly described her own abduction.

"As I was completing my dressing to receive you, two masked men broke into my room and declared that if I wished to see Gabriela alive, I must accompany them. They blind folded me and placed me in a cart. After a short journey I was led from the cart into a room where my blindfold was removed. I saw and spoke to Gabriela and was given a letter from the leader of kidnappers to take to Catarina. Blindfolded once more I was released just near the southern gate."

"Did Gabriela look as if she had been abused?"

"Quite the contrary. She looked better than I have seen her for months."

After leaving Catarina, Luke visited the cemetery, found the relevant grave and flagstone. Lifting it revealed a large, buried metal container which could house quite large objects. On his way to the barracks, he dropped in on Roberto and brought him up to date on the latest developments. On mentioning the flagstone, Roberto who was holding a ceramic plate, uttered a cry of amazement and dropped the plate.

"What is it? asked an alarmed Luke.

"This is definitely an inside job. In addition to the points you made, that flagstone has been used for years by the local authorities for clandestine activities. Only senior officers in the administration know of its existence and use."

"Are you suggesting our kidnapper is Mario, Carlos, Miguel or Gil?"

"A possibility!"

"Why? What would be the motive?"

"Simple greed! None of them are wealthy and their imminent removal from Tangiers may place them in a difficult financial situation. A thousand silver ducats would greatly ease that embarrassment."

"Surely all of them could seek a loan from Catarina?"

"Not at the exorbitant rates she would charge," was the practical reply.

"Catarina is not a charity. I have over the years tried unsuccessfully to convince her that she should adopt a less ruthless attitude to business."

"Which of those four is the most likely?"

"Three of them would have strong motives and opportunity. Carlos is the least likely as I cannot see a motive other than money, and he seems a dedicated servant of the state. It depends also on whether Gabriela is an active and willing participant in the enterprise. With Miguel it may simply be a lover's plot to get some assets. Gil as a former lover may have had more complex motives—frighten Gabriela for deserting him and gain some benefit. If it is Mario, I would have fears for Gabriela's safety. As soon as he receives the silver she might die. In one blow he has immediate financial relief, and a longer-term benefit in his wife obtaining more of Catarina's inheritance."

"So, there are three very different scenarios with vastly different possibilities regarding Gabriela's fate. With Mario she may be killed, with Gil, frightened but probably released, and with Miguel she could be a willing participant."

"What do you intend to do?"

"Put all three men under surveillance."

"To what end? I doubt if any of them would personally collect the ransom. They will pay some pauper or criminal to do it. Your best chance of finding the culprit is further down the track when one of the suspects spends more than usual?" suggested Roberto.

"That will not happen in Tangiers. All three will soon be gone from here, and surely none of them would be foolish enough to start spending in the few months they have left here."

"Another possibility—if Catarina's ransom contained some unique coins any minor daily expenditure by them may provide us with a clue."

"It's a possibility. I will see Catarina immediately."

Luke explained to her the enhanced possibility of tracing the kidnappers if her ransom contained some unique coins. Catarina gave him a big smile. "Colonel, you are in luck. I have a unique set of coins.

My father was paid decades ago with the complete output of an Italian mint which was commissioned by the Spanish crown to produce silver coins to celebrate a victory over the Ottomans that never occurred. These coins to provide most of the ransom. If they begin to surface in Tangiers before we all leave, you may be able to trace their origins. Hopefully you will recover the ransom before the kidnapper has any chance to spend it."

Back at his barracks Luke briefed his men. "Tomorrow from dawn until midnight I want the deputy governor, the commander of the infantry and the police commandant under surveillance If you are asked by any inquisitive local authorities, you are acting under direct orders from the governor. With teams of six to eight we should be able to maintain a comprehensive surveillance. I want another team of six or seven to take up positions after dark tomorrow in the Portuguese cemetery adjacent to the local church. The kidnapper will expect that Catarina's agents will have the cemetery watched in a vain hope of catching the culprit as he collects the money. Arrest is not your aim. Do not reveal yourself unless you have a direct order from me. However, if any suspicious character appears in the vicinity of the collection point, follow him."

The early morning surveillance of Mario was immediately rewarded. He was seen giving a letter to one of his servants who immediately left the villa. One of Luke's men followed. Within minutes Mario and another servant rode out, headed for the southern exit from the city. Luke, after an excruciating delay in procuring horses, finally left in pursuit. Luke's steed was restless and difficult to control.

On leaving the city Luke lied to the soldiers guarding the gate. "I am supposed to be with the deputy governor. Which road did he take—that to the mountains, the southern agrarian areas or the eastern coastline?"

"The coast," was the reply.

On approaching the first village Luke was in luck. The road passed through a small forest and then led down a sharp incline into the village. He dismounted and from the security of the forest could see the whole of village below. The deputy governor entered a house and within minutes appeared on its roof in the company of a woman.

Luke grinned, and thought aloud, "Fortune has smiled on me. That woman is probably Gabriela, and Mario has come to organize her return to Tangiers for tonight's handover."

He stayed in the forest waiting for Mario to leave the village. He would then visit the house.

An hour later Luke was becoming frustrated. Mario and the woman on the roof had been joined by four other persons and appeared to be enjoying a mid-morning drink and eats. In his hurry to follow Mario, Luke had forgotten the required canteen of water. He was excruciatingly thirsty.

Another half an hour on, Luke's flagging spirits were revived. Mario left the building,

Luke changed his plan. He would confront Mario as he left the village hopefully with Gabriela. Any elation was short lived. There was no Gabriela and Mario expressed no surprise or alarm on confronting Luke.

"Getting to know the villages west of the city?" was Mario's opening remark.

"Yes," replied an embarrassed Luke.

"This is a fortuitous! I have just been talking about you with the local tribal hierarchy. The chief is absent, but his wife has heard a lot about you. She is Dona Takama's mother, Jamila—and born an Englishwoman. Come back to the village with me and I will introduce you!"

Luke could hardly conceal his disappointment. So much so that the possibilities created by a meeting with a tribal matriarch who happened to be mother of another suspect woman, seemed to elude him. After introductions Mario immediately departed and Luke soon found himself on the rooftop indulging in the drinks and nibbles which earlier had been lavished on the general. Both Luke and Jamila, speaking in their broad country accents quickly warmed to each other while several villagers joined the gathering. Despite the noise Luke commented, "I am amazed that you can still speak fluent English and have not lost your accent."

"That is why I taught Takama English, so that I would have someone to talk to. Takama speaks highly of you. I am sorry my husband, Majid, is not here. With the withdrawal of the Portuguese with whom this village and our surrounding neighbors have maintained an alliance for the past two centuries, our future will now depend in part on the English."

"Where is your husband?"

"He has gone into the mountains to assess whether our people should take over a village that the Portuguese recently demolished."

Luke was interested. Were the Portuguese arranging to repopulate the Ghailan village where Luke was nearly killed with more friendly tribesmen?

"Why would your people wish to expose themselves by being closer to your enemies—the supporters of Ghailan?"

"As a woman I am not privy to the discussions between my husband and the other tribal leaders, but the general feeling is that if the English do not establish their dominance beyond the city and support us, we will have to choose between the competing local rivals. The village that was destroyed controls a narrow pass into the mountains. If we controlled it, Ghailan and his supporters would be limited in their ability to constantly raid the lowland villages—and Tangiers."

"I will return in a few days to discuss such matters with your husband. We have a mutual interest in controlling Ghailan. Does he have any chance of obtaining one or more of the rings of Islam?"

Two of the fellow guests stopped in their tracks and glared disapprovingly at Jamila.

She saw their reaction and shouted at them in Arabic. To Luke it was clear that some of the gathering in addition to Jamila understood at least a few words of English.

Luke whispered, "I am sorry. I did not expect such an innocent question would cause you trouble."

"Our tribe has suffered over the years because of a false rumor that one or more of its elders knew the location of the fluorite mine from which the gems in the original rings were found. Several have been tortured in the past by both Moroccan and Portuguese authorities to reveal a secret they never had. The current controversy has reignited a fear that a similar period of persecution would occur—and on this issue we do not trust anyone. Takama was to update us on developments within the city regarding the missing emerald ring, but she has been silent for several days."

9

Luke was met at the barrack's main gate by one of his troopers. "Colonel, Captain Moon would like you to join him as soon as possible."

"And where is he, trooper?"

"Outside a house in a seedy part of the town. I will lead you there."

"Your unit followed Colonel Lopez to this unsavory destination?"

"Yes!"

"As an unmarried man he is probably visiting a lady of his choice. Why does Captain Moon think I should be present?"

"We ran into Lieutenant Pickford and his unit. They had followed Captain Serano to the same premises."

"Did Moon or Pickford express an opinion as to why the two Portuguese officers were both in the same house in a dissolute part of the town?"

"Captain Moon suggested that Lopez and Serano had jointly kidnapped Gabriela Sarmento with or without her approval and had hidden her in the house they were now visiting. He awaits your arrival before entering the premises."

"Did Serano have many of his men with him?"

"Not when I left to report to you, but I see almost fifty of them approaching the house as we speak."

Suddenly a few shots were heard and Serano's approaching men ran into the building.

Luke reached his officers, Jack and Greg. They jointly assessed the emerging situation and decided not to enter the building immediately, but await developments. There was much noise and eventually a dozen men were led away by the police. As Miguel and Gil left the building together, Luke pounced, "Can I be of any help?"

Miguel answered, "No, an embarrassing episode in which you were nearly a victim, is now under control."

"What happened and how was I involved?" asked an intrigued Luke.

"Come back into the house and we will explain," said Gil.

On entering a large room, Luke and Jack were overwhelmed by an over-powering odor. The room was littered with half-finished milky drinks and plates of what appeared to be a fudge covered in sesame seed. Miguel eagerly explained. "I have just dealt with a rogue element within my regiment. For some weeks a group of them went on unauthorized raids into mountain villages seeking loot and women. One of their number had second thoughts and informed me of what they were up to and where I could find the ringleaders."

Gil added, "They were part of the group that attacked you and the Sultan's men in the foothills."

"What motivated them to attack us?" asked Luke.

"You English may not recognize the smell in this room. It is cannabis. The men were high on drugs when they mutinied and have just spent several hours completely out of this world. Their favorite drink is bhang—crushed cannabis pods and leaves immersed in milk. The fudge-like sweet is a cannabis infused cake. The local Berbers have used cannabis, majpoun, medicinally for centuries. These men are now addicted to their own more highly concentrated product," explained Miguel.

"Why attack us?" reiterated Jack.

"The drug has a range of effects. They were probably hallucinating when they saw your men in discussion with those of the Sultan. I have no idea who or what they thought you were," answered Gil.

"What happens to them? asked Jack.

"They are subject to military law. I have already found them guilty of mutiny. They have been taken to the tower and should be executed," explained Miguel.

"Delay their execution! I need to question them further. We just arrested less than a dozen men. The group that attacked Tremayne was three times that size. Too many renegades remain within your ranks, Miguel. How could so many men engage in such activity without you being aware? You were specifically appointed here to bring discipline to the infantry and to remove this developing problem," declared a suddenly aggressive Gil.

"You clearly have failed."

Luke was surprised. Had the two former close friends fallen out? Did it have to do with military discipline or the missing Gabriela?

Miguel seemed distracted and hardly reacted to Gil's pointed attack. He limply responded, "With the return of my deputy, Major Dimas Vento, I will be able exert tighter control."

Luke asked, "Where do they get the cannabis?"

"A little is grown locally by the Berbers, but Tangiers has a major trade in the substance from sub- Saharan Africa. Someone in that trade must have illegally sold significant amounts to my men."

"Who controls that trade?" Luke probed.

"Dona Catarina—she imports the substance from the south and her ships take it to France, the Iberian Peninsula and beyond," answered Gil.

The English officers withdrew from the house and returned to their barracks.

"At least we now know that we were not attacked by Ghailan or the Spaniards," commented Jack as they left the premises.

"But being attacked by our so-called allies creates a much more concerning situation," said Luke.

Early that night Luke visited Catarina to collect the ransom he had promised to deliver. He asked her about the cannabis trade. "Some of your shipment was stolen and sold illegally within the city. Any idea as to who is responsible?"

Catarina smiled, "Colonel, you are clearly living up to your reputation. What led you to ask such a question?"

"If you answer my question, I will explain my interest," said Luke in a semi-jocular manner.

"I can tell you precisely. The thief or thieves of any cannabis can only be Takama or Gabriela or both."

Luke was surprised. "How can you be so certain. Such a trade is complex and there would be many aspects of it that could create an opportunity for theft."

"True, but my father in setting up the trade left nothing to chance. To the outside world the cannabis supply comes overland to Tangiers and is then shipped to Europe on one of my ships. It does not happen. As you surmise there would be too many opportunities for such a desirable import to go astray. For decades the cannabis has been collected by local traders from Senegal and Guinea and taken to Casablanca where it was transferred to my ships. Only a few of these cannabis laden vessels dock at Tangiers and those that do unload a miniscule amount for me. The rest of the cannabis remains on board under guard."

"You keep a small portion of the drug for yourself?"

"Not for myself, but to sell to regular customers for medicinal use, both within and without the city. It is a business in which I alone am involved. Somehow Takama or Gabriela came across my private store. I noticed over the last few months that some of it had gone missing. Takama may have taken some to supplement the supply needed by her Berber relatives for medicinal use. Local crops have been decimated by the current drought. Given Gabriela's reported behavior she may have taken and used some of it, or sold it on to her dissolute friends, simply to make money. It might explain some of her outrageous behavior."

Luke collected the ransom from Catarina and headed for the cemetery. As he approached it a figure emerged from the shadows. Luke tensed and drew his sword.

The figure whispered, "It's Jack. Our men are in place, but there is a problem. There are others hidden in the area. Either the kidnapper has a team of accomplices, or someone else is also looking after Catarina's interests."

He disappeared back into the shadows. Luke found the designated grave. He had a sense that indeed he was being watched. He slid the flagstone aside and as he was about to deposit the ransom into the metal box, he saw that it contained a short note which read in Portuguese, *Catarina has too many of her servants ready to pounce on me here. You are to proceed immediately back to barracks. You will be notified later where to drop the ransom. Inform no one!*

Luke rode through the darkened streets of Tangiers with the aid of an intermittent burst of moonlight and the occasional taper burning in the gardens of the more affluent citizens. As he approached the barracks located near the main southern gate the city four men dressed in Arab garb confronted him. Luke asked, "Do I hand the ransom to you?"

One of the men answered in unaccented Portuguese, suggesting that their garb was a disguise, "No, you will be blindfolded, and we will take you to the handover location."

Luke acquiesced and tried to keep his bearings, but without success. His only clue was that he did not hear the gate of the city being opened. He was lost.

Nevertheless, he eventually realized that he was outside the city as his steed picked up speed and appeared to enjoy its nighttime frolic along an essentially sandy road. Was he heading into the mountains, towards the coast or south into the farmlands?

After half an hour as far as Luke could ascertain, the leading abductor announced, "Dismount and hand me the ransom. I will check it to see that the devious Catarina has not tried to trick us."

Luke replied, "I cannot stop you taking the ramson but are there any guarantees that Gabriela is still alive? Where do I find her?"

There was a long silence as the box of ransom coins was removed from his saddlebag and his kidnappers made a quick assessment of the contents. Eventually their leader replied, "We will leave you here. In the morning proceed down this road to the nearest village. Gabriela will be at the second house on the left, just after dawn."

Luke heard his abductors ride off. He removed his blindfold and found himself in a forest. In the dark he could not ascertain whether it was the same wood he had traversed earlier in the day. Given the warmth of the evening, Luke propped himself against a tree and hoped to achieve some sleep before dawn.

With sunrise Luke realized he was in the same wood that he had visited less than twenty-four hours earlier, and as he emerged from it, he found himself on the edge of the village which contained the house of Takama's parents. He was not surprised that the house he had been told to visit to collect Gabriela was indeed the Khirri house.

A servant who answered the door asked if he was the man who was to collect a runaway girl. As they spoke a tall man with a short black beard and wearing flowing light blue robes intervened, "I am Takama's brother, Fadel. Both my parents are away. They offered to have a girl stay here until her parents were willing to collect her. Either you are not after this girl, or my parents have been lied to. The English colonel would not be involved with a runaway."

"No, my interest involves a much more serious crime. A girl was kidnapped, and I paid the ransom demanded last night. I was told to collect the ransomed girl here at dawn."

The tall Berber appeared perplexed, "Both of us have been tricked. The girl did not arrive this morning as promised, and I have received no explanation for it."

"Let us hope that she has only been delayed, —and not murdered," muttered Luke.

As they were speaking at the door two white robed horsemen arrived and immediately chatted in Arabic to the servant who immediately spoke to his master.

Fadel explained to Luke. "These men asked if this was the house where they were to deliver a girl. Apparently, they collected her just outside the city but when they reached the forest, she claimed she had to relieve herself and disappeared deeper into the bushes. She never re-emerged. These men searched for a while without any success and decided to come on here and inform us. I will put together a search party."

"Ask these men in what sort of mood was the girl?"

He did and one the men became very demonstrative, waving his arms around his head and then shaking it sagely.

"They thought she was a mad woman, or at least very high on majoun."

"Where did they collect this woman?"

Luke gained the impression that the men were reluctant to answer Fadel's question but the arrival of two other men of almost identical appearance as the brother seemed to change their mind. After a now heated exchange the men who had lost their charge confessed all and galloped off.

Luke was updated. "Those men are Berbers, but not from here. Their tribe provides a few of the musketeer mercenaries that man the southern wall of the city. We provide most of them. The woman came from within Tangiers and was collected from one of the defensive towers and brought here by two men who are stationed there. This whole operation appears to be the work of the Portuguese army, Colonel. I fear you cannot trust your allies?"

Luke, Fadel and his men began an immediate search of the small forest. Although the canopy of several varieties of oak, and the occasional cedar provided a dense tree top cover, the undergrowth was sparse. There was nowhere to hide. The search disturbed a few birds and surprised a family of European rabbits, and a couple of snakes that quickly slithered away.

There was no Gabriela.

As they completed their search on the eastern edge of forest a group of people approached on foot down the road from Tangiers. Fadel questioned them and quickly informed Luke. "These are some of our people who have been delivering their goods to the market in Tangiers. I asked them did they pass anybody on the road heading back to Tangiers. A demented woman galloped past them shouting and singing. By her dress they assumed she was a Portuguese noblewoman. Clearly a drug affected Gabriela has returned to Tangiers."

"Does she know what she is doing? Is she under the influence of drugs, or is it a giant hoax being acted out by a known prankster?" mused Luke.

10

An hour later Luke entered Dona Catarina's compound to confess that he had paid the ransom—but had failed to find Gabriela.

He was waiting in an antechamber when the door swung open, and Catarina burst into the room. She hugged him and smothered him in kisses murmuring, "One of Pimento's patrols found her just outside the city walls. I assumed that after you paid the ransom they released her. Thank you again.!"

"I cannot claim any credit for her recovery. I failed to rescue her. She escaped her captors and ran away," Luke confessed. "May I speak with her?"

"Not now. Her abductors kept her heavily drugged. When Carlos himself delivered her here an hour or so ago, she was heavily restrained. She was uncontrollably violent and alternatively screaming and singing the most inappropriate ditties."

"I'll return when the effects of the drug have worn off. We must discover every detail of her abduction," warned Luke.

Luke immediately visited Carlos. "Colonel, one of your patrols found a drugged Gabriela returning along the western road from the Atlantic coast. Do you have any information of other traffic on that road for the last twenty-four hours?"

"We do not patrol at night."

"That's a pity. I need to know who used that road between midnight last night and midday today."

"The cavalry does not patrol at night, but each morning I receive the overnight reports from the lookouts in each of the three towers that defend the southern wall. This morning I was concerned that the tower near the gate reported no suspect movements, but the two more westerly towers both reported the same disturbing incidents."

"Such as?"

"In the middle of the night a group of four soldiers from the most easterly tower, that next to the southern gate, escorted a hooded man out the city along the western road. An hour or so later the soldiers returned, and then a few hours later two more soldiers led a noisy woman back along the same road."

"Exactly as I thought," remarked Luke.

Luke explained to Carlos, "I was the hooded man being led to where the ransom for Gabriela was to be paid. They took the ransom, returned to the city and collected Gabriela to take her to the nearest village where the handover was to occur the next morning. In a highly disturbed state, she escaped her escort and returned towards the city where she was apprehended by your patrol."

"Do you realize what you are saying?" asked a concerned Carlos.

"Yes, that elements of the Portuguese army kidnapped Gabriela and are enjoying the proceeds of a ransom."

"More renegades! I thought Serano and Lopez had dealt with that problem."

"The involvement of the soldiers is only one of the issues, another is whether Gabriela was ever kidnapped? Maybe she willingly went along with a plan to exact money from her aunt? She may even have been the instigator."

"I will have Mario stand down the entire garrison in the southern tower. Most are Berber auxiliaries with a few Tangerine- born militia," declared Carlos. "Has Miguel been informed? They are his men."

"No, replied Luke.

"Why not?"

"If this is a Gabriela scam, her partner must have been a high-ranking infantry officer. Miguel was one of her lovers. I will come with you to see Mario," announced Luke.

Mario listened to Carlos's presentation with obvious irritation, which made Luke wonder if Gabriela's accomplice in any scam was her brother-in-law, Mario, and not her lover Miguel.

Mario rejected their request. "Gentlemen, I have no intention of weakening our defenses by standing down so many troops at a time when a Ghailan attack may be imminent. After all everything has ended well. Gabriela is safely back in the arms of her doting aunt. You have not heard Gabriela's account of her adventures and what you have suggested is entirely circumstantial. You have no evidence to involve Miguel in this fairytale. I will await Serano's report into the matter."

Luke was astounded. As far as he knew he alone was investigating the disappearance of Gabriela, not Serano. Catarina had double crossed him. A fuming Luke and an irritated Carlos left the deputy governor. "What is he hiding?" exclaimed Carlos.

"Agreed, a most unexpected reaction! I momentarily thought Mario might be involved, but on reflection if that was the case you would have thought it was in his interest that we continue to suspect Miguel. Can you take the issue to the Governor?"

"Only if you can make a case that it affects the handover of the city to the English. In a month or so the whole Portuguese military establishment will be gone. I doubt if Governor Almeida would wish to be involved."

"Then we must await my interrogation of Gabriela," Luke concluded.

"Not necessarily! Much of the infantry attached to this garrison is unreliable and drawn from several quarters and with very few professional Portuguese soldiers. Consequently, it was deemed necessary some time ago to place a few well-trained Portuguese within those units manning the walls to report any potential problems to the authorities."

"Who are for this purpose?"

"The governor, the deputy governor and myself. I will send for our two agents in the gate tower—the site from which the wayward troops and Gabriela appeared to have emerged."

Carlos was confident that his agents within the infantry establishment would have the answers, but this confidence was immediately destroyed. He asked the two men as he and Luke walked with them along the wall, "We are concerned with the activities of soldiers from this tower last night."

"I knew there was something strange about that special assignment," answered one of the men.

"The trip down the western road to the coast?" suggested Luke.

Both men looked puzzled.

"Nothing of the sort. We had orders in the middle of the night to take a unit from the gate tower to the harbor. We were to board a small merchant vessel and prevent it sailing until midday today."

"So both of you were away from the southern wall for twelve or more hours?" re-iterated Carlos.

"Yes, sir."

"From whom did the order to move to the harbor come?" asked Luke.

"I assume down the usual line of command."

"From Colonel Lopez?" emphasized Carlos.

"I don't know, but it is unusual for the lower level of command to initiate such a major re-deployment. It was either Colonel Lopez or General de Silva."

"This appears more serious than we thought," concluded Carlos. "We must involve Coval and perhaps the governor himself. Neither of us have the authority to act against a deputy governor or commander of the city's infantry."

Leo listened carefully to situation as described by Carlos and supported by Luke.

He rejected their interpretation outright. "Gentlemen there is not the slightest evidence that the security of the city was endangered by any of the acts you describe. The removal of a few troops from the gatehouse tower did not render that tower undermanned. Their redeployment at the harbor was requested by the ship's owner to ensure that the master paid the owner what was due to her."

Luke picked up on *her* and asked, "Is the owner Dona Catarina?"

"Yes," replied Leo. "What you gentlemen have described to me may be part of a criminal conspiracy but does not involve a threat to national security or threaten the transition of authority to the English. You have at this point no solid evidence to implicate either the deputy governor or the commander of the infantry. If you want to take it further, then the police commandant must be involved."

As an angry Carlos and Luke walked away from their interview with Leo the latter remarked, "From our point of view the possible involvement of Dona Catarina in the withdrawal of key troops from the gate tower adds another intriguing aspect to the situation."

"What should we do now? asked a dispirited Carlos.

"I will visit Catarina. I have to question Gabriela in any case. Maybe you should explain what we have just told Leo to the other direct representative of the Portuguese Queen, Father Antonio. He will agree with us."

Luke's intuition was incorrect. Antonio was even more strident than Leo in pouring cold water on the concerns put to him by Carlos. "Even if the deputy governor and the commander of the infantry are involved, it is not a matter that should concern the withdrawing Portuguese authorities. This is a family matter involving Dona Catarina, Takama and Gabriela—potential heirs struggling to gain an increased share of a large inheritance before they all disperse."

He then turned on Luke. "Carlos, you should not be taken in by Colonel Tremayne. He has a reputation for finding conspiracies and murderers where they do not always exist. Without concrete evidence, you have nothing against the senior officers of the administration. Desist from further investigation! —if you value your career."

Carlos was incandescent with rage but remained silent.

A frustrated Luke decided to test Catarina. He would put to her his most extreme fears and hope for an enlightening revelation.

"The abduction of Gabriela and the ransom demand are part of a family plot to deprive you of some assets. It probably involves members of the garrison's infantry, and I suspect your nephew by marriage, Mario; or the commander of the infantry Miguel Lopez."

"And Gabriela a willing accomplice in this endeavor?" asked Catarina to Luke's surprise.

"Most likely, but I have yet to question her. Has she had any visitors since her return?"

"Yes, and they would add some credence to your interpretation of events. Her visitors have been her sister Lidia and husband Mario, Colonel Miguel Lopez, Major Leo Coval and Captain Gil Serano."

Luke was surprised that Leo had visited, and he used the mention of Gil to ask a direct question, "Gil came to report to you, rather than give his best wishes to Gabriela. You took out insurance in the search for Gabriela by asking Gil to find her as well as myself?"

"Fortunate, because in a sense, both of you failed me. How do you know about Serano?"

"My men realized that others than themselves were staking out the cemetery, although I saw none of them in moving through the city with the ransom."

"No, you were followed for a short distance, but your abductors took you into the barracks associated with the infantry manning the gate tower, where Serano's men could not enter."

"Is Gabriela able to be questioned?"

"Yes, but she will not be co-operative. Serano got nowhere with his interrogation. She is clearly a troubled young woman. I have already taken steps for her future, and one option needs your assistance."

"And what is that?"

"Let her tell you, it might help break the ice."

Catarina led Luke into Gabriela's spacious bedroom and announced, "The English Colonel has come to see how he can help us plan your future."

Gabriela took some time to decide whether she would pretend to be asleep, or awake and willing to talk. Eventually she sat in up and indicated to Catarina that she should leave the room.

Catarina obliged, forcing Luke to comment, "Was that necessary. Your aunt is doing everything to help you."

Gabriela chuckled, "So she had pulled the wool over your eyes as well. I thought an Englishman would be immune to her charms, or should I say her trickery, if not treachery."

"Why such a view of your aunt?"

"She is about to leave Tangiers with all her riches and leave me penniless."

"She told me she had raised several options regarding your future, one of which involved me."

"All three involve me leaving Catarina, or rather Catarina getting rid of me."

"And what are these frightening options?" asked the unimpressed Luke.

"That I marry and immediately become the responsibility of my husband, that I enter a convent back in Portugal, or the one where your assistance might be helpful, that I become a lady-in-waiting to your new Queen. My aunt has already written to our Queen Regent for her to put my name to her daughter. However, she has been told that your King and not the Portuguese will appoint the ladies-in-waiting for his wife. According to Catarina if you could mention my name to him, it would assist my selection."

"Of these options which do you prefer?"

11

Gabriela did not answer. Luke pushed further. "I thought your marriage to Colonel Lopez was imminent. He is besotted with you."

Gabriela simply grimaced.

Eventually she spoke, "I will not enter a convent and I will marry later rather than sooner. A move to England with your Queen could be the new beginning that my aunt thinks is necessary."

"I will immediately write to His Majesty on your behalf—but only if you co-operate with me regarding your abduction."

"Resorting to blackmail!" declared Gabriela with an engaging smile. She continued, "I would love to assist but I cannot help you, colonel. My kidnappers fed me with so many drugged drinks and cakes that I remember absolutely nothing."

"Don't lie to me, young lady! Cannabis makes you very elated or very sad, but in the short term does not affect memory. If you are not responsible for your own abduction who is? Who are you protecting?"

Gabriela remained silent. Luke persisted, "You are protecting yourself. When Takama saw you, well into your abduction, you were not drugged. You are complicit in extorting money from your aunt, and your accomplice is either your lover Miguel, or your brother-in-law Mario."

Gabriela's relieved smile suggested to Luke that his interpretation was faulty—but he continued. "Unless they are going to look after you in the future, why protect them now?"

Gabriela suddenly went on the offensive. "And why are you bothering about an alleged criminal act within a Portuguese territory? You have no authority to investigate. Serano has already tried to coerce me into some sort of confession. Your enquiries are illegal and unnecessary."

"They are necessary in as far as your abduction is related to the security of the city. Your display of an emerald ring was seen by many as a threat to this security. I can act if I believe your activity in any way threatens the peaceful transfer of power and the safety of the city before such a transfer. Did you try to sell the emerald ring to Ghailan?"

This question unrelated to Luke's previous line of interrogation brought a chuckle from the wayward woman. "Your imagination is boundless, but it is an issue on which I can help you. I never had the real ring, and my use of a fake was a simple prank to annoy a lot of people. However, during my captivity, I discovered who has the real ring and what is intended to be done with it."

'You continue to lie. You told me earlier that you remember nothing of your abduction and now you claim that you remember who has the emerald ring. Do you really know, have you just heard rumors, or made the whole thing up? And why would you tell me?"

"It's up to you to determine whether what I know is truth or gossip. My motive is simple. During my disappearance, I was betrayed by one or more men I thought I could trust. Simple revenge is now my motive."

"Then tell me!"

"Not at this moment. I need a few more days to consider the situation, but if you ask Takama, everything might fall into place for you more quickly."

Gabriela fell back on her pillow and pretended to be asleep. The interview was over.

Luke discussed developments with his officers. Jack was skeptical of anything Gabriela might say. "She behaves like a child. Seeks attention and lies. The delay in revealing any names is probably to allow her time to blackmail the males concerned. Pay up or I will tell the English Colonel that you are a threat to their ultimate security."

The discussion was interrupted by the arrival of the police commandant, Gil Serano. "What brings you here, Captain?" asked Luke.

"Two matters Colonel! We need to work together as public officials and not act as private agents of Dona Catarina. Secondly the ransom money has appeared in the market."

"Already? The kidnappers must be idiots to spend their loot so soon, especially here in Tangiers. Smacks of real amateurs! Have you traced the source?" asked Luke.

"Two separate occurrences. A souk stall holder received the suspect coinage but his new assistant who took the money could only remember it was a well-dressed servant. When the stall holder saw the unusual coinage, he called in my men thinking that they were forgeries. I recognized it as part of the ransom money. The second incident involved a seller of fabrics who thought the buyer was the wife of one of the city's soldiers."

"Any further useful detail?"

"The souk stall owner said that the only servants of the wealthy that frequent his stall all came from the upper-class residences in the street near the church. And who lives in that area? —Dona Catarina, the deputy governor, and the Pimentos."

"I need to uncover the internal workings of Catarina's complex. Do Takama and Gabriela provision their own areas, or are all resources drawn from a central pool?" pondered Luke.

His plan to immediately follow this line of enquiry was put on hold by the arrival of Father Roberto who whispered, "Luke, another urgent message from the local warlord, Ghailan. He wishes to meet with you urgently to discuss England's attitude to him, and to help prevent any Portuguese attempt in the interim to damage your mutual interests."

"Not another long march into the mountains providing a target most of the way for renegades, Moroccan or Portuguese, to shoot at us?" replied Luke, only half-jokingly.

"No, we will follow a different path. It would be wise, given our experience if nobody, other than Captain Moon, knows where you are. You are paying a secret visit to Ghailan which must be kept from the Portuguese authorities. After you finish here come to the friary! I will provide you with a disguise. We must leave as soon as possible."

Roberto bowed to the gathered officers and departed.

"What was all that about?" asked Gil.

"He wants me to drop into the friary. He may have news relevant to our enquiries," was Luke's half- truth reply.

At the friary Luke was provided with a Franciscan habit. In Morocco, unlike most of the other countries Luke was aware of, this was an original dull grey rather than the more widespread brown. He was given a gleaming white cinture or girdle with three knots to symbolize poverty, chastity and obedience. Roberto spent the time with Luke as he changed, giving a brief outline of the order's history forcing Luke to comment, "Roberto, I am simply disguised as a Franciscan, I am not becoming one."

The two men left the friary. To Luke's surprise they did not head to the southern gate. They walked to the harbor with Luke's face almost completely covered by his cowl. At the far end of the harbor Roberto moved to a collection of the small boats lined up along the beach. He explained that several belonged to his order.

"A bit of exercise for you Luke! You will paddle along the harbor foreshore to the far end and then slip out into the ocean and head east to the next bay."

"Won't the Portuguese suspect something seeing two Franciscans leaving the harbor in a tiny canoe?" Luke asked.

"Not at all! Our regular missionary work along the coast almost as far as your old stamping ground of Benbali is undertaken in part by sea. It is quicker and less dangerous in these troubled times."

Luke faced the direction in which he was heading and took up the broad paddles Roberto sat facing in the same direction in a small craft that was a cross between a rowing boat and a canoe.

As they left the harbor Roberto turned to peruse it, and his faced clearly expressed consternation.

"What's the trouble Father?" asked Luke.

"It may be nothing, but there is a small fishing vessel that appears to be following us."

"Surely fishing vessels come and go all day in this area with its multitude of close fishing grounds?"

"No, Luke. Tangerine fishermen do not leave port at this time of day. Much earlier and much later, but not now. The tides are all wrong."

Luke followed the shoreline rather than risk the potentially dangerous waves, if he travelled directly from headland to headland.

As they reached the bay designated by Roberto, Luke was surprised to find anchored just offshore not the small skiff that he expected, but a medium sized well-armed galley that showed no identifying insignia.

Roberto addressed Luke's rising alarm. "No problem, the vessel is a galley that the Spaniards at Ceuta have loaned to Ghailan to harass the Portuguese."

"There has been no sight of it since I have been in Tangiers. It is much larger than the vessel that tried to eliminate me on my arrival," remarked Luke.

"Ghailan is probably not sure when the English fleet would appear. As it is his only naval weapon, he would not risk it."

They boarded the galley and after a short conversation with its captain, Roberto explained," We will sail further along the coast than usual which will cut the overland trek down by half."

As the galley put out to sea the fishing trawler that Roberto thought might be following them reappeared.

Roberto assured Luke, "A futile surveillance. This galley will very quickly outrun the lumbering trawler. They will have no idea where we disembark. This ship is continuing on to Ceuta to be reprovisioned."

After some time, a concerned shout from the lookout directed everyone's attention further out to sea. Bearing down on the small galley were two large war galleys. Without warning they opened fire on the smaller ship immediately de-masting it. The attackers boarded the ship without any resistance. Luke recognized them. He whispered to Roberto.

"These are my old friends from Benbali. They probably think this vessel is Spanish."

On the quarter deck of one of the war galleys Luke saw a familiar figure—the commander of the Benbali fleet, Admiral Hasan.

After a convivial reunion and much discussion Hasan allowed Luke and Roberto to land, before sailing away with the Ghailan galley in tow and its crew reassigned to the oars of the larger ships.

Roberto was depressed. "Luke, I do not think that Ghailan will view the loss of his only ship without somehow blaming us. In his eyes every failure is someone else's fault. Perhaps we should turn back and hope that we come across that fishing trawler somewhere along the coast to return us to Tangiers?"

"On the contrary, we may be able to use the existence of two anti-Ghailan warships along his coast to apply a bit of pressure. My friendship with Admiral Hasan can be exaggerated to suggest that Benbali may be ready to land troops to bring the whole area under Ottoman control. We can suggest to Ghailan that without English help his territories will be taken over either in the name of the Ottoman Empire or the Sultanate of Morocco. His future depends on England, even if he does not realize it," was Luke's optimistic assessment.

Roberto and Luke left the coastal plain passing through several small villages with stone houses perched on precarious peaks. As they continued to climb Luke caught glimpses of armed men in white robes placed in strategic positions. Roberto explained, "We are approaching the inner sanctum of Khadir Ghailan's domain. The village you see on the peak ahead of us contains what passes for a palace in these mountainous regions."

"Are those Ghailan's men in white?"

"Yes, all the tribes in the upper reaches of the mountains have traditionally distinguished themselves by wearing white. It is a perfect camouflage in winter. As you observed the Sultan's men from the south wore burgundy, and the lowland Berber tribes to the west of the city are resplendent in light blue. The only thing they all have in common is their use of very long barreled muskets."

12

They waited in a large reception hall that reminded Luke of castles in the north of England. The room was eventually flooded by an array of servants and armed soldiers led by a tall man exuding charisma and power. He was accompanied by an older bent-over woman. Roberto bowed. Khadir Ghailan spoke to him which was immediately translated for Luke.

"His Highness welcomes you and trusts he can initiate a lasting and fruitful alliance with the English. The woman with him is English born and is his interpreter."

Ghailan quickly outlined why he wanted a treaty with the English. "The Portuguese leave you with an empty shell which will destroy my people at the same time. They have moved most of their commercial assets to the west coast of Africa. That virago Dona Catarina has already set up her organization in Casablanca and has the Tangerine authorities convince my lowland neighbors to send their goods there and not Tangiers. The agents of the fake Sultan from the south have cut off the overland trade from Central Africa to Tangiers and redirected it to the Portuguese Atlantic ports."

Luke replied that the loss of his only naval vessel emphasized why Ghailan needed an English alliance. "That Benbali attack suggests that the Ottoman Turks aim to extend their influence into Morocco while local leadership is divided. One factor that can prevent this happening is the English fleet."

The ensuing negotiation was eventually disrupted by a senior official resplendent in a flowing white robe with a golden girdle. He excused his intrusion and spoke earnestly with his master. Ghailan turned to Luke and Roberto, "This is my vizier, Ibrahim Yedder. An unknown force has attacked my villages closest to Tangiers. I must strip this palace of most of its troops. Yedder will lead them to confront the enemy. They are currently being held back by a few loyal villagers taking advantage of the narrow passes. Without help they can only delay any advance. Gentlemen, follow this woman into the next chamber where a meal awaits you. I will rejoin you as soon as possible."

Luke enjoyed slices of what he thought was a highly spiced roast of lamb until Roberto pointed out to him that it was goat. His English prejudices against such food immediately took effect. Luke moved to a range of pastries. They were soon rejoined by Khadir.

Luke asked, "An unknown force has invaded your foothill villages. What do you mean *unknown forces*?"

"Early reports indicate that they are concealing their origins. They are dressed in a range of different colored robes."

"Surely their weaponry is a clue? —long barreled muskets of the Moroccans as opposed to the shorter barrels used by the Europeans. What do the intruders hope to gain?" probed Luke.

"If they are Moroccans opposed to me, it could be a strategic move to control the mountain passes and bottle my troops up in these mountains. If they are European renegade troops from Tangiers, it is a raiding party after resources and women. As they are about to leave, it may be their last hope to obtain some paltry assets. I hope Colonel that your English troops are better disciplined. Without their effective cavalry, and their Berber allies led by that traitor, Majid Khirri, I would have taken Tangiers years ago. Its infantry is a rabble."

"Possibly, but I was told that Your Excellency has failed to take Tangiers because you lack two essential weapons in your armory. You have no men or equipment capable of undermining the walls of the city, and you lack a navy that can penetrate the harbor," commented the undiplomatic Luke. "You need the English fleet to survive, let alone conquer!"

Before Khadir could respond the door of the chamber opened and servant rushed in and whispered to him. He commented, "I must leave you gentlemen once again. Enjoy the repast. A delegation has arrived to speak urgently to me. I must attend to them."

After Khadir's departure the older woman commented. "Colonel, it is good to hear a West Country voice after the three decades I have been here."

"Are there not many former Cornish or Devonian women here in the mountains? When I was in Benbali a large proportion of the women the local corsairs had abducted came from the English West Country," said Luke.

For a moment Luke's attention was diverted by the sound of not-too-distant gunfire.

The woman oblivious to the ominous sounds answered, "His Excellency, without a navy was never engaged in pirate activity, and most of his slaves come from rival Berber tribes or from darkest Africa."

Luke then heard what sounded like a large explosion very close by and the room shook. This was followed by intense gunfire. The door burst open and Khadir entered the room with a cohort of troops.

"Relax gentlemen! I have just foiled a coup," he explained.

Roberto noticed that Khadir's robes were splattered in blood. "Let me   look at your wound," he asked.

"No worry Father, my wounds are minor, and our women will dress them as soon as I have properly secured the building."

"What happened?" asked Luke, more concerned with what was occurring than in Khadir's state of health.

"A small delegation wished to speak to me. They claimed to be acting on behalf of Spain and wished to expand their contribution to my attempt to gain control of northern Morocco. I was immediately suspicious because unknown to this group, a delegation representing Spain from Ceuta and Oran, were here only a few days ago. During our discussion I received a message that our troops guarding the road from the coast that you used, that the small delegation that they let through was followed by a large company of troops that left the road and tried to conceal their presence as they progressed towards the palace. Fortunately, our local commander there informed the remnant of our garrison here and then closely followed the foreign troops. Between them my two forces ambushed the invaders in the courtyard of the palace. You heard the gunfire."

"What were you doing while this was happening," asked Luke.

"I had a few troops outside the reception hall, but only a couple in the room itself."

"How many men were in the so-called Spanish delegation?" asked Roberto.

"Four. As we discussed their proposals one of them suddenly threw a device into the brazier that was burning in the corner. There was a mighty explosion which given the thickness of the walls was probably limited to the hall. I was knocked out and remember nothing of what happened. My men filled in the details later."

"What did the invaders hope to achieve?" asked Luke.

"Apparently the explosion was a mistake. It was a signal for their troops which they believed were waiting outside the door to enter the chamber and arrest me and take over the palace. The device used was too heavily impregnated with gunpowder, and it was our troops that entered the chamber, not theirs. My men shot dead the one member of the delegation who was still on his feet attempting to stab my unconscious body. They arrested the other three after they had regained consciousness."

"Do you know who they were?"

"No. If you look out of this window, you can see them being taken across the courtyard to the dungeon."

Luke looked down on Khadir's troops manhandling three prisoners in the direction of the dungeons. He announced prosaically, "You may not know who these intruders are, but I do."

Khadir looked at Luke in amazement, or was it gentle amusement? "And who are our unwelcome guests?"

"Algerians! Whether they are acting alone or on behalf of the Ottoman Empire is an answer your interrogators should seek."

"How possibly could an English officer who has never been here before know that for certain?" asked Khadir.

"When I was English ambassador to the Islamic states of North Africa the government of Benbali, where I was based was being undermined by Algerian agents who wanted Benbali to unite with Algeria. Their plot was foiled, but Algeria sent a delegation to negotiate their way out of the aftermath. One of the men below was part of that delegation."

Later that evening Yedder reported back to Khadir as he ate with his senior officials, Luke and Roberto.

"Your Excellency the intruders have been repelled."

"Excellent work, Yedder!"

"To be honest they simply disintegrated and dispersed. They were not serious invaders."

"No, they were decoys to draw most of our garrison from here, to make the capture of this palace much easier," suggested Khadir.

Yedder looked perplexed and Khadir explained what had happened in the vizier's absence. The vizier commented, "At first I was certain of the identity of these decoys."

Khadir smiled, "They were Algerians."

"How could you know that?" asked an astonished Yedder.

"I ask you the same question?" teased Khadir.

"The Arabic dialect that some of the invaders used was Algerian or Tunisian."

"And our English colonel recognized one of the pretend delegations here as an Algerian," was Khadir's response.

Luke asked, "You said that at first you thought they were Algerian. Did you change your mind?"

"Yes, while there were clearly a number of Algerians scattered through the ranks of the invaders my thorough examination of several bodies, and the weaponry used, indicated that most of the men were

Portuguese soldiers from Tangiers, probably out to take cattle and women."

"Then how did these rogue Portuguese troops come to ally with Algerian agents at the precise time to act as effective decoys to the Algerian attack on the palace?" asked Luke.

Khadir smiled, "That Colonel is your problem rather than mine. A link between the Portuguese and Algerians should be of concern to you. I wonder what other surprises these rogue soldiers have in store for you before they leave?"

Yedder intervened, "Are they really rogue soldiers, or are they acting for elements within the Portuguese government? I suggest Tremayne that you will face a revolt by some Tangerines against their government's decision to hand the city over to you."

Luke felt increasingly uneasy. He intuitively agreed with the vizier.

Next morning Luke attended a session in the dungeons where Kadir and Yedder led the interrogation of the prisoners. It was evident that the three men had been heavily tortured. Red hot irons were clearly evident as an array of torturers gathered around the three inquisitors. Yedder was direct, "Why deny you are Algerians? Your decoy troops in the foothills spoke with an Algerian dialect, and you sir have been recognized by our visitor, the English colonel."

"The named individual just gazed at Yedder as if unaware of the question."

Khadir intervened "As enemies of the state and foreign invaders you will all die today. You have a choice. If you admit that you were acting on behalf of the Ottoman Empire to expand its frontiers into Morocco you may bathe, feast—and then be shot at sunset. If you do not, torture will continue until you eventually die in continual agonizing pain."

Luke was appalled at this barbaric approach but asked, "Whatever the answer regarding Ottoman involvement, the words of tortured Algerians would carry little weight. So why bother?"

"The truth is irrelevant. I will spread the word throughout Morocco that the Ottomans attacked my palace as a precursor to invading the whole country. That should rally many Moroccan Berbers to my cause. It would help if you endorsed this view of the situation to your government."

Luke was frank. "No! your Excellency. I will certainly report that a long-term enemy of English shipping, the Algerian corsairs were involved, but I will not implicate the Ottoman Empire. The Protestant nations of northern Europe including the Dutch Republic and England have an informal alliance with the Ottomans in that we have a mutual enemy, your ally. Spain."

Khadir changed the topic. "Colonel, is your visit to Tangiers short-term, or are you to be its first English governor?"

"I return to England as soon as the transfer of authority is achieved. Under the new Royalist administration, I am not of the social class from which governors are drawn. My role here is simple—to alert the King of any hitherto hidden problems involved in taking over the city. May I ask you a question?"

"Concerning what?"

13

"The three rings of Islam. Tangiers is agog with the prospect that you will obtain the three rings, and fearful that somebody in the city is willing to give or sell you the emerald ring which it once possessed."

Khadir smiled. "You really wish to know whether I am about to take possession of one or more of those rings, or whether the whole idea is one large propaganda lie. You would also like to know who my agent in Tangiers might be, and with whom he or she might be negotiating for the ring."

It was Luke's turn to smile. Khadir had an agent in Tangiers and he or she was negotiating with someone else in the city. Or was this all-false information generated by Khadir to confuse his enemies?

Luke was surprised by Khadir's next comment which revealed a little more of his nefarious activities. "If I do not to receive the emerald ring within the week, I will send you the names of my failed agent, and the Tangerine traitor. In this critical period there is no time for delay. It equates with failure. If I cannot unite the Berber tribes of the north in the next few weeks the religious fanatics from Fez, or the imposter from the south will be upon us. All will be lost."

"I doubt if the so-called Tangerine traitor would see it that way. The Portuguese establishment in the city has nothing to lose. Selling you the ring is not an anti-Portuguese act. It is aimed at us. In the end the united Berbers of the north will be confronting the English, not the Portuguese," commented Luke philosophically.

"Are these the matters you will report to your government?"

"Among others. You have been an irritant to Tangiers for years. Why have you not requested Spanish aid in the form of military engineers to undermine the city walls which is the major obstacle to your success?"

"I have, but Spain was not greatly concerned with Portuguese control of Tangiers. The Portuguese have no concerns in the Mediterranean whereas Spain has vital interests. After centuries of fighting Islam, Spain would not help a Moslem leader topple a Catholic city. However, in the last half century Spain has added to their anti-Islamic campaign an equally determined opposition to international Protestantism. Therefore, with Tangiers under Protestant English control, I anticipate they will more readily grant my requests. To assist their Islamic and Protestant enemies destroy each other would be a brilliant move."

"But England and Spain are now allies," commented Luke.

"Theoretically, but England by the King's recent marriage treaty is committed to defend the Portuguese from Spanish aggression. Your fleet remains in local waters for that very purpose," replied Khadir. "You are also to send 3000 troops to Portugal to fight the Spaniards—hardly the actions of an ally."

Although Luke agreed with this assessment, he said nothing and reverted to a previous subject." Have you had earlier experience of Portuguese troops aligning themselves with other groups to attack you?"

"No, for years Portuguese troops, initially officially, regularly invaded our lands to increase their assets and indulge their lust. Since your arrival so-called groups of rogue soldiers have defied vague orders to desist."

"I am aware that the Portuguese infantry is in disarray. Without the cavalry and the lowland Berber militia, you could walk in tomorrow."

"Unfortunately, my time is running out. I received a report overnight that the returning English fleet is now approaching Tangiers. Once it arrives, my chances of prevailing become more limited."

"Unless it is your ally! emphasized Luke.

Khadir's information was correct. As Father Roberto and Luke descended out of the hills and approached Tangiers, the seaward horizon was dominated by a hundred English man-of-war. The fleet had already divided. Further out to sea, part of the fleet under the Earl of Sandwich, was sailing on to Lisbon to protect Portuguese trade and eventually take the Infanta to London to marry the English King.

The vanguard of the remaining fleet was already entering Tangiers's harbor but given the port's small size and lack of facilities, most of the fleet dropped anchor in the adjoining bay.

Next morning Luke and Jack boarded the English flagship. Luke explained the local situation as he saw it, emphasizing the untrustworthiness of the local infantry. Vice-admiral Lawson acceded to Luke's request that the largest force possible of English troops be landed in the city and that the guns of the ships be continually directed against key city landmarks. It was to make clear that while Portugal retained sovereignty for a few more weeks, the real power now rested with the English.

Luke was delighted that the English fleet could raise over 300 men into two large companies. The soldiers garrisoned on each ship were supplemented with many sailors who had had military experience in the civil war and whose naval skills were not required while the fleet was in harbor. Luke was to exercise overall command and the two new companies formed would be led by Jack Moon and Greg Pickford. After leaving the flagship Luke informed the Portuguese authorities of the increased English military presence. Should the rogue local infantry raise its head, Luke was ready with the local cavalry, to decapitate it.

Later that day Moon and Pickford marched through the city with their newly raised troops to emphasize this English presence. After the march Luke discussed with his officers their immediate priorities. "Following my discussion with Khadir Ghailan our immediate priorities have become clearer. We need to identify within the Tangerine establishment our clandestine enemies. Who among our so-called friends and allies is willing to sell the Islamic emerald ring to Khadir? Who is Khadir's agent? Who has been secretly supporting Algerian or

Ottoman interests in the city? Who, if anybody in authority, controls the rogue elements in the army? How reliable are the lowland Berber, the anti-Khadir tribes, as our allies, and do they have a secret supporter of influence in the city?"

The discussion was interrupted by the arrival of Father Roberto in a highly agitated frame of mind. "What is it Father?' asked Luke.

"An attempted murder, and the would-be victim is beside herself and sought sanctuary in our friary. I gave her a sedative last night and she has yet to awaken. I would like you to be present when I question her."

"Takama or Gabriela?" asked Jack.

"Neither, it is Dona Catarina," announced Roberto.

"And her whereabouts must be kept secret. The failed murderer may try again if he or she can find her ladyship."

Four hours later Catarina had awakened and eaten. She was eager to reveal all to Roberto and Luke. Luke observed that the normally self-assured woman was still shaken.

Roberto asked, "What exactly happened?"

"As is my norm I was to have the midday meal on my rooftop garden. When I climbed the stairs and sat at the table, I was not surprised that everything was laid out before me. But my personal valet who usually serves me was absent. I poured myself a red wine from the carafe provided, while I waited for Angelo to arrive and serve the meal. I accidently knocked over my goblet of wine and some of it ran into in a slight depression in the floor. My dog lapped it up and almost immediately convulsed, frothed at the mouth and died. I called for Angelo and when he did not come, I ran down the stairs to find him. I did. He lay on the kitchen floor."

"Was he dead?" asked Luke.

"I don't know. I immediately went in search of the other kitchen servants who should have been there. I saw them at the main gate haggling with suppliers over the provision of fruit and vegetables. I had almost reached them when a shot rang out. It hit the dust just in front of me. An attempt to poison me followed by a shooting was too much.

I probably had some sort of temporary breakdown. I knew I had to go into hiding. I remember coming here, but not much else until I awoke a short time ago."

Roberto commented, "I sent a message to Dona Catarina's complex informing those present that her ladyship was safe, but not well enough to return. It was delivered by a man who could not be linked with us in the friary."

Luke commented, "For the time being you must stay here. I will go straight to your villa and question the staff. When it is safe for you to return, I will have you guarded by a detachment of English troops that have just disembarked from our fleet, which now dominates the harbor."

"Thank you, Luke! Yes, it best that nobody, not even my relatives know where I am."

Luke muttered to himself, "Especially relatives!"

Next morning Luke arrived alone at the Sarmento complex. As he entered, he was mobbed by dozens of servants who seemed to be under the impression that the English had kidnapped their mistress. Gabriela appeared accompanied by a man Luke had previously only seen at a distance. He introduced himself as Aristotle da Gama, Catarina's steward.

"Where is her ladyship? he asked.

Luke replied, "That is not the most important question. I am here to ascertain who tried to kill her ladyship twice around midday yesterday. She has put herself under English protection until she feels it is safe to return. Co-operate with my investigation and all will proceed as normal. If I find opposition or reluctance, my troops will occupy this complex, and the uncooperative will find themselves in the brig of one of our warships. My first question is on behalf of her ladyship. What is the condition of her valet, Angelo?"

Aristotle was astounded. "I had no idea that her ladyship had escaped poisoning and a shooting. My assumption was that the dog had been poisoned to stop it alerting anybody to her ladyship's kidnapping. The overturned goblet I put down to some struggle during the kidnapping."

Gabriela replied to Luke's question. "He is abed, recovering from a massive blow on the head."

Aristotle added, "I tried to question him yesterday when he first regained consciousness, but his memory had not returned. He is very confused about events. I will take you to him." Luke and Aristotle entered a bedchamber where they confronted a figure with a massively bandaged head and a very small woman sitting beside the bed holding the victim's hand.

"This is Jacinta, Angelo's wife who works in the kitchen," said Aristotle. He turned to her and announced, "This gentleman is Colonel Tremayne, the English envoy. Her ladyship has sought his protection until she feels safe to return. He wishes to question you."

"Was her ladyship harmed?" asked Angelo.

"Not physically, but the double assault on her within the sanctuary of her own home has left her very shaken. What do you remember of the events leading up to the attack on you?"

"I set out the midday meal on the roof garden. The edibles were laid out on various platters with I had covered with napkins. I provided two carafes of wine ready to pour on the arrival of the mistress. Just before she was about to arrive, I was called downstairs. I did not respond immediately as I expected her ladyship to arrive at any moment. When this did not occur, I finally walked down the outside stairs. I reached the entrance to the now deserted kitchen and I was hit from behind. My next memory was waking up here. I was unconscious for almost a day."

"Why were you called downstairs?"

Jacinta spoke, "I can answer that. Just after Angelo went upstairs the housekeeper arrived and called the head cook and most of the kitchen hands to leave what they were doing and move to the main gate."

"Was this usual?"

"Not at all. When I was the only one left in the kitchen, I called Angelo down. When he didn't come, I joined the others at the gate"

"Why were most of the staff called to the main gate?"

14

"Most of our regular suppliers appeared there to sell and deliver their produce," said Jacinta.

"Is that usual?"

"Highly irregular. Normally one or two of the staff visit particular stalls in the souk at a prearranged time during the week to inspect and purchase what the villa needs."

"Why did the suppliers all arrive together around midday?"

"They claimed they had all received a note from the mistress saying that their goods were urgently needed, and if they could oblige by delivering around midday yesterday, they would receive a bonus."

"No one here knew anything about the note. Did the mistress send it?" asked Angelo.

"I suspect not," replied Luke.

"Certainly not!" added Aristotle. "Her ladyship is never involved in such mundane matters. These were left to the housekeeper and me."

"After your people negotiated with the suppliers, did any of the latter accompany them back into the villa?"

"Yes, several! Most of them carried the goods that we had purchased to the kitchen and pantry," replied Jacinta.

"So, one of these outsiders could have been in a position to hit Angelo, and poison the wine before her ladyship arrived on the roof garden?"

"But most unlikely. Most of the staff returned to the kitchen area with the suppliers. I doubt if any of them were wandering around unattended," replied Aristotle.

"Can I see the body of the dog? I would like to get some idea of the poison used."

"No. Egipcio was buried almost immediately."

"That's a strange name for a dog. What breed was it?"

"It was a local breed known as a Sloughi. Very similar to your English greyhound. It originated in ancient Egypt, thus the name," responded Aristotle.

A new concern raised its head and Luke asked with some urgency, "What happened to the carafes or decanters from which Catarina poured her wine?"

'With no knowledge of any poisoning they were returned to the cellar by the servants who cleaned up the roof garden," answered Jacinta. "I was one of them."

"Can they be easily retrieved? It is possible the poison was introduced to them and not to the goblet."

"Yes, I know which ones they are. Take me to the cellar and I will find them. If they are poisoned, the whole villa could be in danger," said a now very worried Angelo.

Deep in the cellar, Luke sniffed at the contents of the two recovered decanters. "It is none of the usual poisons that I can identify by smell."

"There are many poisons obtained from darkest Africa of which we Europeans have little knowledge," explained Aristotle.

"I will get some experts to examine the contents. They may come up with an answer."

"There is a quicker way," said Angelo. "Let an animal sip up the wine as did Egipcio."

"What animals did you propose to sacrifice to this task? asked an alarmed Aristotle.

"None of value, and if it is poison it may help remove some of the vermin that have overrun part of this cellar—rats. Several saucers of wine can be placed along the tunnels into which this cellar extends—red wine in one and white in the other."

Luke expressed the opinion that given Catarina's account of Egipcio's demise, the death of any rats should be almost immediately after drinking. Luke, Angelo and three other servants spread out around this subterranean labyrinth and watched. Within a quarter hour there were six dead rats, all had drunk the red wine. The white wine was consumed by dozens of rodents with no ill effects. The red wine carafe had been poisoned.

Luke asked Angelo, "Is the cellar locked? Who has access?"

Angelo was aware of the significance of this latest development. "Many in the household have access to the cellar. The critical question is who would know which carafes are used by her ladyship? And who would be so callous as to endanger the lives of the whole complex?"

"Only someone who has dined at Dona Catarina's table or yourself, my love," muttered a concerned Jacinta.

Luke assessed the situation and concluded, "This attempted poisoning of her ladyship may have less to do with the supplier's turning up at midday than I thought. A family member may be responsible, creating those supplier activities simply as decoys. I must turn this investigation over to Captain Serano."

Later that day Luke accompanied by Aristotle talked to the chief of police. "I will co-operate with you in every way, but Catarina's location must remain a secret—until you find who tried to kill her," commented Luke.

After they left Serano, Luke asked, "Where is Takama? Why is she absent in this time of crisis confronting her companion and employer?"

"By now she is in southern Morocco. I put her on the first ship available heading south after the trauma of her abduction."

"Why have the authorities been kept in the dark? Is the mission concerned with Catarina's commercial empire, or with the political disposal of one of the Islamic rings?" asked Luke provocatively. Without waiting for an answer, he continued, "Who would have benefitted most if Catarina had died?"

Aristotle smiled. "A most pertinent change of focus! Forget Takama's mission! Concentrate on the attempt on Catarina's life. Who benefitted most depends on which of two wills is current? What I can reveal which is pertinent to your investigation is that for months she has been discussing with me revisions to her will. All the landed property in Portugal that was controlled by her late husband reverts to a distant male great nephew. Her ladyship's immense wealth here derives from the commercial enterprises of her late father which she has expanded greatly. This was to be split three ways. Her nieces were to receive a third each, and the remaining third is split evenly between Dona Takama, myself and other employees."

"And the proposed changes?"

"Denying any inheritance to her nieces."

"Did either of them know of this potential change?"

"They have been warned for several months that their aunt was not happy with their behavior and that a variation in their inheritance would be the likely consequence of such activities."

"I can see her reasons for this regarding Gabriela, but surely her older sister has not stepped out of line?"

"No, not directly—but her husband has. Our deputy governor has upset and irritated her ladyship on two fronts. He has argued to her face that all the inheritance should go to her eldest living relative, his wife, thereby depriving Gabriela, Takama and myself of everything. When this failed, he asked for an immediate advance of thousands of ducats to help him and his wife to adjust to life after Tangiers."

"Which will do you think is current?"

"I don't know. I drew up the new will some weeks ago, but I do not know if Catarina has had it witnessed, thereby making it the valid will.

Luke thanked Aristotle for this crucial information, but he was immediately suspicious. Changes to the will cast suspicion on the nieces, but at the same time appeared to free Aristotle and Takama. They would gain more if Catarina lived to alter the will, but what if it had already been changed?

Luke returned to the friary to update Catarina on developments, and to question her further. She was not surprised that Luke now suspected a family member or a recent recipient of her hospitality for tampering with the decanters, rather than someone associated with the midday visit of the villa's providers.

"I hope it is not family or friends. Blood is thicker than water. Let's hope it was a servant who has been bribed by one of my personal or more likely commercial enemies." Luke tried to catch Catarina off guard. "I may be mistaken in concentrating on the beneficiaries of your inheritance. Is the area of contention more immediate and more political? Are you trying to sell the Islamic ring to the highest bidder? Is that why Dona Takama is in Casablanca and elsewhere in the south? Is she selling it to the emerging Sultan based near Marrakesh to forestall the ambitions of local warlord Khadir?"

Catarina laughed. "For once colonel you are absolutely wrong. I am not trying to sell the ring. I am trying to buy it."

Luke was surprised. Such a possibility had never entered his head. "With any success?" he limply added.

"Not up to the present. The seller's go-between is different at every meeting. They tell my agent that rival bidders have increased their offer, would I do the same? Your wild imagination has hit upon one element of fact. Takama is in southern Morocco to ascertain whether the Sultan would assist us to buy the ring."

"Why didn't you tell me Takama had left Tangiers?

"I was not sure. Aristotle simply implemented a pre-arranged agreement to get Takama to the south as soon as possible."

"I know Khadir has an agent in the city who is negotiating with the current owner. Do you know who the owner and Khadir's agent might be?" probed Luke.

"I do not know who has the ring. I have pondered that question for years. All my suspects have long left the city. Khadir's agent could be a member of our military, political or religious establishment. My own nephew in-law, the city's deputy governor is very short of money. He is desperate to create some assets before he leaves. He will not have to confront a more powerful ring-possessing warlord. Any consequence from this sale of the ring to Khadir or the Sultan will be felt by the English."

Luke immediately confronted the deputy governor.

"What can I do for you colonel?" was Mario's opening remarks.

"Since my arrival I have adhered to the fundamental principal that until formal transfer is made, you continue to be the only government of the city. My role is simply to observe and try to ensure that any changes that occur in the city before the transfer do not negatively affect our takeover."

"And now you have observed such a detrimental change?"

"Yes."

Mario smiled, "Or is your visit due to the arrival of the English fleet. You now have at your disposal the most powerful coercive force in the area. What is the alleged anti-English activity you wish to highlight?"

"The frenzied activity within the city to buy and sell the emerald Islamic ring and eventually sell it on to the highest Moroccan bidder— the consequences of which will have to be faced by us and not you."

"And you think a senior Portuguese official, unhappy with the transfer, is determined to make it difficult for you?"

"Not necessarily a deliberate anti- English action—more simply greed or need. Many of you will face a financial loss when you are forced to leave Tangiers. And according to rumor, you are one of most seriously disadvantaged by the move."

"Rubbish! My wife is the heir to the wealthiest woman in the city."

"That is a most misleading statement. Your wife may be in line to inherit the small amount of property owned by her late uncle, Dona Catarina's husband, but the latter's wealth is derived from her commercial properties whose future will be determined by the vagaries of her will. My information is that this is about to be changed. The recent attack on her could have been an attempt either to stop her changing her will, or to seize the benefits of that change."

"More rumor! Why would Catarina change her will? I understand that half of the business would be left to my wife, a quarter to her sister Gabriela and the remainder in small amounts to Dona Takama, Aristotle and various charities."

Luke decided to be diplomatic and not focus on the possible dilemma confronting Mario over the nature of Catarina's new will. "Given her behavior, hasn't Catarina threatened to reduce Gabriela's inheritance?"

"You don't think my sister-in- law is behind the attack on Catarina?"

"She has everything to gain, especially if she was to lose everything in a revised will."

"Colonel, you seem to be confusing two separate issues—the attack on Catarina and the sale of the ring. While it is clear that Gabriela, and for the same reason myself, could be agitated over a proposed change of will, neither of us have the money to buy the ring."

15

"Agreed, but Gabriela and yourself, given the lack of ready funds, may be acting as the paid agent of another. Someone in your circle is Khadir's agent whose identity if he or she does not deliver the ring quickly, will soon be revealed to me."

Luke scrutinized Mario's reaction to this comment. There was none. Perhaps he was not the agent.

Mario commented, "That is typical of Khadir—betrayal, double crossing, denial, lies, feigned friendship and meaningless alliances. My advice to you, Tremayne, is that you treat Khadir as a permanent enemy. Ignore any advances he makes and ally yourself with his opponents!"

"Who would you suspect as Khadir's agent?"

"Miguel Lopez."

Luke expressed surprise. "He was one of the last on my list, giving his lack of opportunity to talk to Khadir. You are often outside the city, as military commandant, but I assumed Miguel's duties confined him to the city."

Mario laughed. "He has fooled you, but I have been aware for some time that he has created a cover for his illegitimate activities. The so-called rogue soldiers that break discipline and raid Khadir and other local territories for women and loot are no such rebels. They are a private army that Lopez has created within his largely undisciplined troops. His enforcer is master sergeant Bruno Costa—probably the most dangerous man in Tangiers."

"Why create such a clandestine group?"

"Simple! To maximize their accumulation of assets before they leave. The infantry is the most impoverished group within the city. It has been the only occupation available in the city for its poor and untrained."

"Do you have equally clear views as who has the ring, and is willing to sell it?"

"No, but I can share with you a piece of information that few have. When it disappeared from the church a decade or more ago there were several suspects. A month or so ago Father Diego, prior of the Dominican friary and representative of the Inquisition in the city came to see me. He confessed that the Inquisition had confiscated the ring as part of its concern for the security of the city. The ring was recently stolen from them and one of the key agents in the city trying to buy it back is the Inquisition."

"Thank you, Mario! That is indeed useful information."

"I am that agent trying to buy the ring—but as a representative of the Inquisition, not Khadir."

"Does the Inquisitor know who stole it?"

"Yes, but his views have to be taken with a grain of salt. He hates Moslems, conversos, Jews and anybody descending from such types. He hates Dona Catarina. He suspects someone in her pay stole the item and that through Takama, she is negotiating its sale to the emergent Sultan."

"You do not believe this?"

"No, the seller is still within the city and seeking the best price. If Catarina, had it, Takama would have already put it into the hands of the Sultan."

"How exactly is this sale being conducted?"

"Through an agent several times removed from the real seller. He meets the representatives of the buyers once a week on the edge of the slave market. I send one of my servants there to inform the seller's agent of my latest offer on behalf of the Inquisition. This agent receives all the offers and on the following week returns the seller's decision. So far there has been a continual escalation in the asked-for price."

Luke had an idea. He asked, "And what is the current asking price?"

Luke's thought that the English should put in a bid of their own was immediately scuttled. The current asking price for the ring was probably ten times more than the financially embattled English monarchy would be prepared to pay, —and well beyond the assets of its agents on the spot.

He then asked, "Have you had the seller's agent followed?"

"On several occasions. It is a different person at each meeting— usually local traders. The seller's network is constantly changing and is well concealed."

Luke returned to his earlier focus. "If Gabriela or you are not responsible for the attack on Catarina to prevent a change of will, who is behind the attempted murder?"

"My aunt has created many enemies over her years of trading in the city. Maybe someone with an old grievance seeks revenge before she leaves the city. The transferring of her assets and activities to Casablanca has infuriated many locals. Her ruthless methods over the decades have destroyed many a family."

Luke was not convinced by Mario. The former remained wedded to the probability that the attack on Catarina was by close family— most likely Mario or Gabriela and not by hardly done commercial rivals.

Luke decided to question the Inquisitor, but Jack protested. "He won't see you; you have no authority to interrogate him, and even if a meeting occurs, why would he want to help you in any way? The only way to deal with that cleric is to abduct him and keep him on one of our ships until he talks."

"If only! I am not authorized to provoke our new ally Spain or embarrass Portugal. I will ask Father Antonio to make the initial approach."

Antonio informed Luke two days later that Father Diego would be delighted to meet him. They had apparently met before. This last fact intrigued Luke as he mounted the steps to the Dominican friary. He could not recall any earlier meeting.

Ushered into the inquisitor's library, Luke was greeted by a tonsured priest in a white habit who said, "You obviously do not recall our earlier meeting, Colonel. You were then a general and English ambassador to the North African cities."

Luke now recognized the priest. "And you were the Inquisitor in the Spanish enclave of Oran when I made a visit there on behalf of England, and the Islamic state of Benbali."

"Yes, you and the Spanish governor there knew each other. How can I help you now, especially as our countries are at peace? Not that I can help you much concerning recent events. I have just returned from six months in Rome, Lisbon and Madrid. While I could not miss the English fleet, I was unaware of your presence here, until Father Antonio enlightened me."

"My role as special envoy is to ensure nothing occurs in the months leading to the transition that will endanger the English position."

"I would have thought the presence of that large war fleet guarantees your position."

"Not completely. My main concern is the state of the Moslem tribes that surround the city. If anyone of their local leaders can unite most of the tribes, they will be a major danger to our occupation."

"How do we Dominicans fit into this concern?"

"The emerald ring was in your custody for decades and is now on the market for the highest bidder."

"We rescued it during the brief period of trouble when Tangiers declared for Portugal and not Spain for the very same reasons that you wish to recover it—prevent it falling into the hands of Ghailan and his ilk."

"When did it disappear?"

"Just after I left on my trip. It had been concealed under the altar in our chapel."

"Who knew it was there?"

"Some of the friars who were here when the rescue occurred. They were all Spaniards like me. Most of our friars are now Portuguese born."

"You are not suggesting that your fellow countrymen may having stolen the ring and put it on the market to thwart the Portuguese decision to hand the city over to us heretics?"

"No, their obsessive concern is to be relocated within Spanish controlled territory, but over the years they have probably talked to our recruits and supportive laity."

"Who include?"

"Most of the establishment, but our outstanding defenders and donors are the deputy governor, Mario de Silva and Aristotle da Gama, Dona Catarina's steward."

"Should I treat them as suspects?

"No, unless you have evidence that I am not aware of."

"Only possible motives. It is common gossip that Mario is short of funds and has no clear future once the transfer takes place."

"Surely Dona Catarina will look after her nephew by marriage?"

"Not if she believes he is behind the attempt on her life."

"Any attempt on Catarina's life is motivated by racial and commercial tensions, not personal feuds within her family," Diego revealed. "She has converso ancestry and secretly supports the clandestine Jewish community within Tangiers and Morocco in general. Her commercial ethics leave much to be desired and there are many within the city who feel aggrieved and taken down by their financial encounters with her and her unscrupulous manager, the brilliant, but manipulative Aristotle da Gama."

"And what are you doing about the theft of the ring?"

"Absolutely nothing, except bid for its recovery until we leave. The Dominican mission in the city ends in less than a fortnight as will my position as an agent of the Inquisition. During my trip away I negotiated the future of my brothers who would not be tolerated by your Protestant government. The Portuguese born friars will relocate somewhere in Brazil, the Spaniards to the enclave of Ceuta. I will return to the mother house of the Dominicans in the Spanish province of the order in Madrid. We will all leave Tangiers in exactly twelve days from now. We then become completely irrelevant to your mission."

Conditions for Catarina, settled in protective custody within the English barracks, improved when Luke agreed to the arrival of several of her servants. She also continued to run her enterprises through daily missives to Aristotle, delivered by Luke's men.

Luke's own investigation into the source of the ransom coins that had begun to circulate, led nowhere. They had gone through several hands before they were discovered, and the more recent owners had no idea where they had been obtained.

A few mornings later Takama surprisingly appeared at the barracks wishing to see Catarina. Luke was blunt. "Have I been lied too again? I was told you were in Casablanca."

"I was, but returned on the first available ship with urgent news for my mistress. I would like to report to her in person on my brief visit south."

Luke took her to Catarina. He left the two women alone with each other but with two guards at the door. After half an hour of discussion the women asked him to join them.

Catarina spoke, "Takama has returned unexpectedly from southern Morocco with alarming news, verified locally by her own father. As a result, I will leave Tangiers immediately, but want my departure to remain a secret as long as possible. The ship that brought Takama back from Casablanca will return there the day after tomorrow. I need to board it without being recognized. Only Aristotle and Takama should know that I am no longer in Tangiers. My absence may help you capture my would-be killer."

"What has Takama revealed that has determined this decision?" asked Luke.

"Elements in the Portuguese administration are planning a coup with the aid of the populace to turn Tangiers into a city state. This would be a danger in itself, but several Moroccan elements are preparing to attack the city when this occurs. That is when Tangiers will be at its weakest. The one inhibiting factor at the moment is the English fleet. If it leaves port to protect the Portuguese sugar fleet, or to attack the Spanish treasure ships, one or more Moroccan factions will strike," explained Takama.

"Colonel, you must ensure that the English fleet does not leave port until your full garrison arrives. The moment it leaves port, Moroccan elements will attack the city with considerable internal support," reiterated Catarina.

"That is most unlikely. The part of the fleet that is now in Lisbon is tasked with the defense of Portuguese trade, the fleet here will remain until the garrison arrives."

Luke changed the focus of his discussion with Catarina. "Were you not in favor of the city state solution? When did you change your mind?"

"When Tangiers was a thriving port, I fully supported the idea that should Portugal withdraw, Tangiers could stand on its own. But times have changed. Future trade will ignore Tangiers, and Takama has played a major role in convincing Sultan al-Rashid to direct Moroccan African trade to the Atlantic coast, especially Casablanca. His forces are at the moment pushing the Sufi Brotherhood out of that town's hinterland. I am relocating there. Here in Tangiers, you English will inherit an empty commercial shell."

"This city state idea has no legs unless its supporters have won over a major ally. Did any of the rumors name such an ally?"

16

 "Two groups were mentioned—one of which I reject outright. Some suggest that the Sufi Brotherhood based at Fez and currently with troops not far from Tangiers, is eager to have a port from where they can deal with the fleet of the Ottoman Empire and particularly its Algerian corsairs. These Moslem purists detest the relatively lax attitudes of the Ottoman sultan and deplore his attempts to infiltrate Morocco, but people who believe this option are ignorant," replied Takama.

"In what way?" asked Luke.

"The Sufis detest the Ottoman, but they hate the European more. Tangiers leadership is aware of those attitudes. Seeking Sufi help is suicidal. As soon as the city declared its independence, the Sufis would move in and remove all Christians. The interest that would gain most by being associated with an independent Tangiers is Spain. The English would be deprived of a local base from which to attack Spanish shipping. My father thinks that Ghailan, with Spanish help is negotiating with the one or more treacherous military officers within the city to achieve such an independent Tangiers," continued Takama.

"Which officers?"

"I don't know, but it has be one or more of the four senior men- de Silva, Pimento, Lopez or Serano. Father is in two minds. De Silva and Pimento have had more opportunity to talk to Ghailan, and perhaps Spanish representatives, whereas Lopez and Serano are closest to the common people and are in daily touch with their problems and anxieties. If you look at their personal situations, Pimento is the only one with an assured future after we all leave Tangiers," concluded Takama.

"We will get Catarina to her ship in the morning. Takama, come here early tomorrow wearing capes and hoods to conceal your identity! Catarina will leave here dressed in such garb, and we will get her to her ship. I was about to visit your villa, Catarina, to interview Gabriela and others regarding the attempt on your life. Are you returning there now Takama?"

"No, we have further mattered to discuss," replied Catarina. "Before you go, there is the matter of the emerald ring. I asked you to act for me, but events have forced me to change my mind, and the latest information may make its possession less important."

Takama intervened, "While I was away, I persuaded Sultan Al-Rashid to finance a joint bid for the ring, and his representative Colonel Zammit returned with me to bid for it."

"Why is possessing it not as vital as we thought? After all, it is the major focus of my mission," exclaimed a surprised Luke.

"Al Rashid claims to possess the amethyst and citrine rings, therefore the most that Ghailan could have, if his bid is successful, is one ring—hardly enough to rally the doubtful tribes."

Luke was both skeptical and alarmed.

"But can you believe the Sultan's claim? And if it is true, and he obtains the third ring with your help, it creates a major problem for us in the future—a leader with all three rings. Do you hate the English that much?"

"An irrational, emotional outburst, colonel. Completely irrelevant. Al Rashid will eventually attack Tangiers with or without the help of the rings. His African regiments carry all before them, and his miners will have walls of Tangiers demolished overnight. You must persuade your King to sell the city to him, sooner rather than later. England has nothing to gain by staying here. Even the port is third rate and not suitable for a fleet of warships. You will need to completely rebuild the harbor," responded Catarina.

Luke was dispirited. There was no point in pursuing his investigation into the attempts on Catarina. She was removing herself from any further danger, and the matter rightly belonged to the Portuguese authorities. Serano could carry on alone, if he thought it appropriate. Even more depressing, the rings seemed no longer vital to English interests. Rumors of a coup to create an independent state however did create an urgent new focus.

He briefed Jack on what he had been told by Takama and Catarina. His deputy was unimpressed. "Don't believe a word of it!"

Luke admitted that on the contrary, he was inclined to accept what he had been told but given Jack's doubts he would modify his plans for Catarina's departure.

"After Takama leaves in a few minutes, take Catarina and two of her maids to the harbor, and conceal them not on her ship, but aboard one of our vessels. We will transfer her to her own ship in the morning. Keep their identity well concealed. To the outside observer it should be seen as an English officer taking three local women aboard a ship for his pleasure. I will not tell Takama or Aristotle of this change. This way Catarina remains under our protection, until minutes before she actually leaves Tangiers."

"What will you do," asked Jack.

"Question Gabriela again! Before that, inform the vice-admiral of the need to conceal Dona Catarina aboard one of our ships and then secretly transfer her tomorrow. I will take Smith with me as interpreter while I interview Gabriela."

Two hours later Luke and Thomas Smith entered Dona Catarina's complex and were immediately accosted by Aristotle. "Did Takama manage to speak to the mistress?" he asked.

"They were still in conversation when I left them some time ago, but I would have thought that Takama would have returned by now," Luke replied.

Aristotle ignored Luke's comment and announced, "A gentleman that serves the Sultan, and who returned here with Takama wishes to speak to you. I was just about to have one of the servants take him to your barracks."

It was Colonel Zammit. He warmly embraced Luke and thanked him most profusely for saving his life. With Thomas translating, the two soldiers quickly dispensed with chit chat.

Zammit explained, "My Sultan is now in a position to buy the emerald ring and put to an end the ambitions of local warlords. He reiterates his offer to buy Tangiers from England. This will add to English coffers and save you a fortune in future expenditure on a city that will give you no benefit."

"That request has already been forwarded to Whitehall. For the time being I will compete with you to buy the ring. I have not the funds to offer any real opposition, and my sole intent is to uncover the seller, and perhaps lay bare the machinations of some of my so-called Portuguese allies."

"I may be able to help a little. Since my arrival here the Sultan's agents in the town have reported a ground swell of support for a popular uprising to create an independent city state."

"By whom?"

"Elements in the Portuguese infantry, and long-term inhabitants of the city who will have nothing with the withdrawal of Portuguese trade. The idea apparently received strong support in the final sermon of the Inquisitor."

"The devious Diego de Cisneros! Do your sources have any idea who might be the seller of ring?"

"Yes, but you won't like it. The ring was never stolen from the Dominicans. Under pressure they gave it to the Portuguese government in the person of either the powerful Franciscan friar, the Queen's secretary, Father Antonio, or their secret agent Major Coval."

"To what end?"

"The Portuguese hoped to increase their coffers by selling it on to the highest bidder. The Dominicans were happy that it would make heretical England's hold on Tangiers less secure."

Luke and Tom made their way to Gabriela's part of the complex. The latter commented, "Colonel, don't believe a word of what you have just been told. I lived with these people for decades. To sow division among their enemies is a time-honored approach."

Luke smiled, "Tom, you have spent too much time with Captain Moon. He suspects everything he is told. I don't have your experience of Moroccan attitudes and tactics, but I did find the concept of the struggling Portuguese government selling the ring a little fanciful. They are perforce our closest allies. If they want our naval protection, it is hardly a friendly act."

Luke and Tom neared Gabriela's part of the complex. They heard a bell ring.

Above the locked gate that led into Gabriela's courtyard was a large bell which summoned a servant to come and open it. Since her kidnapping Serano apparently had two of his men stationed outside the gate.

They recognized Luke and gave him a formal salute. He asked in his improving Portuguese. "Who is ahead us with Dona Gabriela?"

One of the policemen gave a knowing look and commented, "Colonel Lopez, sir."

"Let's interrupt the lovers!" Luke remarked half- jokingly.

The male servant who answered the bell protested that Dona Gabriela was in no position to receive guests.

While Luke was deciding whether to wait for a more convenient time, or against protocol force his way into her ladyship's presence, he heard a male cry of alarm and Miguel Lopez burst out of the room— abusing a couple of maid servants in the process.

Luke confronted the fleeing Lopez and asked, "What's the problem, Miguel?"

"I am glad you are here. Come back with me!"

While Luke followed Lopez, Tom spoke to the servant girls who were now crying and comforting each other. "Why did the Colonel abuse you?"

"He is furious. He and the mistress have been meeting, often twice a day for the last week. They were about to announce their wedding plans after today's meeting. The last time they reached this stage, her ladyship was kidnapped. Colonel Lopez entered her bedchamber a few minutes ago, but immediately stormed out," answered one of the girls."

Luke followed Miguel back into the reception hall, half expecting to find the body of a murdered Gabriella. Miguel led him into Gabriela's bedchamber where her clothes and the bed looked as if an afternoon of lovemaking had been anticipated.

A distraught Miguel turned back to Luke, "It has happened again. At the eleventh hour she disappears."

Luke was unsympathetic. "Let's not fret unnecessarily. Your immature lover may simply be playing her silly games. Her kidnapping on the last occasion was dubious. She may have been a willing accomplice who was quite happy to desert you at that critical time. She may be repeating the game."

"No, Gabriela needs me. Her aunt has cut her off without a penny. Even if she did not love me, marriage will solve her problems. What else can she do?"

"Forgive me Miguel, she may have been using you to achieve some unknown end, but when marriage comes too close, she conveniently disappears. She has three other options—enter a convent, go to court as a companion of the Queen Regent in Lisbon or of the Infanta in London, or marry someone else."

"You must have talked to my sister to have such a low opinion of Gabriela. She would not move to England simply to serve the Infanta. She is no courtier."

"But that Miguel may be the very destination of the disappearing Gabriela. Dona Catarina has approached me to assist in such a move."

Miguel gasped, "I do not believe you. Gabriela never mentioned any such possibility, even in our most intimate moments."

Luke wondered to himself what Gabriela had to gain by her cruel behavior towards Miguel, but he addressed the immediate problem. "I will inform Serano, and he and I will try and find Gabriela."

Gil Serano was not impressed. "Another childish prank by a stupid girl. Miguel's a fool to stay attached to her. She has now pulled the same trick twice. It must make you suspicious?"

"Yes, but what if we are wrong? What if she has been abducted, or worse? I half expected when Miguel took me into her bedchamber that I would find her body."

"Why think that?"

"She was about to reveal to me the details of her initial kidnapping, and name who had stolen, and was about to sell the emerald ring."

"Probably this was also a figment of her imagination. Put more bluntly a pack of lies! She is incapable of telling the truth. Let's question her maids!"

Luke turned to a male valet who had discreetly stood at the door and asked, "Would you fetch the two maids who were here when I first arrived?"

"That would be Dina and Fada. I will bring them to you."

A few minutes later he returned in a flustered state, "Sir, I cannot find them. I went to their quarters, and another servant, Rachel, showed me a wooden trunk that contained all their possessions. It was empty. Two maids have also disappeared."

17

"This is a voluntary disappearance by Gabriela and her maids. A kidnapper would not risk adding servants to his catch," suggested Gil. "Let's talk to Da Gama. He runs a tight ship and should know something."

Aristotle was dismissive. This was another of Gabriela's pranks. He was not alarmed and suggested that both English and Portuguese authorities should simply ignore what had happened.

"How did Gabriela and later her maids leave the complex without being detected? They cannot exit through the courtyard gate without being seen," asked Luke.

"No problem! Gabriela's villa can be accessed through the adjacent apartments—Takama's on one side and the servants on the other.

Dozens of people arrive or leave through the small southern gate all the time."

"Is there a servant responsible for that gate?" asked Gil.

"Not since the attempt on Catarina when you placed your men there, captain."

"I placed no men there. Did you Luke?" said the surprised police chief.

"No! They must be Miguel's. I thought their formal salute when I arrived was a little too military for your more relaxed police. He must have been protecting his lover," concluded Luke.

"Or spying on her," countered Gil.

"Or neither. Miguel may have staged all of this to confuse us. Where is he now? Has he disappeared as well?" asked Luke.

"Possibly, Miguel is obsessively besotted by Gabriela— abnormally so. She must have something over him. Her tainted charms are not a sufficient explanation for his stupidity," added the cynical Aristotle.

Luke and Gil were about to leave when the valet returned. "Gentlemen, come quickly, Dina and Fada have returned in a highly agitated condition. I have been unable to elicit any sensible comments from them."

Luke, Gil and Aristotle followed the valet into a large bedchamber where both girls lay on a very large bed and were being given a calming liquid by Rachel. Sensing that the two distraught girls were in no state to be questioned., Luke asked Rachel whether they had told her anything.

"A little! They were to meet their mistress aboard Dona Catarina's ship, *Rainha de Tanger*, to start their voyage to England, but Dona Gabriela was not on board waiting for them as she had promised. The ship's captain had no knowledge that Dona Gabriela was to board his vessel. His only instruction was that Dona Catarina herself would board the ship in the morning to travel to Casablanca, not England."

"Why then are they so distressed? Missing out on a trip to England could hardly be that distressing?" said Aristotle with a wry look at Luke.

"They fear for Dona Gabriela. They saw Colonel Lopez coming away from the wharf. They fear that maybe he caught up with their mistress and has kidnapped her for the second time."

Luke was struck by this final comment. Was Lopez was behind the first kidnapping after all?

Gil concentrated on the comment that the captain was not aware that Gabriela was to board his ship. "Where did Gabriela receive her false information and why? Was it simply to entice her to the waterfront where she could easily be abducted by a range of suspects, not necessarily Miguel Lopez?"

"Why would anyone want to kidnap that young woman? She has no assets, her aunt's new will leaves her penniless, and her behavior has cut her value in the marriage market. From her point of view Miguel's obsession was her last chance. Why reject it?" asked Aristotle.

"Perhaps the opportunity to start afresh in England was too strong a temptation for the wayward lass. Why would anybody want to prevent that?" suggested Luke.

"Why would anybody want to leave the perfect climate here to travel north, especially to England?" responded Aristotle, half in jest.

"There must be something else causing the girls' level of distress. Let us question them again, right now," announced a determined Luke.

Dina and Fada appeared more relaxed as the medication that Rachel had provided had taken its effect. Luke was direct.

"You were both very distressed when you first returned. Your explanation was a lie. What really troubles you?"

The two girls looked at each other and Dina nodded to Fada to reply.

"Since Dona Gabriela returned from her initial kidnapping, she has been under pressure from both the Lopez siblings. Colonel Miguel's love for her became obsessive and on more than one occasion he told the mistress that if he could not have her, no one else would. That is why she decided to escape to England."

Dina added, "At the same time she received horrible letters from Catia demanding that she cease seeing Miguel or she would suffer severe consequences. The women hate each other."

"So, you think that Miguel, realizing that Dona Gabriela was leaving him, has carried out his threat?" asked Luke.

"Or that Catia's own besotted lover has harmed the mistress," added Fada.

"And who is that besotted lover?" Gil whispered.

"Major Dimas Vento," was the joint reply.

"He has only been back a little over three weeks. He returned to Portugal with the previous governor to organize the future of the Portuguese infantry here, especially Miguel's own company," explained Gil.

"Catia Lopez wasted no time ensnaring him once again," muttered Aristotle.

"She is as obsessed with matters of the heart as her brother," was Gil's interesting comment.

"Were you not yourself one of her lovers?" asked Luke undiplomatically.

"As I am a bachelor, she was often my partner at official engagements, nothing more," Gil uncomfortably replied.

And in Luke's eyes, not a convincing response.

"Gentlemen, I will talk to Major Vento and then question Catia," Luke announced.

Luke found Major Vento at the infantry barracks and asked, "Have you seen your Colonel today?"

"Yes, he was here when I arrived this morning."

"What sort of mood was he in? Was he more troubled, or more elated than usual?"

"I did not notice anything unusual at the time, but later in the morning the duty officer commented that the Colonel was unusually buoyant proclaiming to a subordinate that he was about to put an end to a persistent problem."

This alarmed Luke. Did Miguel mean that finally he was putting an end to the on and off relationship with Gabriela by officially announcing their engagement, or was it more sinister? Was he was getting rid of an unpredictable and two-timing woman?

Vento asked, "Do you need to speak with the Colonel, or can I help?"

"I need to find him. He has disappeared."

"What do you mean *disappeared*?"

"He has either disappeared after being engaged in a possible crime, or he has been kidnapped or even murdered. Serano's men are looking for him now."

"What led to his disappearance?"

"The flight, abduction, or possible death of Dona Gabriela Sarmento."

"I should have known that predatory virago would be involved. Since I returned from Portugal, I noticed that the Colonel is a different man to the one I knew before I left. His sister is convinced that this change in personality is due entirely to his obsession with Gabriela."

"You are close to Catia?" Luke asked.

"Not as close as I was—but that is water under the bridge."

"Has Catia asked you to rescue her brother from the clutches of Gabriela?"

"Yes, but her request came too late. Catia claims that Gabriela bewitched her brother, and I should report it to the Inquisitor, but he has, or is about to leave Tangiers for good. For an Inquisitorial investigation of young Gabriela, she would have to be in Portuguese or Spanish territory, and Tangiers is about to become neither."

"It seems as if you have given the issue some thought."

"Yes, but I am more concerned for Catia than Miguel. Both Lopez siblings are obsessed with that girl. It has turned Catia from a sweet enticing young woman into an embittered old maid before her time. I will not resume any close relationship with her until Gabriela can be exorcised from her consciousness."

"Does this bitterness extend to her brother? Could she have organized his abduction to stop his betrothal to Gabriela?" asked Luke.

"She certainly harbors such intent, but I doubt if she could organize a meal for herself, let alone the abduction of a senior military figure."

"She could have had assistance. My impression is that Catia competed with Gabriela for the favor of many young men. She may have inveigled one of these besotted fools into assisting her," suggested Luke.

Dimas was clearly not pleased to hear such a comment, but Luke continued, "In fact elements of your infantry regiment were involved in Gabriela's original abduction. At first, I thought she had used her favors to get the assistance of some soldiers in obtaining a ransom from her aunt. On second thoughts, it could have been Catia using her links with the infantry behind the kidnapping. After all, the Lopez's have few assets to see them into their post Tangiers future."

"Not true. Their father is able to leave Miguel a reasonable inheritance and provide Catia with an acceptable dowry. Until his father's death. Miguel will continue to hold a high-ranking military position which is well paid. His infantry company is about to be transferred to the defense of a Portuguese castle on the Spanish border —the result of my recent negotiations in Lisbon. Before his obsession with Gabriela, Miguel's future looked stable and prosperous. He is a professional soldier, not a would-be politician or courtier. I will have my men join Serano's in the search."

Luke was about to leave when one of Serano's men appeared. "My commandant requests both of you to accompany me to a semi-demolished house on the edge of the slave market."

"What's the emergency that requires both of us to attend?"

"The body of Colonel Lopez has been found outside a house following an explosion which demolished most of it."

"An unexpected turn in events!' muttered Dimas.

On arriving at the scene Luke asked Gil who was supervising the situation, "You found the body of Colonel Lopez. What happened?"

"Good news, Miguel is not dead. He appeared badly injured and was unconscious. He is now coming in and out of consciousness. He appears to have regained his faculties. He has been taken to the Franciscan friary. He now appears in no danger."

"I will send my surgeon there immediately," said Luke. "What have you ascertained about the explosion?"

"The nearest stallholder to the house, the reliable Miriam Barros, says it is occupied by five non-commissioned infantry officers—most of the infantry sergeants. She saw Lopez whom she knows well arrive and enter the building. Then a few shots were heard followed by an explosion."

"Are all the occupants dead?" asked Dimas.

"Three of them are. We are yet to find the fourth and fifth inhabitant."

"Let us try and recreate the crime scene, —if it is a crime. It could be an unfortunate accident. Soldiers tend to help themselves to weapons and ammunition," suggested Luke.

Luke, Dimas and Gil analyzed the scene. Gil placed three of his men where the victims would have stood and placed himself just outside the door where Miguel must have been.

A few minutes later the searchers found the fourth man covered by a considerable about of masonry. Luke examined the body and exclaimed, "He is still alive."

Gil put his finger to his lips and then shouted, "You are mistaken Colonel Tremayne. My men will take him to barracks to be interred with his comrades."

When Gil and Luke left the demolished house, a furious Luke exclaimed, "What was the meaning of that. The man **is** alive."

"Of course, he is alive, but it will enhance our investigation if nobody else knows that —not even Dimas. The body has been sent to your barracks, not to be interred, but to be looked after by your surgeon. It will be interesting to see if his recollection of events is the same as that of Colonel Lopez."

The fifth man was not found.

Dimas caught up with them and commented. "Gentlemen, this may have been an attempt to destroy Colonel Lopez and his most devoted men. The dead are his closest aides—the administrative corps of the regiment. They are his trusted sergeants This could be a security issue and given that everybody is involved, perhaps the investigation should be carried out by the deputy governor as commander-in -chief."

Serano was incensed and Luke immediately sensed an attempted cover up by the army. Serano spoke quietly, "Dimas, I will hand over the investigation to Mario as soon as soon as I ascertain that it is what you suggest."

Luke could not contain his ire, "And I am sure that the Queen Regent would prefer that the army did not investigate itself, especially as many elements in the infantry are guilty of a number of illegal activities."

18

After Dimas left, Luke suggested that he and Gil interrogate Miguel immediately. They arrived at the friary just in time. Miguel was about to leave.

"Good to see you up and about. How do you feel?" asked Gil.

"Apart from a few cuts and bruises from the impact of the flying rubble, I am unharmed. What about my men? Did any survive?"

"No!" lied Luke.

"That is why we are here to find out from you what actually happened," said Gil.

"Tell us what you did from the time you left Dona Gabriela's villa until you were found unconscious outside your sergeants' demolished house," probed Luke.

"I was determined to find Gabriela. Your comment Luke that she might be headed for England worried me. If she left Tangiers she could be gone forever. I knew there was one of Catarina's ships in the port, and about to leave either today or tomorrow."

"So, you visited its Captain?" Gil asked.

"Yes. He told me that Gabriela was not on board and was not expected but that Catarina was—and that she had not yet arrived. He then told me I was not the first to have been given false information. Two female servants had been there before me looking for Gabriela. This increased my anxiety. Both mistress and maids were supposed to be aboard a ship—and were not. The captain then revealed that his destination was Casablanca, not England or even Portugal. It was then that I saw the light. Gabriela was probably hiding in the city until a boat bound for England arrived."

"Did you not think that she may have used her charms to get aboard one of our English warships in the harbor?" asked Luke.

"How would that help her?" asked a confused Miguel.

"The fleet receives regular instructions from Whitehall brought by a fast frigate. On its return journey it often carries passengers. After I leave you, I will contact the fleet on your behalf. She could be aboard one of our vessels."

"You said *you saw the light.* What did you mean?" probed Gil.

"What I tell you now must go no further. If it does, I will deny I said it, and accuse you of trying to frame me."

Both Luke and Gil nodded that they would keep the confidence, although both were already considering how they could ignore this commitment—if the need arose.

Miguel continued, "Some time ago Gabriela persuaded my sergeants to join her in a supposed abduction by saying it was a prank, and that I was fully supportive of it—a situation she escalated when she demanded a ransom, promising my men a substantial share each. Whether she blackmailed them into the ransom part of the plot, or they were attracted by simple greed, I do not know."

"So, it was your sergeants who abducted me, took the ransom and left me in a small forest, and who returned later with Gabriela who escaped them?" reiterated Luke.

"Yes!"

"Why didn't you act to stop all this?" asked Gil.

"I knew nothing about it at the time. Gabriela convinced my men that I did, but that they must never raise the matter with me, so that if it came to light, I could honestly deny my involvement."

"Then how did you find out?"

"During one of our more torrid lovemaking sessions in which she consumed a considerable amount of cannabis, she boasted of her achievement in not only obtaining the ransom from her aunt, but in misleading and manipulating my men."

"How does this information relate to you *seeing the light?* persisted Gil.

"During her alleged abduction Gabriela stayed in the house occupied by my sergeants, I suddenly became aware that as she wasn't at home or on the ship, she may be repeating history by hiding in their house."

"How does the simple enquiry into the whereabouts of Gabriela turn into a shooting match followed by an explosion?"

"I have known these men for years. They were my most trusted aides. I explained the situation that Gabriela had disappeared again. When I asked were they hiding her, two of them became very shifty. I suspected she was there and asked could I search the premises. When I tried to enter the next room, one of them blocked my way and a third turned his back. When he faced me again, he had primed his pistol and fired directly at me. It missed, but as another of them primed his pistol, I ran to the door. Then I saw one of the sergeants light the fuse of a grenade which he held aloft and was waiting until the last minute to throw it in my direction. I shot him and as he fell to the ground the grenade ignited and I was knocked out by the flying debris. I was saved by being mainly behind the well-built entry."

"Why did your trusted men attack you? It doesn't make sense," asked a skeptical Luke

"It does, if they had Gabriela."

"Or if they thought you would reveal their part in her earlier abduction and ransom activity," suggested Luke.

"You found no woman's body in the remnants of the house?" asked Miguel.

"No."

"Thank goodness! She must have left before I arrived."

As Luke and Gil walked to the English barracks to see the surviving sergeant, the latter expressed his disbelief in what he had been told. "Why would his sergeants turn on him? If the details of their assistance to Gabriela was revealed, they could very easily involve Miguel in their story. They were in a perfect position to blackmail Miguel. Maybe that's why he killed them. I hope the survivor, master sergeant Bruno Costa, is in a position to tell us his version of what happened."

He was not. Surgeon Pickering was not optimistic. "Costa is in a coma occasioned by massive blows to the head from the falling masonry. He is most likely to die. There is a possibility he will eventually come out of the coma, but remember nothing of the events surrounding it. There is a slight chance he will recover with memory intact—but that may be days, weeks or even months away."

"What should we do now?" asked a disappointed Gil.

"I will question the stallholders in the souk, and then visit the fleet on the off chance that Gabriela did find her way there," replied Luke.

"Then I will search the debris in the house to uncover anything that may prove Gabriela was there—and hopefully remnants of the fifth man. Let's meet at noon tomorrow to update each other!"

Luke, Jack and Tom arrived at the souk. Luke asked the nearest stallholder, Johanne Barros, had he seen a Portuguese noblewoman enter the house that had been destroyed by an explosion on that day.

Luke was delighted with the reply. "The house is occupied by soldiers and attracts an array of unsavory women. I was surprised to see a lady of such quality arrive earlier on the day of the explosion."

"Did you see her leave?"

"I did see her leave the house a quarter hour before the explosion. She passed our stall heading for the harbor."

"Did she meet anybody after she passed you?"

"I did not see her after she passed here. I was too busy serving my customers."

During Luke's discussion with the stallholder Tom chatted to the former's wife in Arabic. As Luke and Jack moved to next stall, Tom stayed engrossed in his discussion at the conclusion of which he gave the woman a big hug.

As Tom caught up with the officers Luke asked, "Why the discussion in Arabic? Was she hiding something from her husband? And why the hug? Have you met before?"

"I speak Arabic with an accent of the people around Fez where I was a slave for twenty years. This woman was born in Fez and probably thought I was from there. She was certainly willing to tell me more than you would have obtained. In fact, she has solved your problem Colonel. Therefore, the hug at the end."

"What do you mean, solved my problem? Which particular problem?"

"I can tell you the movements of Dona Gabriela in the vicinity of the demolished house, her movements after she left, where she is now—and who helped her get there."

Luke was gob smacked. "Tell us all!"

"My new friend Miriam is no humble stall holder. She owns the freehold to most of the souk and leases individual plots to the various stall holders. She is a wealthy and powerful woman in this part of Tangiers. She said that an affluent well-dressed woman arrived at the house several hours before the explosion and left about a quarter an hour before it occurred. She left by the back door and proceeded up the main street of the souk passing Miriam's stall."

"We got that much from her husband," commented Jack.

Tom continued, "She moved through the souk and was confronted by a group of unruly English sailors. After some discussion she proceeded towards the harbor with one of them. The others dispersed through the souk, but one of them came to see Miriam. He told her that the woman had offered them a fortune, if they could get her aboard one of the English ships. He even told her the name of the sailor who went off with her—Willie Street."

"Amazing work, Tom. Here, take some money and spend up big at her stall. You can give her another hug from me. Jack and I will visit the Admiral as a matter of urgency."

Luke explained in detail to Admiral Lawson the saga of Gabriela's disappearance and the strong possibility that she was aboard one of His

Majesty's ships. He pointed out to the Admiral that this could blow up into a major diplomatic row as the woman concerned would probably become one of the new English Queen's lady-in-waiting. He needed to interrogate a seaman, Willie Street, immediately.

Lawson had his aide establish on which ship Street served. It was *Rupert's Revenge* which was anchored only three ships away from the flagship. The Admiral commented, "She is simply trying to join her aunt. I placed Dona Catarina on *Rupert's Revenge* because it had an unused cabin.

"No way!" responded Luke abruptly.

"She did not know where her aunt was. For that matter nor did I."

Luke and Jack accompanied by the admiral were rowed to *Rupert's Revenge*.

Its captain apprised of their mission defended Willie Street. "He simply re-united this missing girl with her aunt. They are both in the cabin next door."

"Nevertheless, I would still like to speak with Street," said Luke.

The sailor was overawed by the presence of the Admiral, but it was Luke who made the first comment, "Street, I came here to charge you with the kidnapping of a Portuguese noblewoman. Maybe of her murder. Your captain has explained the situation. How did you happen to bring her here?"

Willie's face brightened. "When I met her in the souk, she told me she feared for her life and that her would- be husband was violent towards her, and her only hope was to escape to England. I told her we already had one Portuguese noble woman aboard, a Dona Catarina. She said that woman was her aunt, and she would like to join her. I informed the captain as soon as I came aboard. She gave me this ring as payment for what I had done."

Luke recognized the ring immediately. It was one of many fake emerald rings that Gabriela had obtained. While not of great intrinsic value in Portuguese circles, it was still a valuable asset for a common English seaman. Luke put Willie at ease.

"I accept your story. You may have saved the younger woman's life."

Luke next visited Catarina and Gabriela. Catarina did not hold back, "Why have your men kept me prisoner here, instead of taking me to my own vessel?"

"For your own safety. Already potential enemies have enquired of your captain concerning your whereabouts. You will be escorted to your ship in the morning, and I will not withdraw my protective guard until it leaves the harbor."

He then turned to Gabriela. "You young lady are lucky to be alive. You left the house of your soldier friends less than half an hour before it was blown up, and all of them killed and Colonel Lopez injured."

"What was Miguel doing there?"

"Looking for you."

"What actually happened?"

"We don't know. We have heard Miguel's version which implicates you and the dead men in an earlier escapade. He suggests that they thought he was about to reveal the details of this to the authorities and they tried to kill him. There was a shootout and one of men tripped as he lit a grenade which destroyed the building and its inhabitants."

19

"His explanation is an outright lie. That earlier escapade as you diplomatically called it in front of my aunt was a stupid prank that I played on her. It was Miguel who suggested that we raise the tempo by demanding a ransom. And it was he who ordered his sergeants to become involved, although it was I who decided they should be paid for their services."

Catarina interrupted, "Gabriela confessed all of this to me sometime after her return, as Miguel became more obsessive and potentially violent."

Luke asked, "What happens to Gabriela now? Will you take her to Casablanca?"

"No, I leave for Casablanca tomorrow. Given Miguel's unpredictable behavior he might follow us there. I have already arranged with the captain of this ship for Gabriela to stay here, hopefully with the protective guard you provided for me. The regular frigate from England bringing mail and instructions for the fleet is due to arrive in the next few days. On its return voyage to England, Gabriela hopefully will be aboard. Will you make sure that this happens?"

"Of course. Your transfer tomorrow will be a little more complex than you would have hoped. Your would- be murderer is still out there and if he has picked up rumors of your departure, he will be watching the only Sarmento ship in port."

"How do we avoid any unwarranted attention?" asked Catarina.

"You will not board your ship while it is anchored portside. I will board it and guide your captain as close to the English fleet as possible. My men will row you from here to your own ship, by then well away from the docks. You will thereby be obscured by dozens of English ships from any prying eyes or more pertinent, potential musket fire from the shore."

Next morning Luke, Jack and two of their men boarded Catarina's ship. Luke explained the slight change of plan to the captain who remarked, "A wise precaution. There were a few strangers hanging around the pier which the soldiers you provided turned away."

"So, nobody has boarded the vessel this morning?" asked Jack.

"Only a group of Dona Catarina's servants who are moving with her."

"Did anybody arrive, and then leave?" probed the ever-thorough Luke.

"Yes, the men who loaded a number of chests, the paperwork for which was signed by Aristotle Da Gama."

"What did these chests contain?"

"Largely household utensils. I need to get underway now to take advantage of the tide, but I need your direction to maneuver through the English lines."

Luke and the captain moved to the bridge while Jack and the two soldiers with the ship's manifest went to check the holds.

As the ship entered the English lines and a boat carrying Catarina came into sight there appeared to be a major disturbance below decks, followed by a bell being rung ferociously followed by Jack shouting to abandon ship. He screamed at the helm.

"There is a trunk full of explosives about to ignite and blow us to smithereens! It is in the middle of the fire and unreachable."

Luke yelled at the approaching longboat, "Turn back, we are about to..."

Luke did not finish his sentence as an explosion sent debris flying in all directions. The ship was quickly ablaze from stern to prow. Those passengers not killed in the explosion were throwing themselves overboard. Jack with help was trying to launch the vessel's boat into which they were guiding the female servants who survived.

There was now a major calamity in the offing. The disabled and burning ship was drifting straight towards several vessels of the English fleet, which had no time to weigh anchor and avoid the inevitable collision.

A large longboat suddenly appeared beside the burning ship. It was commanded by the admiral who declared, "Get off the vessel immediately! I am about to hit it with dozens of grenades, and it will be blasted shortly by cannon fire. It will be sunk before it reaches our ships."

The water around the burning vessel was now filled with boats picking up those who had jumped into the water. Luke and the captain were the last to leave and as they treaded water, the continuing avalanche of exploding grenades split the hull, and it began to sink before the flagship's battery of guns opened fire. The burning ship sank before Luke was rescued.

Three hours later the admiral convened a meeting aboard his flagship with Luke, Jack, Catarina and her captain. At Luke's request Gil Serano also attended.

Catarina asked the men present how many of her servants were injured or killed.

It was Jack who replied, "Four persons aboard the ship were killed—a male and two female servants who took the full brunt of the blast and a third woman who drowned before she could be taken from the water. Nearly everybody else luckily suffered superficial wounds from the flying debris."

"Where are the survivors now?" asked Catarina.

"They have been taken back to your villa where Luke's surgeon and two or three others from my ships are attending to their wounds," answered the Admiral.

"And my men?" asked Catarina's captain.

"Only two died and the injured only have minor problems. Those with homes in Tangiers have gone there—the others are being currently monitored in the Franciscan friary," continued the Admiral.

He then turned to Jack, "What exactly happened?"

"While Luke and the captain were guiding the ship out of the harbor through the English fleet, I went with two of our men to the holds to make a casual check of the cargo. I became aware of the smell of fire which was coming from behind a closed door which was locked. After much difficulty, it was battered down and we were confronted by a massive conflagration. There were two trunks in the middle of the room surrounded by burning wooden planks ripped from the floor. The fire had taken such a hold there was no way we could reach it, let alone extinguish it. One of the now lidless trunks was filled with the grenades and the intense heat had clearly ignited the fuses of some of them. We ran, alerting the ship's company and passengers as we went."

Luke commented, "We can only assume that the men who delivered the last two trunks supposedly containing Catarina's house goods placed the trunks in position and placed the combustible goods where it might take a while for the fire to develop and ideally the ship would be out to sea before it went up. The door was locked so that the initial small fire would not be detected too soon. It had to gain a hold before being detected."

He turned to the captain, "You saw these men. Did you recognize them?"

"No, I know many of Catarina's servants, but I did not recognize these men. I took the paperwork they had, signed by Aristotle da Gama, as their authority to board the ship and deliver then goods."

Gil Serano's contribution to the discussion stunned the group. "I suspect nobody will be able to question these four. Just after the explosion, my men discovered in a narrow alley leading off the harbor, the bodies of four men. They had all been garroted. I will ask the captain to identify them, but the circumstances suggest that these are the four arsonists who have been removed subsequently by a very professional assailant."

"What do you intend to do now?" asked the Admiral of Catarina.

"Move to Casablanca! My captain here will go there and collect one of my ships undergoing repairs, and will return here eventually to move the remainder of my people and possessions."

"And what of the intervening period?" asked Luke. "You have three options—remain on board an English ship until your captain returns, return to our barracks where I am in the best position to protect you, or sail in our communications frigate on its return to England. You can disembark in the safety of Lisbon and wait there for your captain to pick you up."

"And what about a fourth—that I return to my villa under your protection, Colonel Tremayne?"

"No, I do not have enough resources to give you complete protection in your network of villas—and I am not sure whether our elusive would-be murderer is not one of your household," was Luke's blunt response."

"Luke's suggestion that you escape Tangiers for the safety of Lisbon has merit," added the Admiral.

"I will discuss the situation with Aristotle and Takama before I make a decision. May they be brought to the ship tomorrow. I will let you know my decision after that meeting."

Next morning Jack escorted Takama and Aristotle to the meeting with Catarina, while Luke accompanied by Thomas, discussed the developing situation with Gil who informed him that the captain had identified the four bodies in alley as the men who boarded his ship.

Luke expressed the view based on no evidence that Aristotle was emerging as a possible suspect.

"Rubbish!" countered Gil. "He certainly has opportunity, but what's the motive?"

"It depends on which of Catarina's wills is current. Under the newest will he is well catered for, on the earlier will he gets very little. I have to clarify with Catarina, which will is valid, and whether Aristotle is privy to that information."

They were interrupted by Jack who returned from the harbor and informed them of Catarina's decision. "She will return to our barracks under certain conditions which I approved, namely that three of her servants come with her, and that Takama and Aristotle may visit her there regularly so that she can maintain her commercial enterprises and household."

A second interruption occurred. It was Major Vento. "Gentlemen, I have heard rumors about the latest attempt to kill Dona Catarina. If you can fill me in on the details, I may be able to help you."

As Luke explained what had happened the smile on Dimas's face broadened. "Take me to the bodies of these four men. I may be able to identify them."

"Why do you think that?" asked the cynical Jack.

"At roll call this morning there were four unaccounted absences. One of their friends said he saw them on the docks earlier in the day."

"This could be the break-through we needed," commented Gil.

"What could be most disconcerting is that my missing men belonged to the same unit that tried to kill Colonel Lopez," added Dimas.

"Someone seems intent on wiping out a specific unit of the infantry. Lopez in part removed four men and then another four from the same unit are murdered after they successfully fire Dona Catarina's ship. It is worrying scenario," surmised Luke.

"This returns suspicion onto your commander Miguel Lopez, and not Aristotle da Gama as Luke is suggesting," commented Gil.

"Don't jump to conclusions until Dimas identifies the bodies," cautioned Jack.

The men went to the friary. Dimas looked at the bodies. His face fell. "These are not my missing men." Luke, Jack, Thomas and Gil could hardly conceal their disappointment. Luke looked intently at one of the bodies.

"What is it?" asked Gil.

"The small tattoo mark behind the left ear!"

Gil checked the other bodies, "They all have the same mark."

"And I have seen it before," remarked a worried Luke.

Thomas noticed Luke's increasing stress and remarked, "Of course you have."

He pulled back his hair and there, behind his left ear, was a similar mark.

There was a gasp of astonishment from the group as Thomas continued, "This mark is that of the slave market at Fez. Like myself, these men were at some stage of their lives sold as slaves in Fez."

Dimas exclaimed, "Then forget family and commercial rivalries in this attack on Dona Catarina. Look at the broader picture! This latest attempt on her has nothing to do with her family or elements in Tangiers. The answer lies in Fez."

"Why?"

"Garroting is the favorite method of assassination of an extreme branch of the religious fanatics based there and these men with their slave market tattoos have most likely been sent from Fez," explained Dimas.

"Why would the Islamic brotherhood at Fez want to kill Catarina?" asked Gil.

"Fez is about to be invaded by the army of the Sultan. One thing he lacks is a navy and ports to keep him supplied during his campaign to destroy these Moslem brotherhoods. Catarina has the ships and is about to move to Casablanca from where she has made it clear that she will help the Sultan."

Luke whistled, "A plausible interpretation."

Later when Luke and Tom were alone the latter commented, "It does not add up, sir."

"What doesn't add up—the Fez involvement?"

"Not their involvement, their demise."

'What's the problem?"

"Garroting is not a run- of-the- mill form of execution. For the Fez fanatics it is ritualistic form of killing—not used in removing agents who have only partly succeeded in their mission. I knew there was something amiss with those corpses. The ritualistic garroting is done using a rope with three knots. None of those bodies showed any mark of knots. These men were killed by Europeans, wishing to trick us into thinking it was done by their disappointed Moslem leaders."

"Could this have been a joint enterprise by Fez extremists and rogue Portuguese troops?" asked Luke.

"Not likely! The Fez fanatics are Moslem idealists who hate Europeans. I cannot see them in alliance with the Portuguese and the mixed blood low life represented in part of the local infantry."

20

Next morning Luke received a surprise visit from Colonel Ibram Zammit who asked, "May I speak with Dona Catarina."

"Why?" asked Luke abruptly

"To express my concern at another attempt on her life, and to discover when she now intends to move to Casablanca. This is of vital importance to my master, the Sultan. Do you know who destroyed her ship?"

"Yes, I first thought that the attempt was a family affair, then that it may have been commercial rivals within the city. Four garroted bodies were found near the harbor, later identified by Catarina's captain as the four men who loaded trunks onto the ship at the last minute. All these bodies had the tattoo mark of the Fez slave auction. The Islamic Brotherhood was the probable instigator of the attack, but my valet argues their murder was the work of Europeans."

Luke outlined Tom's evidence.

"It is not unusual for extremist elements at Fez to eliminate their own agents by garroting, but I agree with your man that their failed attempt on Catarina is hardly an appropriate case. Maybe this attempt was not only against Catarina and her move to Casablanca, but against me. Nevertheless it is still not appropriate procedure."

"Why could the attack have been aimed at you?"

"I was supposed to be on that ship."

"Why did you fail to board?" asked a suspicious Luke.

"I was due to return to the Sultan with the emerald ring that he and Dona Catarina were buying from a mysterious seller, who confirmed a few days ago that our bid had been successful. It was to be delivered to Dona Catarina's villa yesterday, but this did not occur."

"With Catarina under our protection at a secret location to whom was it to be delivered."

"To any one of myself, Aristotle da Gama or Dona Takama. None of us received it."

"Did the three of you discuss what you should do in the circumstances?"

"Yes, Aristotle suggested I accompany Catarina to Casablanca and explain the situation to the Sultan. Takama disagreed. She wanted me to stay and assist her investigate the non-arrival of the ring."

"You took Takama's advice?"

"Yes. The non-arrival of the ring could be the beginning of a prolonged set of new negotiations, and I am sure the Sultan would want me here. That is why I need to see Catarina."

"Have you paid for the ring?"

"I am not stupid. Part of the letters of credit drawn on a Florentine bank were to be transferred on receipt of the ring, and the remainder after it had been examined by the Sultan's experts. We have only paid a low deposit in coin, of a few thousand ducats."

Luke was about to lead Ibram to Catarina, when Tom burst into the room.

"Colonel Tremayne, I have more information regarding the murder of the four Moslems who blew up Dona Catarina's ship."

"You may speak freely in front of Colonel Zammit. He may have been the intended victim."

"I have just returned from the souk."

"Where you will have had an intimate conversation with the attractive wife of the fruit seller Barros?" teased Luke.

"Not the alluring Miriam?" asked Ibram.

Luke noted this comment. Was Miriam a secret agent of the Sultan?

"And what did you discover?"

"That the murdered Moslems and members of the Portuguese infantry knew each other. Soldiers who frequented the house that was blown up, met the Moslems in the souk on several occasions, and Miriam claims she saw some of them leaving that house a day or so before it blew up. She said these Fez visitors claimed to be carpet sellers and she had seen them carry carpets into the bombed house before it exploded."

"Excellent work Tom! We can now construct a possible scenario. The Moslems carried the ammunition in carpets into the house where it was placed in trunks that had come from Gabriela. These were then carried to the ship. On completing their mission, they were killed by their military accomplices to hide the latter's role."

"No! There are too many gaps in that interpretation, Luke. I cannot see how the Fez militants would become entangled with the Portuguese military. It suggests an undertaking that convinced the Moslems that they could participate in the joint venture to their advantage. The only scenario that fits this is ominous— the infantry will open the gates to supporters of the Islamic Brotherhood," announced Ibram.

"No, I cannot see the Portuguese of any status giving any grounds to the Fez insurgents," said Luke. "It would be suicidal."

"My guess, gentlemen is that someone in authority in Tangiers is an agent or ally of these Islamic militants who would prefer the city to fall to Moslem extremists than to Christian heretics," exclaimed Tom.

"But the killing of their four agents would not give the Fez group much confidence in their Portuguese ally," said Luke. "The only scenario that would make sense is that the four men were killed by a Portuguese faction opposed to activities of the Fez agent. The killing would certainly put an end to any further co-operation between the unknown Fez supporter in Tangiers, and the Islamic Brotherhood authorities."

Suddenly Tom exclaimed," Colonel, there may be a simpler explanation. Why would the Sufi agents who were leaving the city immediately to return to Fez have had to die?"

"And why would they?" asked Ibram.

"It has nothing to do with their failed mission to destroy Catarina Sarmento," answered Tom.

"What else occurred that would necessitate the killing of four men, and the subsequent attempt to put the blame on the Fez authorities?" questioned Luke.

"Someone in Tangiers supplied the ammunition to those fanatics. The supplier could not risk his identity being revealed. It was imperative that any link between the supplier and the bombers had to be eliminated. Find the supplier and you have your murderer," concluded an elated Tom.

Luke was about to take Ibram to Catarina when the surgeon Pickford entered the room.

"Colonel, the survivor of the grenade blast, Bruno Costa has at last regained consciousness. He is capable of being questioned."

Luke sent Tom to bring Gil Serano to the infirmary.

"We will wait for Gil. It is officially his enquiry."

Within a quarter hour Gil and Tom arrived and the four men followed Pickford into the infirmary where Costa was just finishing his first proper meal for some time.

He confronted Gil, "Did any of my comrades survive?"

"No one in the house, but the Colonel was found outside, and has fully recovered, and we never found any trace of the fifth man that we were told lived there."

"You wouldn't. My deputy, Gigante, lance sergeant Cornelio Rios was very lucky. He left by the front door almost at the same time as the Colonel entered."

"Why Gigante?" asked Luke.

"He is six foot six and of gigantic build. He started his working life as a wrestler in which his physical advantages made him unbeatable. In addition to this advantage, he quickly developed skills as a musketeer. He is now one of the most capable marksmen in the city."

Luke wondered if Gigante's timely departure was because he was in league with the Colonel. Diplomatically he simply said, "What happened?"

"We were used by our colonel. My comrades died for no reason."

"Describe the events leading up to the explosion?" asked Gil.

"It all started weeks ago and at one stage involved you, Colonel Tremayne."

"The kidnapping of Dona Gabriela?" Luke suggested.

"There was no kidnapping. Dona Gabriela approached us to help her in a little prank she was playing against her aunt. Could we hide her for a few days to see how her aunt would react to her disappearance? As she was our commander's sweetheart, we went along with it. Then without warning she changed the whole nature of the game by demanding a ransom. None of us were happy with this development, but her offer to give us half the amount obtained, won us over."

"If she was not kidnapped, why did you have to drug her."

"We didn't. While she was staying with us, she took an excessive interest in our cannabis infused cakes and drinks. For someone who had not imbibed or eaten drugs before it did create an extreme reaction with the young Gabriela. That is why she ran away from us when we were delivering her, but she has absolutely no memory of that last day."

"But she returned to your premises a day or so before the explosion?" asked Gil.

"Yes, she arrived in a very disturbed state. She claimed that our colonel had threatened violence against her, and she needed a place to hide until she boarded a ship to leave Tangiers."

"Why didn't she stay?"

"Fear that Colonel Lopez would find her. I told her that the most secure place was to come here under English protection, or even better board an English ship. I suggested that she confront some of the English sailors in the souk and ask to be taken aboard."

"Which she did?"

"Yes, I followed her into the souk to see that she was not molested. After her meeting with the sailors, I approached her, and she told me that the English tar beside her would take her to her aunt who was already on board an English ship. I followed at a distance to ensure that this happened."

"How did your group become temporary accomplices of the Islamic brotherhood from Fez?" asked Luke.

"Miriam the owner of the souk who I believe is an agent for Sufi Brotherhood and whose own stall is in sight of our house brought a man to me just after I returned from seeing Gabriela safely board an English warship. He said that Miriam suggested we might be able to help him."

"Why was he in Tangiers?"

"He told me that his group had come to buy weapons and ammunition, urgently needed in Fez to hold off the imminent attack by the Sultan."

"Did you find him the weapons?"

"We would not be able to lay our hands on much. In any case he said they already had the weapons and ammunition required. They wanted help to get it aboard the first ship about to leave for the Atlantic coast. And he would pay us a substantial sum. My four companions were ecstatic. The money was very tempting, and we would be removing weapons from Tangiers."

"You found a way to assist them?"

"Gabriela had arranged that trunks of her belongings would be sent to our house because at the time she did not know where she would finish up. We would hold them until this was known. Not long before the explosion Gabriella's trunks and several carpets in which the Islamic ammunition had been concealed, arrived. We transferred Gabriela's possessions into other cartons we had, and the Fez agents filled the trunks with the ammunition and weapons which they took to the harbor and loaded it on Dona Catarina's ship, falsely using Da Gama's authorization that these were household goods. The ship was due to leave for Casablanca the next morning. We had no idea that they proposed to blow up the ship. We were misled."

"All this explains a lot. Now the vital information, what happened when Colonel Lopez arrived at your house?" asked Luke.

"The Colonel burst into the room and demanded that we release Gabriela into his care. I told him she was not with us and had joined her aunt on an English warship. He would soon be rid of her. He attacked us verbally about how we had undermined his standing with Gabriela. This was too much for one of my comrades, who threatened the colonel that if he did not leave, the authorities would be informed of his part in Gabriela's abduction and the ransom extracted from Dona Catarina."

"Not the most calming of comments towards a man already enraged by his sweetheart's desertion." commented Gil.

"At first I thought it had had a positive effect. The colonel strode to door as if to leave. As he reached the exit he turned and with his two pistols now primed, he shot two of my comrades dead, and then he produced two grenades, with their fuses burning. I managed to get one shot away which I think hit him, but the last thing I remember is two lighted grenades thrown in my direction."

"The only question remaining which you cannot answer as you were in a coma under the rubble and then here in the infirmary, is who killed the four Fez agents and why?" posed Luke.

Costa's pragmatic answer agreed with Tom's assertions

"Whoever supplied the ammunition would want their part kept secret. Where is Colonel Lopez now?" he asked.

"He was in the friary but discharged himself," answered Luke.

"I had him under surveillance since he left there, but my men lost him early this morning," Gil advised.

"The man who killed my comrades is not the Miguel Lopez I knew. His obsession with Gabriela has turned his mind. There is no accounting for what he might do next. The deputy governor must remove him from his post—and you must detain him for his own as wellbeing and for the safety of others," said Costa.

Luke turned to Ibram, "You may see Dona Catarina now. Feel free to update her with what you have just heard."

<h1 align="center">21</h1>

Luke was determined to uncover the renegade who had sold the ammunition to the Fez agents. As one or more of the senior officers must have been involved, he took his concerns to the governor and asked, "Who controls the arms and ammunition of the city?"

"Up until my arrival the military commandant, General de Silva had absolute and sole authority."

"What changed?"

"I had orders to send all arms and ammunition not required over the following two months back to Lisbon as a matter of urgency. It was a task which I delegated to Major Coval. It would have been more convenient if the English had bought some of the contents of the arsenal, but given the collapse of your military regime and the demobilization of tens of thousands of troops and hundreds of ships, you have a glut of arms and ammunition. My government hopes that some of this surplus will come to Portugal with the three thousand troops you have promised. In the meantime, every musket and accompanying shot and powder are urgently needed at home. I will call in Major Coval who can update you on the situation."

Leo explained, "I personally supervised the removal of all arms and ammunition from the arsenal in the tower until they were secured in the holds of ships bound for Lisbon. I watched every ammunition laden vessel leave the harbor. The last shipment leaves tomorrow. The Fez agents had no access to our arsenal since I arrived here."

"Does that mean the city is now without reserves of arms or ammunition?"

"Not at all. As soon as we arrived, I explained to the general what was to happen to the arsenal and asked him to remove what he needed over the remaining month or two. He has his reserves stored in the basement of the southern gate tower."

"Apart from this stock for de Silva's current use, is there anybody else in the city who would be in a position to sell ammunition?"

"No, the importation of arms and ammunition by private citizens has been banned for decades. With half the population soldiers, most households would have a musket or two—but all ammunition is controlled by the authorities."

"I need to question de Silva, yet not arouse his suspicions."

"Yes, for a foreign officer to be probing the quantity of arms and ammunition we have in Tangiers would certainly alarm me. But there is a way. Major, take the colonel with you to the general. You will ask as the last shipment of material leaves for Lisbon tomorrow whether he has any arms and ammunition in excess of requirements," suggested the governor.

"But how do I explain Colonel Tremayne's presence?"

"That he is interested in buying some of the surplus, as English supplies have been delayed."

Leo carried out the governor's suggestions. Mario claimed he had no excess.

Leo persisted. "General, I am sure you have put aside more than you need. Take me to your mini-arsenal so that I can assess the situation for myself?"

Leo and Luke followed the general to the basement of the gate tower. Even to the casual observer there was a plethora of arms and ammunition.

Leo was diplomatic. "General, do you have the paperwork relating to the supplies you received from the arsenal on my arrival? I can then more fairly assess what you have used since then, and more accurately assess what you will need in the immediate future."

"My aide will have the necessary papers, let's return to my office," replied Mario.

Back in the office Leo asked, "Did you have an unusual demand on your resources last month?"

"I re-equipped my Berber auxiliaries who man the southern wall with new muskets."

Luke was dying to ask, "Did you sell any ammunition in recent weeks."

But he remained diplomatically silent.

After spending some time over the papers that Mario's aide had produced, Leo declared, "I doubt that you need all the ammunition you have, but if there is any left when you leave the English might buy it."

Luke interjected, "We would certainly buy the ammunition, but we have no need of the muskets.

After Leo and Luke had left Mario's office the latter asked, "Well does that clear Mario of any sales?"

"He certainly has not sold any of the ammunition he drew down from the arsenal although there was a discrepancy in muskets. Fifty muskets, even allowing for those distributed to the Berbers, seem to be missing."

A despondent Luke bemoaned the fact, "Then Mario is not the man who sold ammunition to the Fez fanatics."

"Don't feel so low, Luke. It does not mean that at all. I do not know what supplies of ammunition Mario had before I arrived. He could have secreted away for his private benefit over a decade, a considerable amount of arms and ammunition. He could still be your man. He may have been supplying arms and ammunition to Moroccan groups for years. The Fez agents obviously knew who to approach for such material."

An hour later Gil arrived at Luke's headquarters with one issue dominating his thinking. "We must find Miguel before he kills someone else. Father Roberto has informed me of his escape. The friar is on his way here."

"I will alert the barracks to the necessity of restraining Colonel Lopez for his own good. I will also inform the deputy governor that given recent information that elements in the infantry may open the gate to an influx of Fez militants, the English will occupy the gate tower, and that I will transfer as many ship's cannons as possible to that site," Luke explained.

The two men were interrupted by the arrival of a blood-stained Father Roberto.

"What exactly happened Father?" asked Luke.

"Miguel Lopez!"

"Did he try to kill you?" probed Gil.

"No, but you must send men to the deputy governor's house and office. Lopez may try to kill him."

Gil ordered his men to go immediately to Mario's home, and Luke set his troops to Mario's office in the barracks which he had left an hour or so earlier.

"What happened, Father?" Luke asked again.

"Miguel came to the friary in a high state. He accused me of being part of Catarina's conspiracy to separate him from his one true love, Gabriela. He was not himself. I endeavored to calm him down. The subject of his vengeance kept changing—myself, Catarina, the English, his own sister, Major Vento, and a cohort of his own men. He suddenly stopped his rambling, battered the wall with his fists, and announced that he now saw things more clearly. The one person who had orchestrated his current misfortune was Mario who was determined to get his hands on Gabriela's rightful inheritance, and who wanted his sister-in-law dead, or at least out of the way. Miguel would settle with this arch enemy once and for all. As he strode out of the friary, I tried to stop him. He threw me to the ground, and I hit my head on a low table. By the time I recovered and reached the street I could not tell whether he had headed for Mario's home or his office."

"Our surgeon will have a look at you Father, and we will follow our men to their respective destinations," announced Luke as he and Gil departed.

Halfway across the barrack square Luke met Major Dimas Vento and asked, "Have you seen the Colonel today?"

"No, but according to my men he came in while I was talking to you and mentioned that he had an appointment with the deputy governor, and after ascertaining that Mario was not in his office headed for his home."

"Serano is already moving to that location. I will join him. Come with me! Did he take any men with him?"

"Yes—do you expect trouble?"

"At the worst he may kill Mario, at best try to arrest him. There is no accounting for a troubled mind."

On arriving at Mario's villa, Dimas and Luke were met by Gil whose men had already surrounded the complex. He explained, "Most of the servants have been expelled by Miguel at gunpoint and told if they tried to reenter the room, their mistress would be shot. Miguel has Mario, his wife and two or three female servants bailed up in the library. He has a man stationed at the main door and within the building two men outside the library door. The fourth man must be in the room with his colonel."

Luke turned to Dimas. "Talk to the three soldiers at the door! Explain the situation and order them to stand down or more positively to help you calm the situation."

The man at the outer door only needed a few words from Dimas and he moved away from the door. The two outside the library required more convincing but eventually followed Dimas back to where Luke and Gil were waiting. Gil asked, "What did your colonel tell you was his mission in confronting the deputy governor in the way he has. After all General de Silva is his and your ultimate commanding officer. At the moment your actions can be construed as mutiny, which after a brief court martial could lead to your immediate execution."

The soldier who had stood at the outer door responded. "Colonel Lopez said we must save Tangiers from an Islamic takeover. The deputy governor and others in authority preferred Moslem control to that of the English and we had act decisively now to prevent an infidel victory."

"Did he explain further?" asked Luke.

"He didn't need to. He is our commanding officer."

"If so, why did you leave your post when spoken to by Major Vento?" probed an irritated Gil.

"He persuaded me that Colonel Lopez was not himself. We had our own doubts as during the trek over here he kept mumbling about a woman who was behind all his and Tangier's troubles who must be dealt with first."

"Did he mention a name?"

"No, but constantly referred to a greedy sister."

"It looks as if Miguel maybe targeting Lidia, Gabriela's sister, as much as Mario," said Luke.

Dimas turned to the men who had guarded the library. "Is the library door locked?"

"Yes, just after the colonel and our comrade entered, we heard the lock being turned."

"It is an impressive door which will not give way easily—and the hinges are on the inside," added the second man.

"Let's question the staff on the layout of the library and whether there is another way of entering it," suggested Dimas.

Luke asked, "In the meanwhile should Gil knock on the door and suggest to Miguel that we are here to take over his prisoner, Mario."

"Too dangerous!" replied Gil. "In his state of mind Miguel's reaction might be that given the corruption of the authorities, handing Mario over to us is simply freeing him. It might provoke him to execute the deputy governor on the spot."

"Something needs to be done immediately. We need to distract Miguel until we can confront him," persisted Luke.

"I can do that. I will knock on the door and claim a crisis has arisen which I need direct orders to deal with," announced Dimas.

"What crisis would be sufficient to gauge their attention?" asked Gil.

Dimas turned to Luke, "I will present my superiors with a combination of truth and lies, claiming the English have moved to take over the city. I will tell them that with the help of our own cavalry, the English have confined our infantry to their barracks, have occupied the gate tower, and installed half a dozen ship's cannon on it, and above all seek to arrest both of them."

"Take the three soldiers with you and try to get all of you into the room. Ideally if Miguel unlocks the door to let you in, try to keep it unlocked. If the door is unlocked, we can then make a frontal assault and take over the room," advised Gil.

Dimas gathered his men and instructed them, "Our aim is to rescue the colonel before he harms himself or the de Silvas. Once inside, our aim is to calm the situation not to escalate it. However, if I wipe my brow, disarm the colonel. If such an opportunity does not arise try to station yourself between the colonel and his captives, while I try to distract them all. If we can keep the door unlocked, Captain Serano will storm into the room shortly after we enter. If it remains locked, they may take some time finding other points of entry."

The plan failed at the first obstacle. Dimas knocked on the door and explained that given English aggression, he needed to discuss the matter with his two superiors. Miguel dismissed Dimas by ordering him to take his concerns to the governor—the deputy governor and himself had others matters to resolve.

Dimas tried a new line. "Gentlemen, in addition to the move of the English, Captain Serano is headed this way to arrest both of you."

This did bring a response. "On what grounds?" Miguel asked.

"You for murder and the deputy governor for treason."

"Then you and your men must stay at this door to defend us from such an illegal police action."

22

Meanwhile Luke and Gil questioned the staff regarding alternative means of accessing the library. Unlike many houses that were made of dried brick in which the walls could be cut through, the de Silva's villa including internal walls was of stone brought down from the mountains. Smashing their way through the walls was therefore not an option.

All was not lost. There was a small antechamber leading off the library that contained stairs that led to the roof. Gil sent one of his men to see if the roof door was locked. It was. Gil addressed the staff. "We believe that your master and mistress are in danger. If we try to force entry into the library this may lead to their death. Is there any way we can get into that antechamber without alerting those in the library?"

There was a prolonged silence and then a young boy of seven or eight came forward and announced, "You can get through the roof door."

"But we can't. It is locked from the inside," repeated an annoyed Gil.

"I will unlock it," the child replied.

There were murmurs of disbelief and the odd derisory remark.

Luke gently asked the boy, "How can you do that when you are on the outside?"

"Simple sir! There is a ventilation outlet with a loose grill. I am small enough to squeeze through it and drop onto the internal stairs—and then open the door."

Luke scooped up the boy and headed for the roof, followed by Gil and several of his men.

The ventilation grill was in the side of the wall and quite tiny. Luke was concerned for the boy. "The drop from this grill to the stairs is too much. It is too dangerous."

The boy whispered to Luke, "I have done this many times before. I swing myself towards the higher steps and then there is no problem."

The grill was removed, and the group became concerned that the hole was too small. Perhaps an attempt should be made to enlarge the hole. Luke lifted the boy to the hole, and he began to wriggle his way through. Luke called for a trunk on which he could stand and hold onto the boy's hand to ease his fall. Luke could feel the boy beginning to swing just before he let go.

As Luke jumped down from his trunk, he heard the door leading down into the antechamber next to the library open to reveal a grinning child. Gil suggested Luke not take part in the exercise about to occur. It might strain relations between Portugal and England if an English officer arrested a Portuguese deputy governor while the city was still under Portuguese administration.

Luke waited with some of Gil's men outside the library door. A shot was heard and a short scuffle. Luke hoped that it was not fired by Lopez and had not killed Mario or Lidia.

He need not have worried. The door was opened. Miguel and Mario were led away. Servants streamed back into the house and several escorted Lidia back to her room.

Luke congratulated Gil on a mission accomplished and asked, "What happened in there?"

"We were in luck. The door between the library and antechamber was wide open. Miguel had his back to the open door with a pistol pointing in Mario's direction. I hit Miguel from behind, knocking the pistol from his grasp. A shot was accidently fired as the weapon hit the ground, but no one was hit. My men flooded the room, freed Lidia and have taken Mario and Miguel into custody. I will inform the Governor immediately of this delicate situation."

Later that day Luke learnt that the Governor had placed Mario under house arrest while charges against him, if any, were examined by Major Coval. Miguel was returned to the Franciscan friary for examination and treatment. The Governor endorsed the English seizure of the gate tower and its strengthening by several ship cannons. He noted in an aside to Leo Coval that in this process the English had also seized Mario's supply of arms and ammunition. He asked Colonel Carlos Pimento with Major Dimas's advice to clean out rogue elements of the infantry, and that they would be replaced gradually by the English. Luke would have to wait until morning to discuss with Gil whether further questioning of Miguel and Mario could occur. But he could question Lidia now.

As the current Governor had not brought his partner with him, Lidia de Silva nee Sarmento was formally, as the wife of the deputy governor, at the top of Tangier's social ladder. This first lady of Tangiers in reality was overshadowed in power and influence by her aunt Catarina Sarmento and in popularity and notoriety by her younger sister Gabriela Sarmento. Rumor suggested that Mario and his wife Lidia faced a very uncertain future when his role in Tangiers ceased. Such a situation suggested to Luke that this provided a motive for Mario to act illegally in the search for additional income. To supply arms and ammunition to conflicting groups in such a volatile area as northern Morocco would be a profitable clandestine activity.

Luke hoped that he might use Lidia's probable resentment against her Sarmento relatives to facilitate his enquiries. He also risked breaking the basic rules of Portuguese social relationship. He would visit a married woman in the absence of her husband and without an invitation. Thomas told him in no uncertain terms that such an act could be counterproductive. His answer was just across the courtyard—Catarina. They agreed that Catarina should send one of her servants to her niece's villa asking if she was willing to receive Colonel Tremayne.

Next morning Luke was received by Lidia in a room full of male and female servants. He expressed his thanks and immediately explained that he wished to question her on two issues—what happened during the de Silva's confrontation with Miguel Lopez, and where did she see Mario fitting into the last days of Portuguese power in the city.

A good sign was that she immediately dismissed all the servants from the room except for a very large man who remained standing behind her mistress who remained seated on a lavishly decorated sedan. Luke was asked to draw up a chair which he placed adjacent to Lidia's. He began his interrogation gently.

"My lady, I hope you have recovered from your ordeal. If you do not feel up to answering my questions, I can come back another day."

"Thank you, Colonel, for your consideration. The English are not renowned for such civility. Regarding yesterday, it was not as traumatic as you might think. For most of the time I was not concerned with Miguel's visit because I thought that he had come to announce he was to become my new brother-in-law. When he dismissed all the servants at gun point and installed one of his armed soldiers in the room, which he then locked, I sensed a little drama."

"To be invaded in your own house by an armed man is hardly *a little drama*," said Luke.

"I probably inadvertently diverted Miguel from his initial aim and calmed him down by assuming he had come to tell me that he and Gabriela were engaged. I even gave him a hug and welcomed him as my one and only brother. I went on to say as I hugged him that he would be my only male relation in Tangiers apart from my husband. He began to weep during which he began to relate how Gabriela had disappeared again and that he had spent most of the last few days trying to find her."

"He didn't threaten you or Mario?"

"Not at this point. I kept my arms around him and tried to comfort him. Looking back, I could have at that stage removed the pistol from his grasp."

"From outside the door we heard a heated argument. What went wrong?"

"Mario in his most undiplomatic manner suggested that Miguel should simply forget Gabriela. She was a cruel manipulator who had been playing him along while having her way with many a married man in the city. Miguel's personality suddenly changed. He started to breathe heavily, and his eyes glazed over. He strode over to Mario, and I thought he would hit him with the butt of his pistol. He declared that Mario's comments were proof that we had deliberately destroyed his relationship with Gabriela and were probably behind her disappearance."

"Did the situation escalate further?"

"Not then. Luckily Major Vento was heard at the door asking to be admitted as he needed advice from his two superior officers. This diverted Miguel from his anti-de Silva tirade for a few minutes."

"And after the major had been dismissed?"

"Mario took the initiative and demanded to know what Miguel intended to do. He suggested that if Miguel shot us both, he would not survive. The villa was surrounded by troops and police. Before Miguel answered, Serano and his men burst into the room from the antechamber disarming Miguel. The door was opened, and Major Vento and his men also entered the room. You know the rest."

"Thank you, Dona Lidia. I must now ask you questions on a broader issue."

"Not just yet Colonel. I have not eaten today. Join me for a range of smoked fish, cold chicken, olives and various fruits!"

Luke acquiesced. As he ate and chatted, he considered the woman next to him. She was as beautiful as her younger sister, more statuesque and oozed sensuality. She was probably in her early thirties with deep green eyes. Her sober dressing concealed much of her body, forcing Luke to imagine large breasts and a tiny waist. Given her obvious attraction to men, Luke wondered about her fidelity to Mario and the true nature of their marital relationship.

The diners completed their breakfast with what was obviously the best of sweet Portuguese red wine. Luke resumed his interrogation in a more relaxed atmosphere.

"All the charges against your husband are circumstantial, and largely based on an assumed motive—the need for money. How is it that the second ranking official in Tangiers is rumoured to be short of money and apparently without any clear appointment after his term here ends? As a general, surely, he can revert to his military career. Portugal is still fighting for its independence in Europe and for its empire in Asia and the Americas?"

"He had no previous military career," was Lidia's surprising answer.

"How then does he hold then rank of general, is deputy governor of Tangiers and still short of funds?"

"Very simple! Mario is the illegitimate son of one of the late King's favourite courtiers and generals. His late father refused to acknowledge him, let alone legitimise him. He has no family inheritance. However, his father did use his influence to have Mario appointed to a few administrative positions and ultimately as commandant of the garrison here with the nominal rank of general. Soon after his appointment the role of commandant of the garrison was combined with that of deputy governor. Both King John and Mario's father are long since dead. He now has no one of influence at the ever-changing court. His half-brother who has inherited the family title and wealth refuses to acknowledge him in any way, although other family members are seeking a reconciliation. Consequently, when Mario ceases to be deputy governor here he has nothing. He will even lose rank of general."

"He will survive that. I experienced a similar demotion with the change of regime in England. Given the pressures he is under, would have been behind the attacks on Dona Catarina, attempts to sell the city to local warlords, Moslem fanatics or Spain, and the theft and resale of the Islamic emerald ring?"

"Colonel, I will not incriminate my husband in any way regarding that list of outrageous rumours, but I will comment on my family situation. I have nothing but admiration and regard for my aunt. How do you think Mario has retained his position here for so long especially after his father's death? Dona Catarina used her position to ensure he was not replaced. Mario holds his position here due to the continued good will of my aunt. In addition, she pays me a substantial allowance."

"Could this not lead to resentment?"

"It would be self-defeating. Our best hope for the future is the continued benevolence of my aunt."

These revelations suddenly opened a new line of enquiry for Luke which might totally change his perspective on events. Could Mario in all his alleged misdoings have been acting for his aunt? Was Dona Catarina Sarmento and not General Mario de Silva the clandestine mastermind of potentially anti-English activities. Was Mario her agent rather than her ineffective would- be murderer?

On reflection Luke wondered if Lidia's comments regarding her aunt were genuine. Why of all the issues that he raised against Mario did his wife concentrate on how well he got on with her aunt.?

23

L uke continued his questioning of Lidia.

"Why did you come to Tangiers, and then almost immediately marry Mario?"

"My parents died when I was nine and Gabriela was one. We were initially brought up in a convent in northern Portugal. Ten years after our parents' death, my father's brother who was then governor here remarried—to Dona Catarina. They adopted us and we arrived here about eleven years ago. Uncle Raphael had me married to his deputy within a few months. When uncle died soon after, his much younger wife Catarina continued to look after us—despite my marriage."

"Where will Mario and you will be in a month or so?"

"Aristotle da Gama hinted that Mario might stay here as Catarina's Tangerine agent or move to Lisbon and act in the same role there. Neither Mario nor Catarina seem ecstatic about that scenario."

"Have you discussed with Father Antonio a government appointment?"

"Mario talked with both him and Major Coval. He came away from that meeting incensed. They suggested an inferior administrative position in Goa in India, or a military position at a much lower rank in Brazil. He was asked to decide on the spot as Father Antonio claimed that the Queen Regent, who would make such an appointment on his recommendation, was about to relinquish power to her son King

Afonso. The new King may not respond in the same positive way. Mario declined both offers."

Luke began to feel some sympathy for the De Silvas. Perhaps the English could utilise Mario's experience, at least in the short term? He was well pleased with his interrogation. Issues were much clearer, suggesting that the De Silvas as more likely to be innocent than guilty.

On reaching his barracks Luke recounted his interview with Lidia to his officers.

Jack was not impressed. "Don't believe a word of it! She is a Sarmento and like her younger sister prone to lying. She confuses what she hopes to be the case with reality. I am surprised that you are so gullible."

Luke retired that evening a little concerned about his own situation. Was he becoming too soft—too sympathetic to those he considered to be unfairly treated? Were his prejudices overcoming his grasp on reality? Miguel Lopez's mental decline suddenly became more personal.

Early the next morning Luke received a message from Gil to meet him at Mario's villa at ten when they could both question the suspect deputy governor.

On arriving they were met in the reception hall by Lidia who immediately asked a servant to inform her husband that his visitors had arrived. A white-faced servant returned within minutes. He whispered to Lidia who shouted at the two investigators to follow her. "Mario has disappeared, and there is a body in his room."

Mario's bedchamber was in disarray. Chairs and tables were overturned, and furnishings dragged to the floor. A body lay at the foot of the bed. "It is Mario's valet," said Lidia.

A quick look established that he had suffered a heavy blow to the head and received a dagger or sword wound to the chest. He was dead.

Lidia began to sob. Luke suggested she retire. Gil and he would come back later that day for a few questions. Luke and Gil returned to the bedchamber and searched the room thoroughly. Nothing was found that helped explain the situation.

"The dead valet suggests that Mario has been abducted or killed rather than simply disappeared to avoid our questioning," concluded Gil.

"Not necessarily. His valet may have objected to Mario disappearing and in order to escape, the master had to kill the servant," suggested Luke.

"Rubbish! Maybe in England servants stand up to their masters, but a valet in Tangiers is not going to confront the deputy governor. This valet died trying to save his master."

Later that afternoon Luke and Gil returned and were received by Lidia who offered them the finest in Portuguese red wine. Luke asked, "Did you discuss our conversation of yesterday with Mario last evening?"

"Yes, in detail."

"What was his reaction?" asked Gil.

"He was pleased, and armed with the information I had provided, he retired to the library to put together a few thoughts on what he would to tell you today."

"Have you been in the library since?" probed Luke.

"No."

"We will search the room. He may have jotted down a few notes," Luke remarked as he headed out the door.

A few minutes later a jubilant Luke returned. "There was nothing on his desk or in his drawers of any consequences, but in his bin, I found this crumpled piece of paper."

"And what does it say?" asked Gil.

"Elcano!" was the reply.

"And what does that refer to? The word appears to be Spanish rather than Portuguese," commented Gil.

"I have never heard it before," said Lidia.

"Maybe Mario was kidnapped to prevent us investigating Elcano?" mused Luke.

Suddenly cheering was heard from an outer room and within minutes a blood splattered man entered the room with three soldiers.

Lidia embraced her husband.

Mario attempted a humorous comment, "I am sorry gentlemen. I am late for our morning appointment."

"And what kept you?" asked Luke in the same spirit.

"Three men broke into my bedchamber and insisted I accompany them. I resisted and after some swordplay I was slightly wounded and then disarmed. My valet Juan tried to stop them and was ruthlessly struck down and then unnecessarily stabbed. Did he survive?"

"No," answered Lidia.

"How did you escape the clutches of these kidnappers?" asked Gil.

"My loyal bodyguard! I was led out into the street through the wine cellar and immediately bundled into a covered wagon which had clearly carried dried fish. You must be able to smell it still. In the seconds between exit from the building and concealment in the wagon, one of my men who must have been looking out into the street recognized me. He reported the incident to his commanding officer. He had seen the deputy governor being bundled into a wagon. The officer quickly rallied my bodyguard who eventually caught up with the wagon. They whipped off the cover, threw me a sword and engaged the kidnappers."

"Good, we will have a few men to question," Luke commented.

"I am afraid not. They refused to surrender, and my enraged men killed them. I have a wagon load of bodies which might tell us something about them."

"Did you pick up any clues while you confronted them or from what you might have heard in the wagon?" asked Gil.

"They were not Portuguese. They spoke Spanish between themselves, but it was not a dialect I recognized. They were clearly not locals."

"We are delighted that you were freed and have rejoined your wife. Given the circumstances, there is only one question I will ask you now—who or what is Elcano? I found it written on a paper in your study," asked Luke.

"It may completely change your thinking on the attempts to kill Catarina, but I am not feeling too good at the moment. Could you defer your interrogation until tomorrow? I have sent the bodies to the Franciscan friary in case detailed inspection of them can reveal anything."

Luke and Gil arrived at the friary after the midday meal. Roberto led them into the chamber where the bodies were laid out. The surgeon Greg Pickering had just completed his examination.

"Well, do the bodies tell you anything," asked Gil.

"All were sailors. Their bodies suggested they led an outdoor life, their hands that it was arduous, and their clothes were imbedded with salt. My guess is that these men were ocean going mariners," replied Greg.

"And Mario said they were Spanish speaking with an accent not from the parts of Spain with which he was familiar," added Luke.

"Which means the accent was from the far north of Spain—Galicia or Navarre," contributed Roberto.

Gil looked worried, "Nothing fits. If these men were common seamen, they would not be able swordsmen. Mario claims he indulged in swordplay until overcome by numbers."

"Your concern may be supported by my examination of Mario's valet. The wounds to his body were not from the thrusts of a sword, but from multiple stab wounds. On the other hand, the bodies of the kidnappers were penetrated by swordsmen who knew what they were doing. They went for the kill with thrusts to the heart," added Greg. "Mario's bodyguard was ruthless and determined to take no prisoners."

Luke turned to Roberto and asked, "A word that has come up in our investigation of the attack on Mario is Elcano. It is not known by those we have consulted. You have been in Tangiers longer than anyone else, is it known to you?"

Roberto beamed, "Eureka! This may be a break you need. And if these kidnappers were sailors, it does fit. When I first came to Tangiers the bulk of the city's trade, shipping and banking was in the hands of Dominic Elcano. His monopoly was being challenged by an ambitious converso family the Falcones. Abram Falcone played a masterstroke in offering his beautiful daughter, Catarina, to the then recently widowed governor, Raphael Sarmento. Very quickly the Elcanos lost their position to the Falcone with government assistance flowing towards the newcomers and drying up for their rivals. Not long after Abram achieved dominance he died, but his daughter Catarina continued the pressure on her family's rivals, forcing them to leave town."

Luke whistled, "So Catarina destroyed the Elcanos?"

"You could say that," confirmed Roberto.

"What happened to the Elcanos?" asked Gil.

"Again, it fits the pattern that is slowly emerging. The Elcanos were based equally in San Sebastian in Basque country and Tangiers. Dominic had a few friends left at the Portuguese Court and as he was seen as anti-Castilian, he obtained permission to trade with the Portuguese Empire. This was all twenty years ago at least."

"Did the Elcanos have a big family?"

"The sea took its toll on the wider family but Dominic when he left here had two small children—a boy and a girl."

"How do you know so much about this family?" asked Luke.

"One of Dominic's brothers was a fellow friar at the time, and Dominic donated heavily to our order," answered Roberto.

"Let's see if Mario gives us a similar story," muttered Luke to himself.

Next morning Luke and Gil questioned Mario at his headquarters in the barracks.

"Tell us about the Elcanos?" asked Gil.

Mario's account was similar to that of Father Roberto although the former emphasized that the Elcanos had subsequently made a fortune through trading with the outposts of the Portuguese Empire.

"Why have you suddenly alerted us to the Elcanos whose role here ceased twenty years ago?" asked Luke.

"Because they seek to destroy Dona Catarina."

"In what way?"

"Father Antonio informed Catarina that the Elcanos, now the largest trading company in Portugal had petitioned the King for rights to establish trading posts in the one part of the empire from which they had previously been excluded- the African Atlantic coast, particularly Casablanca."

"Surely the wily Catarina can compete successfully with a rival company?" said Luke.

"Perhaps, but the Elcanos petition seeks a monopoly of all Portuguese trade out of Africa."

"Surely the Queen Regent will protect her friend?" posed Luke.

"That is exactly the problem. The Queen Regent would never agree to the Elcanos request, but she ceases to have any authority anytime soon. The young King with new advisers may readily agree to it, as I am sure that the Elcano petition will be accompanied by a very large donation."

"Surely Catarina has the wealth to counter this," commented Gil.

"Money isn't everything. According to Antonio, the Elcanos have waged a very successful propaganda campaign with royal advisers that Catarina is a security risk. She is too close to the Moroccan sultan, whose interests she may place before that of Portugal."

"And you think that the Elcanos have brought their campaign to discredit or destroy Catarina to Tangiers?" commented Luke.

"If they are out to destroy Catarina, why did they attack you?" added Gil.

Mario blushed. "In my discussions with Antonio I have created the false impression that when I leave here, Catarina might make me manager of her West African enterprises. This must have got back to court at Lisbon which has made me a target for Elcanos assassins. They attacked me, because you English have Catarina under such heavy protection."

Luke suddenly changed the topic. "Why did your bodyguard kill your abductors? They were not even competent swordsmen. They were dagger wielding assassins. What could they tell us which you wished to remain secret?"

"I will not answer any more questions after such a slanderous innuendo from the English Colonel. Please leave my office!"

24

They left. Gil was furious with Luke. "Why provoke him? What did you hope to gain?"

"I don't know, but his story is just too convenient in transferring suspicion from the family regarding inheritance to a long absent rival trading family. Mario's message to us is clear. Look for her attempted killers among agents of the Elcanos and for good measure examine his aunt's loyalty to the Portuguese state. Above all, I reject Mario's explanation for why he was targeted, and why he had his abductors ruthlessly killed. Is he was copying his sister in-law Gabriela? Was this a pretend abduction which went wrong?"

Gil laughed, "You are certainly living up to your reputation of finding convoluted explanations for simple events. Catarina is leaving Tangiers. For internal enemies she will soon be gone. Why try to kill her? The answer lies in finding out who does not want her in Casablanca. We have already been made aware that enemies of the Sultan may be out to destroy Catarina. Mario has given us another possibility—the Elcanos."

Luke informed Catarina of the attempted abduction of Mario and asked, "Were you aware that the Elcanos are seeking to trade along the Atlantic coast?"

"Yes, Father Antonio told me when he arrived with you several weeks ago. That is why I brought my departure to Casablanca forward. I need to firmly establish my position there before the Elcanos arrive. My unofficial alliance with the Sultan stems from a similar fear. Hopefully if the Sultan only permits trade to Casablanca through us, it will not matter how many licenses the Elcanos obtain from the young King."

"A disastrous political association my lady. Your enemies are already using your friendship with the Sultan as evidence that you are a security risk to the Portuguese state. Nevertheless, they cannot be confident of their success if they need to murder you and your nephew-in-law before you move."

"The Elcanos are not behind the attack on Mario, or the earlier attempts to kill me."

"Why not? The three men who kidnapped Mario were sailors probably from the Basque area of Spain, the homeland of the Elcanos."

"When the Elcanos left Tangiers, it was put about that my father, Abram Falcone, had on my marriage to the then governor, used his new political influence to transfer the Elcanos operations to him."

"Yes, that is what I have heard. In addition, after your father's death you were even more involved in their destruction."

"This pretense was to cover a very different reality. My father and Dominic Elcano were friends and commercial allies."

"Why create the opposite impression?"

"To help Dominic."

"Explain!"

"Dominic was ambitious. He wished to expand beyond a few coastal traders working out of San Sebastien and Tangiers. He wanted to get a share of the trade of the Portuguese Asian and American empires."

"A difficult task for a Basque citizen of Spain during the Portuguese wars of independence."

"Exactly, but as a Basque, he was not admitted into the trade of the Spanish Empire dominated by the Andalusian towns of Seville and Cadiz, and as a Spaniard, Portugal would not have been interested in him. My husband the then governor had considerable influence in Lisbon and persuaded the authorities to allow the Elcanos to trade out of Oporto with Brazil and Portuguese India. They made a fortune. Years later Dominic told me leaving Tangiers was the turning point in the family's shipping and banking history. As part of the deal with my father and husband, Dominic willingly handed over to father their local assets and trading contacts. Father simply took over the Elcanos now unwanted local network."

"If all this was a cordial arrangement, why the pretense of a forceful takeover?"

"Father did not think an image of a powerful marauding Falcone family network that had demolished the Elcanos so decisively would do any harm."

"Why would Dominic Elcano go along with it?"

"Internal family issues. Dominic was the eldest of three brothers who had equal interests in the company. He wanted to expand into the Portuguese empire, his brothers strongly opposed it. To his brothers and the rest of the local community the Elcanos were forced out of Tangiers by an alliance between the government and the Falcones."

"So, you do not believe that the recent attempts on your life come from them?"

"Neither should you. It is too convenient. It is designed to draw attention away from enemies much closer to home."

"I agree. You must take no risks and I will increase your protection."

Later that afternoon Luke revisited Mario at his barrack's office. Unfortunately, according to Major Dimas, he had just left for his villa accompanied by four bodyguards. Luke decided he would follow Mario on foot.

A street away from the villa Luke heard a commotion and then several shots being fired. As he turned the corner, he saw a large crowd in the middle of the road.

Had the deputy governor been assassinated?

On reaching the crowd the cause of the commotion was obvious. A bull camel had run amok trampling several people before being shot. A serious altercation was developing involving the owner of the camel, relatives of those injured, and the men who had shot the animal. Serano's men were trying to sort out the situation.

Luke's reception by Mario was not warm. Luke apologized for his behavior earlier in the day when he suggested that Mario may have faked his own abduction. The deputy governor half nodded an acceptance of the apology, and asked curtly, "Why have you returned?"

"I have had a long discussion with Catarina. She is certain that the attack on you and her has nothing to do with the Elcanos." He then exaggerated, "She believes the enemy is within the city, and that you may be in further danger."

"I am well protected. I have my own gubernatorial bodyguard who hardly leave my side—and Serano has posted extra men around the villa."

"Have you during your long term as deputy governor upset any individual or group that may seek revenge before you escape the city.

"You think the motives for my abduction stem from my past actions?"

"Revenge appears the only motive that makes sense. You are about to leave Tangiers for good. If you and Catarina were not attacked to prevent you doing something in the future, then revenge for past activities must be the prime motive. Such action is urgent as both of you will soon be gone."

"But until very recently I played little part the running of Tangiers. My basic role was military commandant, and nearly all my dealings were with and within the army. Previous governors were control freaks involved in every government action. It is only since your arrival with the new Governor who has limited himself to dealing with the transfer of power to the English that I have been personally involved in the daily administration of the city."

"Would your financial support of the Spanish dominated Inquisition and the Dominicans have created any fanatical enemies?"

"I doubt it. Who would know? Cisneros was pragmatic, not a fanatic. He never probed the one issue which other Inquisitors focused on, and which would have divided the Tangerine community—the loyalty of former Jewish families, the conversos, to the Christian faith. Ironically most of my donations to the Dominicans and the Inquisition came from my aunt, Dona Catarina, who is of converso stock."

"Within the army, you must have created enemies?"

"No more than any other senior officer. In fact, the only complaints I received as military commander was that I was too lax and allowed colonels and captains to do their own thing. I never tried to stop elements in the infantry raiding the surrounding countryside as long as they ransacked pro-Ghalain villages and not those of our more friendly Berber tribes. Despite my alleged laxity the city resisted all attacks during the decade or more I have been here, and relations with surrounding Moroccan groups have, apart from Ghalain, remained good."

Luke thanked Mario for his cooperation and the two of them walked towards the exit gate closely followed by two of Mario's bodyguard.

Shots were heard and before Luke could ascertain what was happening, he was tackled from behind by one of the bodyguards and rolled behind a low retaining wall. Mario suffered a similar fate being rolled in the opposite direction. The open ground between the four prone men erupted as a hail of shot raised the dust for over a minute.

The gunfire brought musket carrying troops out of the villa who immediately directed their fire towards the source of the attack— the roof of a villa further up the hill. Serano's men outside the gate now ran in that direction.

When the firing ceased, Luke and Mario returned to the house where the host poured Luke and himself the finest of French brandy. Sometime later Serano arrived.

"What did you men discover?" asked an anxious Mario.

"Three or four men were stationed on the roof of the villa up the road. It has been deserted for a week or so, as the owners returned to Portugal in advance of the handover. The shooters were gone by the time my men arrived. The spent shot that covered the ground where you were shot at was of Iberian not Islamic origin, which suggests European rather than Moroccan assailants. Mario, you would be wise to have more of your men armed with muskets stationed outside the house, although I cannot be sure that you were the target. Tracing the trajectory of the attack on you both, most of the shots were levelled at you Luke, not Mario. I will have my men escort you back to the barracks. You should not go abroad without an armed guard—anti-English feeling is escalating."

The following morning Luke was explaining his previous night's encounter to his men when they were interrupted by Major Dimas Vento. "Horrendous news from Captain Serano, Mario de Silva is dead."

"There is probably some misunderstanding. Mario was attacked last night, but survived. I was there. We had a drink together to celebrate our good fortune."

"Nothing to do with last night. Mario was trampled to death this morning with two of his bodyguard on his way here. They were mown down by out-of-control wagons rolling down the narrow alley up which Mario and his men were riding. Serano would like you, to meet him immediately, just up from Mario's villa."

Luke and Jack arrived at the scene where the former commented, "Mario's number must have been up. He escapes a deliberate attempt on his life and dies in an accident."

"This was no accident. Mario was assassinated by a coordinated attack using two wagons racing down the alley. One was slightly behind the other but between them they covered the whole width of the road. Mario and his men could not escape," explained Gil.

"Using a horse and wagon for this purpose in this way would be suicidal for the horses," commented Jack.

"It was. Look at the scene! Five horses were killed or injured—Mario's and those of his two men, and two of those pulling the wagons. The injured had to be put down. They were raced down the hill at breakneck speed, deliberately colliding with the three horsemen. The lead horses of the wagons took the brunt of the impact trampling those they hit; the killing task completed by the wheels of the wagons. The two drivers alone were unharmed and probably jumped before impact. They quickly disappeared from the scene. It is possible that there were no drivers."

"Have you traced the horses and wagons?" asked Jack.

"Removed from Dona Catarina's property earlier this morning."

"Any witnesses?" Luke asked.

"A woman on the roof of an adjacent villa heard the noise and saw the carnage below her, but did not see any drivers or men moving away."

"The horses are still lying where they died. Where are the humans?" continued Luke.

The two bodyguards have been taken to the Franciscan priory where your surgeon can inspect them, Mario's remains have been taken to his villa."

Greg inspected the bodies and ascertained that their injuries and resultant death were consistent with being trampled down by hooves and run over by heavy wheels. Their heads were so mashed that identification rested largely on their dress.

25

Early next morning Luke received a message from Gil for he and Pickering to meet at Mario's villa at nine. At the gate Gil explained, "Last night Lidia sent a servant to inform me that while dressing Mario's body for burial it had been noticed that it had what appeared to be stab wounds in addition to those created by the trampling. You are here to confirm or reject this additional assault."

After a half hour of examination Greg and Luke emerged and informed Gil, and Majors Coval and Dimas who had joined him, "Mario was stabbed several times, but not by a dagger. Three sword thrusts were administered as he lay on the ground—thrusts that went through the body."

"Any conclusions from this fact?" asked Coval.

"Yes, this is a crime of passion—a frenzied finishing off of a man, possibly already dead. One thrust would have been sufficient. Secondly the weapon was a long sword, not the usual weaponry of a wagon driver. This whole operation was overseen by a gentleman who made sure his agents completed a successful mission," answered Luke.

The governor called an emergency meeting following the assassination of his deputy. It was attended by the leading Portuguese and English officials. "Given that this tragic event has occurred in the last months of our administration, my actions seek to combine the need to maintain law and order, and to continue the gradual transition to English rule. I will separate the role of deputy governor and that of military commandant The new last Portuguese military commandant of Tangiers will be Colonel Pimento who will also retain command of the cavalry. The new deputy governor with direct responsibility for law and order will be the current police commander who I promote to the rank of Colonel—Gil Serano. The local Portuguese infantry plagued by desertions and insubordination and without their effective commander Colonel Lopez, and much of their former role already taken over by the English, is immediately disbanded."

"Won't this lead to increased disorder?" asked Luke.

"Exactly, Colonel Tremayne. That is why I am creating two temporary special units to monitor the disbanded infantry. Major Vento will select a group from these men to form an additional special police force under the overall command of Colonel Serano to monitor the behavior of their former comrades, and Major Coval will organize the removal of these disbanded troops and their families from Tangiers as soon as possible but a small group will become a special police. A few may wish to join the English army, but I do not sense any enthusiasm for this from either Admiral Lawson or Colonel Tremayne."

"As a permanent solution your comments are correct. In the short term, if the English are taking over the current role of the infantry an increase in our manpower may be necessary. Recruitment from England is not immediate. I would be happy to talk to Major Vento concerning the temporary inclusion of some Portuguese infantry into the English forces. The more of these men who remain under army discipline the less problems will be created for Colonel Serano," responded Luke.

After leaving the Governor's meeting Luke and Gil discussed the situation.

Gil explained, "Given my promotion and extended responsibilities I cannot continue my hands-on investigation into the attacks on Catarina and Mario, nor on the fate of the emerald ring. You are more experienced than any of my assistants and any solution to these cases is of more benefit to the incoming English than the outgoing Portuguese. Given that both Major Coval and Major Vento have new responsibilities, any on-going investigation of these three issues now rests solely with you."

"If the two attacks are more to do with the present and future rather than the past, it is in England's interests to solve them. As we have now taken over completely from the Portuguese infantry, I will speak to the Admiral for more men from the fleet, and additional cannons to mount on the walls of the city. I will delegate the military aspects of our enhanced role to Captain Moon who will co-ordinate the defense of Tangiers with Colonel Pimento. This will free me with the help of my valet, given his language skills and local knowledge, to continue with the investigations."

Four days later, after overseeing the deployment of additional English troops and guns, Luke resumed his investigations by questioning Catarina once again. He did not waste time with chit chat.

"My lady who do you think murdered your nephew- in- law and was the attempt on your life part of the same plot?"

"It would make your task easier if all the problems that you confront stem from a common motive—the destruction of the Sarmentos. Unfortunately, you cannot assume that. Getting rid of me would force major changes, but killing Mario hardly affects anybody. He was a nobody, sustained for over a decade by my money and support."

"What if all of this is simply an attempt to reduce the beneficiaries of your will and speed up the distribution of its largesse. The terms of your will are a vital factor in this investigation, but I am not certain which of your wills is current."

"Nor will you. The uncertainty is my form of defense. My original will left one third of my estate to Lidia, a third to Gabriela and a third to be divided between Takama, Aristotle and a host of other employees. Mario lobbied for the lot to go to the eldest niece Lidia and therefore to him. In recent times I made it known that I am preparing a new will in which the family gets nothing. I told Lidia and Gabriela that husbands should provide for their future, and not their aunt. A new will could leave half of the business to Takama and the other half to Aristotle."

Catarina surprised Luke with her next comment. "There is a new factor that will eventually affect the details of my will which I have revealed to no one. Juan Elcano, Dominic's eldest son and now in charge of their operations contacted me. He made me two offers—a merger of our enterprises or an outright sale of my network to him."

"How have you kept these discussions from Takama and Aristotle especially since we have had you locked away here?"

"Juan sent a personal envoy on a recent ship from Casablanca who was brought here dressed as one of my servants. Takama and Aristotle thought he was from the Sultan."

"If either of them know they would not be happy. It could be enough to turn loyal subordinates into dangerous enemies."

"They do not know."

"What are your plans for Lidia? I am about to visit her."

"My nieces continue to surprise me. It took me years to accept that Gabriela was a predatory woman with a host of affairs and liaisons. Whether she was the blackmailer that some suggest, I have still not really accepted. Lidia has revealed herself in the last week as unfaithful as Gabriela. She just confessed to me to a long-term affair with another man."

"Who?"

"One of Gabriela's discards, and a friend of yours, the new deputy governor Gil Serano."

Luke was momentarily speechless. Eventually he spoke, "You know this could be a vital factor in the murder of Mario. The lover of unfaithful wife removes the husband and will soon marry the potentially rich widow. He had armed men stationed all around Mario's villa and knew Mario's every movement. You started by telling me nobody cared about Mario, and who would have a motive to murder him. You have now given me someone, or perhaps two people who had a motive."

Luke could hardly wait to question Lidia. He was direct, "My lady, I have been tasked with investigating your husband's murder, and I have just received news that could implicate you. I gather that you are having an affair—a motive for either you or your lover to arrange your husband's demise."

"In your position I would have similar suspicions, but there was no need to kill Mario."

"Why not?"

"He was leaving me, and I am seeking an annulment of my marriage."

"Mario was aware of the annulment application? How did he react to it?"

"This was nothing new. I have been working through Father Roberto to have my case put to His Holiness for over a year. Mario did not oppose it."

"On what grounds?"

"Mario's impotence. We have been married for a decade, and I have never become pregnant."

"It is generally believed that such a situation is the woman's fault. Surely Mario would have wanted to take the lead in breaking with you. Most males would not be able to cope with the blow to their manhood should such details become public. I cannot believe that the military commandant of Tangiers went along with his wife's destruction of his manhood when there was no evidence of his guilt."

"There was not at the time, but in recent weeks the truth has emerged. I am pregnant although apart from my lover, you are the only person I have told. Mario probably felt all the things you suggest, but he had already decided to leave me. He would be long gone from Tangiers when the news of my annulment breaks. I suspect that he also had a lover."

"Where is Mario going?"

"Who would most likely want to recruit a long-time military commandant of Tangiers? Someone who wished to capture the city. There are at least four Islamic groups who might attack when you take over—Ghalain the local warlord, the anti-Ghalain tribes in the local area, the Sufi brotherhood at Fez and the Sultan, my aunt's new favorite."

"And you do not know which of these it was? How was Mario going to disappear as military commandant and become adviser to a group about to attack the city?"

"I do not know which of these groups, but I have my suspicions. I do know how it was to be achieved. Now that Mario is dead, I can reveal all. His abduction was faked. We both saw how Gabriela had used a fake abduction to her advantage, so we decided that Mario should use the same ruse. He employed three men to stage this fake kidnapping and take him out of the city."

"Things went astray?"

"Yes, one of Mario's bodyguards saw the attempted kidnapping, alerted the troops stationed here and they rescued Mario. Mario panicked and fearing that the pretend kidnappers might reveal all, ordered his rescuers to kill them."

"That might be the simple explanation of his murder. Someone in the city that was aware of the situation took his revenge on behalf of the pretend kidnappers. Do you know who his lover is?"

"My suspicions were first aroused by Mario's failure to get distressed over my demand for an annulment. I began to think that he too had taken a lover and was glad to be rid of me. For a while I suspected he was having an affair with the queen of the souk the powerful and charismatic Miriam Barros, and local agent for the Sufi Brotherhood. He visited the souk daily over a few weeks but following the failed attempt to blow up my aunt and her ship and the killing of Sufi agents, he has not gone near the souk. I asked him about his concentrated obsession with the souk and he declared he had business with Miriam that was now concluded."

"So, you have no idea whether he has a current lover or not?"

"For years he has been spending a lot of time in one of the nearer anti-Ghalain Berber villages—in fact the village of Takama's parents."

"That would be a very dangerous pastime if discovered. It would bring instant death to the woman and a lingering painful demise for the male. You have certainly provided me with some astonishing evidence. Will you marry your lover?"

"After due mourning for Mario, and before my pregnancy becomes obvious, we will marry in Portugal, where I will await my lover's arrival after he finishes his time here in Tangiers."

26

Lidia's comment that she thought Mario had a lover within the neighboring Berber community opened a new line of investigation regarding his murder. Luke discussed this new information with Thomas. "Given your years living among these people, would it be possible for a well-known figure like Mario to carry on an illicit affair within a Berber village in total secrecy?"

"Absolutely impossible, and if discovered he would not have made it back to Tangiers alive."

"But he was on very friendly terms with Takama's family. We will visit that village again. I have to talk to her father regarding the use of his men in defense of the city, now that we are totally responsible for the infantry."

Later that day Luke and Thomas arrived at the Khirri house. The local chieftain, Majid, was at home. He welcomed Luke by commenting, "I hear that the English have taken over the defense of the city following the death of General de Silva."

"Almost, but the Portuguese cavalry are still dominant, and its commander still has ultimate control, but we have now taken over the role of the infantry."

"And about to dismiss my tribesmen from their role as auxiliaries?"

"No! That is why I am here—to negotiate an agreement with you regarding their future role as allies of the English."

"At the moment I can see no long-term future in any such alliance. Within a few years the city will be in Moroccan hands and the future of my people lie in my right selection of an Islamic ally, not a distant European power."

"And have you made that choice?"

"Yes, I recently signed an agreement with one of the emerging groups. In fact, it was signed in this very room in the presence of Mario, probably one of his last acts."

"Why was Mario involved?"

"Not as Deputy Governor of Tangiers but an agent of his aunt by marriage, and my daughter's protector, Dona Catarina."

"In that case I assume the agreement is with the Sultan, whom Catarina and your daughter strongly support."

"Yes, Colonel Ibram Zammit signed it on the Sultan's behalf. But in the short term this alliance is not anti-English. For the present we are to assist you in preventing Ghailan or the Fez fanatics from taking the city. To be blunt we are here to help the English against its enemies until our Sultan is ready to strike. Hopefully your government will accept his offer to buy the city. It is of little value to the English."

"Are you strong enough to hold out for the Sultan against his local opponents?"

"Hardly if Ghailan and the Fez mystics combine, but in such a case the English in their own interest will have to come to our aid. In addition, so that you and the remaining Portuguese authorities will not be alarmed the next Sarmento ship from Casablanca which on its return will take Catarina, Takama and Zammit south, is bringing a company of the Sultan's troops to be stationed in our villages. They will be disembarked along the coast before they reach the city port."

"Thank you for your frank discussion. I personally am strongly recommending that my government sells this empty shell of a city to the Sultan, but it will not be accepted. Ignorance and self-interest will prevail as key political allies of the King seek to make their fortune in occupying the city."

"May I ask you a favor Colonel Tremayne? I and members of my family would like to attend the funeral of Mario de Silva. Will you give us permission to enter the city?"

"I will do more than that. I will send you an escort of English troops to bring you to and from the city."

"May I ask you a personal question.? Mario seemed to have a special interest in this village. Was there a reason for this?"

"Yes, but not the one that has been circulating in the city. My men picked up the rumor years ago that Mario had an illicit affair with a woman of my tribe. That would have brought death to both of them."

"And the less fatal link?"

"When Mario first became military commander and before the arrival of Colonel Pimento to head the cavalry, Mario himself led regular patrols into the hinterland. On one such patrol he came upon a group of horsemen leading a covered wagon from which squeals and sighs emanated. They were Ghailan's men heading back to their mountain village. When asked what they were carrying they replied that they had a load of young lambs."

"And what were they carrying?"

"On removing the cover Mario found three young girls who were gagged, and half a dozen babies. One of those girls was Takama and one of the babies her brother Fadel. Ghalain facing the depopulation of some of his villages had sent his men to raid distant villages for babies and young girls."

"You were grateful to Mario?"

"Yes, and he took a strong interest in Takama and eventually introduced her to his aunt by marriage. That is how she became part of Catarina's family."

"Surely her move to Tangiers, and becoming a Christian must have led to conflict between you and Mario?"

"Not at all! Mario tried to convince Takama that she did not need to convert to Christianity to enjoy the benefits that Catarina offered. To be fair Catarina would not have insisted on it. Takama has always had a mind of her own. To be honest with you I believe Takama's very successful dealings with the Sultan indicate she has not loss completely her Islamic heritage."

"Why do you think Mario was murdered?"

"As part of the plan to disrupt the movement of Dona Catarina's organization to Casablanca where she will give much needed support to the Sultan in his attack on Fez."

"You suspect the Sufi brotherhood based."

"It has to be a group that has little understanding of the situation within Tangiers. Ghailan and we would know that Mario, although the figurehead of the administration and by marriage part of Catarina's network, was dispensable. His death would alter nothing."

"It is that last fact and the nature of his death that makes me incline to look at Mario's family and personal relations for motivation. After being run down, Mario's body was stabbed through the heart. How did he cope with his wife's infidelity?"

"Not a problem. That marriage was forced on both parties by Catarina and sustained by her generous allowances. Mario was as anxious as Lidia to end their relationship. In recent years Mario found a partner, not in this Berber village but among the elite of the city."

"Do you know whom?"

"No, but his choices were very limited. She could only have been in a place where his visits did not arouse suspicion. The female relatives of his senior officers would jump to mind. He often talked about his sister-in-law Gabriela and Colonel Lopez's sister Catia. The fact that he never mentioned Micaela Pimento may be a clue."

"Not necessarily! She is the only woman in the ruling elite that I have not had any reason to question. She may simply be the retiring sort."

"My wife raised a most unlikely possibility, but given the constant and generous allowances he received, could it be Dona Catarina herself?"

"I have received no information touching on the love life of Dona Catarina. While she is a very sensuous woman, I have not heard a single piece of gossip concerning her personal relationships."

Another possibility flashed into Luke's mind, but he dare not mention it in the presence of Majid Khirri—could it have been his daughter Takama Khirri?"

While Luke talked with Majid, Thomas chatted to the servants. As he and Luke trotted back to Tangiers the latter asked, "And did you discover anything from your enquiry that helps in our investigation of Mario's death?"

"Their overwhelming reaction filled me with sadness. None of them could see any point in murdering Mario. His existence apparently was not seen as having any importance to anyone and in any case, he would soon be gone."

"Did any suggest that it could be related to his personal life?"

"They certainly believe that it could have nothing to do with his love life. According to rumor he had none. They claim he was the most passionless man they had ever met. And he constantly refused the offer of the occasional slave girl. He appeared to have no interest in women."

"How did they account for his regular visits to their master?"

"Two reasons! As their tribe provided the bulk of Moroccan mercenaries to serve in the defense of Tangiers the Portuguese military commandant Mario de Silva monitored the situation with the tribal chieftain every month."

"And the second?"

"This could be of some significance. Mario was the regular contact between Takama and her family. He kept the family up to date on her achievements and took messages to her especially from her mother."

"That could be significance. Mario's relationship with Takama needs further investigation."

"And what did you discover Colonel?"

"That Mario was not the loner depicted but may have had a lover within the Tangerine establishment—the identity of whom we must uncover."

"And you think that it could have been Takama?"

"Or Gabriela, Catia, Micaela or even Catarina herself? We go past Catarina's lodgings in the barracks. I will visit her."

Luke was well received by Catarina who invited him to eat with her.

"You may withdraw that invitation when you hear the questions, I wish you to answer."

"Ask away!"

"I am aware that your next ship out of Casablanca will contain a unit of the Sultan's army who will locate themselves among the anti-Ghailan tribes just outside the city."

"Yes, in the short term it will help the Portuguese and then the English retain control against Ghailan and the Fez fanatics. Colonel Zammit will be stationed here as its commander."

"The next question is very personal. You have given, especially as you did not like the man, the late Mario very generous allowances over the years. What exactly was your relationship with him?"

"What are you implying Luke?"

"There are rumors that Mario was your secret lover," lied Luke.

"The man had not an ounce of sensuality and behaved like someone twice my age. I cannot believe he had a secret lover. He probably started the rumor himself to protect his manhood, given Lidia's promiscuous behavior. Who else do you suspect as this mysterious alleged lover?"

"Takama?"

Catarina appeared shocked and looked Luke directly in the eye, "I hope not!"

"You do not immediately reject the suggestion?"

"Mario has had a long and changing relationship with Takama over two decades. After rescuing her as a child from abductors, he was a constant visitor to her family. As she grew up, he became a mentor and adviser which led her entering my household. It was then that Takama told me she felt uncomfortable with Mario. He often came close to touching her inappropriately. If he had had a more forceful personality, I doubt if Takama would have escaped."

"Given Takama's awareness of Mario incorrect thoughts about her, why did you not reject my proposition outright?"

"In recent months, ever since we began our move to Casablanca and our alliance with the Sultan in which Takama has played a major role, her attitude to Mario has changed. I have seen them often in pleasant conversation, and she included Mario in the signing of the agreement with Zammit in her father's village."

"Are you suggesting that a newly confident Takama may have changed her attitude to her long- time friend, and sought comfort in his arms?"

"All I am suggesting is that if anything had developed between the two of them in recent months Takama would have been the instigator. Mario was going further and further into his shell as the time for his departure from Tangiers approached."

"Then I must speak to Takama first thing in the morning."

27

He did, and immediately explained, "The Portuguese have given me the responsibility of investigating Mario's murder. Do you have any views on the matter?"

"Catarina has warned me that you had some fanciful idea that in recent times I might have been closer to Mario, than considered appropriate. For over two decades I was the little girl and Mario a grandfatherly figure that I grew up with. It was only in my late teens that his concern for me seemed obsessive, but in the last three months that relationship finally changed—perhaps all in my mind. I was now an independent successful woman with several political and commercial successes to my credit, and Mario appeared as the sad elderly unloved loser. I felt sorry for him."

"If he had taken a lover in the last days, who would it be?"

"If he had taken a lover, he would have been a much happier man. The last few times I spoke with him he was very unhappy. He took no lover. He arranged his own death because he had nothing to live for."

Luke persisted with his line of enquiry ignoring Takama's suicide explanation.

"If you and Catarina deny any such personal relationship with Mario, is it at all possible that Catia or Micaela may have succumbed?"

"Succumbed to what? A penniless old man with no personality— and no future! Neither of those women are stupid—or desperate."

"How do you reconcile your suicide theory with the earlier attempt to kidnap him?"

"Easily. It was a voluntary kidnapping that he planned to end in his death."

"If you are right, I must direct my attention to who assisted Mario to execute his suicidal wishes. However, my enquiries into the attacks on Catarina cannot be dismissed so easily. Do you still believe they were the work of the Fez brotherhood out to prevent the transfer of her organization to Casablanca?"

"Yes, and I know who killed them."

"Who?"

"Supporters of our new ally, the Sultan."

"Who were?"

"Soldiers in the Portuguese infantry, but under orders from Mario, Miguel or someone else."

"Not agents of your father, also now an ally of the Sultan?"

"I doubt if my father's men would have bothered creating a false trail by having them garroted in the manner of some Islamic fanatics. Given the activities of many Portuguese infantrymen in rogue activities, who directed them? Miguel is now restrained; Mario is dead, and Carlos appears beyond reproach. Find their real leader and most of your problems might be solved!

Takama had been informative and incisive, and certainly portrayed a confidence which had been lacking in his earlier interviews. Then it struck him. Was Takama taking over the Catarina network with the aid of the Sultan and possibly her father? Was she the instigator of the events he was investigating? The 'new' Takama was certainly capable of effecting such a coup.

Perhaps the authorities including Mario been correct in questioning her loyalty to the Portuguese state and the Christian religion

Luke next visited Catia. He was surprised at her relaxed almost warm personality. Her anti-Gabriela bitterness of his last visit had disappeared. He explained that he was looking into the murder of Mario de Silva.

"What was your relationship with Mario over the last month?"

Catia giggled, "Don't be so coy, colonel! Word has spread that Mario had a lover and you are trying to find out who it might be. It was not me and I doubt that the rumor is true. Mario never showed any interest in women, even his own wife. He preferred men, perhaps young boys."

It had not taken long for the malicious streak in Catia to return.

"Did Mario's attitude to your brother Miguel change in recent times?" asked Luke.

"You are not suggesting that Mario and Miguel were lovers?"

"No, it is a possibility I had not thought of. Given Miguel's reputation I would reject it outright. My question was much broader. Did you notice any change in Miguel's general attitude to Mario?"

"Yes, for most his time here, Miguel considered Mario a hands-off general. He rarely interfered and allowed Miguel absolute control of the infantry. Miguel and Carlos organized and maintained the defense of the city without any contribution from the commander- in-chief. He seemed just as disinterested in his troops, as he was in women"

"And this changed?"

"Only slightly. During the problems he had with rogue troops, he sensed that they were obeying the orders of someone else. At one point Miguel thought he had seen Mario in deep conversation with some of the leading troublemakers including his coterie of sergeants. However, at this stage my brother's mind, as a result of his obsession with Gabriela was declining, so I do not how much weight you can attach to that observation."

"If Mario was the leader of that small band of special troops it would explain a lot—the success of their rogue activities, the kidnapping and assaults on various people, his own pretended abduction and finally his murder. These trusted men may have turned on him."

"Yet most of the men that Miguel mentioned Mario was close to, were killed in the explosion. I do not know why you are bothering to investigate Mario's death. It will achieve nothing. All of us will soon be gone."

"You will be, but the English remain and the circumstances surrounding Mario's death may have some bearing on the ability of England to defend Tangiers."

"Have your enquiries progressed far?"

"My interviews have certainly raised several interpretations of Mario's death. Some see it as the work of Fez fanatics, others that it was an assisted suicide, and you suggest the work of alienated troops. Personally, I still think it is family related."

In visiting Micaela, Luke decided to play the diplomat rather than the investigator. Micaela Pimento was now the first lady of Tangiers. The governor had left his wife in Portugal and the new deputy governor, Gil Serano, was still a bachelor. The wife of the military governor, even if it were only for a few months, now presided over the social life of the Tangerine establishment. Luke explained his visit in such terms. As the English envoy, he wished to congratulate Dona Micaela on her elevation.

"Colonel Tremayne, I should thank you. My husband is a much more relaxed and happy man that the defense of the city is now being shared between his cavalry and the English infantry. Your continued choice of local Berbers, but now all drawn from the tribe of Takama Khirri, to provide part of the guards on the southern wall, Carlos considers proof of your military acumen."

"The safety of the city still relies heavily on the intelligence gathering and military prowess of your husband's cavalry."

"You can drop the pretense Colonel! You are not here on a formal diplomatic mission. The ladies of Tangiers are not fools, nor are we isolated individuals. We talk daily. You have systematically interviewed all our leading female citizens regarding the murder of Mario de Silva regarding their relationship with him during the last months."

"And do you have anything to contribute to my enquiry?" asked a relaxed Luke.

"No, I have never spoken to Mario outside formal social events. I had no relationship with him at all. But I can help you regarding the emerald ring. Your visit is timely as only last night Carlos and I discussed what I am about to reveal and agreed that you should be informed as soon as possible. Come with me!"

Micaela led Luke through several rooms. Finally, she withdrew a set of keys from somewhere in her clothing and opened the door of a very small windowless antechamber. In the middle of the room was a large metal multi-locked trunk. Further keys were isolated, and Micaela methodically finally unlocked the trunk. She lifted the lid and produced a small case which she presented to Luke.

"On one of few occasions on which we did meet, it was emphasized by the governor that the initial focus of your mission was to find the missing emerald Islamic ring, the possession of which would help unify our Moslem enemies. Here it is."

Luke opened the small jewel case and there lay a large green fluorite ring that flashed its lighter colors even in the dim light of the antechamber.

This was no emerald fake—but was it the genuine ring? He thought Takama had successfully transferred that to the Sultan. He turned to Micaela, "Before I ask you a host of questions regarding this revelation, could you send a servant to my barracks and request that my valet return here immediately. He can verify the ring's authenticity."

Thomas spent ages examining the ring with the aid of a large lens and constant referral to a dog-eared drawing. Both Micaela and Luke were increasingly agitated.

Finally, Luke exploded, "Well man, is it a fake or not?"

A slightly annoyed Thomas gave a non-committal answer.

"It could be. If it is a fake, it is an excellent copy of the real thing."

"Why can't you decide one way or another?" asked Micaela.

"On this piece of paper, I have a drawing of the lighter and darker striations on the original ring. I copied it from a copy that my master at Fez had copied from an ancient book held in the mosque there. As my drawing is a copy of a copy of a copy the detail may be slightly out. This ring would fool everybody except the experts at Fez."

"Let's assume that it is the real ring. I had assumed that Takama had already taken it south to the Sultan, cementing his alliance with her family and the Catarina network. How did you get it?"

"A servant found it very early one morning inside the niche just inside the door of this reception hall where letters and messages are left if there is no servant handy to receive them."

"When did this occur?"

"Earlier last week."

"Was there any letter explaining the deposit?" asked Luke.

"No! The jewel case was hidden in a leather pouch."

"The niche was empty the night before?"

"Yes, when the pouch was found, I asked the servants whether there had been anything there when they retired. They all said no."

"Did you have any visitors that evening who might have slipped the pouch into the niche before they left?"

"We entertained the local establishment as our teenage daughter Andrea had come to stay with us."

"I did not realize that you and Carlos had a daughter."

"We have seen very little of her. When we went to Brazil she stayed in Portugal with her grandmother and since we have been here, she has been educated in a convent just outside of Oporto. She is here for an extended stay as her convent was recently burnt to the ground."

"Who was here on the night of that reception?"

"The governor, Major Coval, Catia Lopez, Mario and Lidia de Silva, Gil Serano and Dona Takama Khirri."

"Great! That does not make my task of finding the source any easier. I had hoped you could have said that you only had one visitor that night."

"Perhaps I can pinpoint the source more precisely for you. One guests returned after he had left and told the servant who re-admitted him to the reception hall that he had come back to collect his wife's parasol."

"And who was it?"

"Mario de Silva."

"Very interesting. The story about the parasol does not make sense. A deputy governor is not going to retrace his steps to collect an item that a servant could have repossessed in the morning. Your assumption may be correct. If true, Mario may have been murdered by someone who knew he had the ring."

"On the other hand, if you believed that Takama had the real ring, she may have left it here and not with the Sultan."

"To what end? If the Sultan has been given a false ring, it could destroy the recently announced alliance with the local Berbers and Catarina's network."

"Maybe the Sultan's troops who are about to arrive in the area have been sent to punish the Berbers and Catarina for providing a false ring," mused Micaela to Luke's alarm.

"Thank you for this astounding information. I will talk to Catarina and Takama as soon as possible. Thomas will complete detailed drawings of the ring's striations and seek advice from Fez. I will keep it under lock and key aboard our flagship until I can return it to you."

Luke and Thomas immediately visited Catarina. She asked, "Have your enquiries into Mario's death yielded anything useful?"

Luke could not resist a dramatic gesture. "It has yielded this!"

Thomas showed her the ring. "One of many fakes that circulate from time-to-time. Gabriela had a collection of them," she commented.

"What if this is not a fake, but the one you have transferred to the Sultan is? It would surely destroy your recently created alliance with him, and your rosy future in Casablanca?"

Catarina began to show signs of concern. "It cannot be the real ring."

"Our expert here, Thomas, was trained in Fez. He has an accurate drawing of the striations on the real ring. This ring conforms to those patterns. Did the one you sent to the Sultan?"

"It must have."

"You had it checked?"

"No, I took the word of the highest authority—the office of the Queen Regent herself."

28

"Tell me all you know about the transfer of the ring from the care of the Dominicans in a local church into the hands of the Sultan—and what role did the Portuguese government play in this farce."

"You know part of the story already. The ring was never stolen from the Dominican chapel. On orders from Father Antonio, it was handed over to me to get to the Sultan to cement good relations with him and our developing Atlantic ports such as Casablanca. This was done while a charade of false auctions was carried out to conceal the real situation. The ring that Takama sent to the Sultan may be a fake, but it is the ring that the Dominicans had here for the last few decades."

"If it is not the real ring, then the Dominicans and the Portuguese government have been misled for years," stated Luke

"And our diplomacy with the Sultan as you suggest, will be seriously undermined," murmured Catarina.

"Inform Colonel Zammit immediately, and send Takama back to Casablanca to smooth things over. The Sultan may have already had experts examine the ring you sent him," suggested Luke. "Let's hope it is not a fake! If this is the genuine ring why did its owner not use it to deal with local Moslem leaders? Ghailan would have paid a fortune for this."

"Is the appearance of this ring relevant to Mario's death?" asked Catarina.

"Possibly! Mario may have left it with the Pimentos. His murderers may have thought he still had it. His body was raked over by his assailant—perhaps looking for it."

"But what is the point of giving it to the Pimentos? He could have hidden it in a thousand places."

"He must have wanted it to come to light."

"To what end, Luke?"

"The obvious answer is to destroy the local alliance with the Sultan, and even more personally, to destroy your future in Casablanca. Did Mario hate you that much?"

Catarina did not answer.

Thomas carefully closed the jewel box and slipped it into its leather pouch and commented, "Colonel, this may not be directed against Dona Catarina and the Casablanca enterprise, it could be a Ghailan move to destroy the local alliance of the lowland Berbers with the Sultan. Catarina's agent Dona Takama could be seen as acting as much for her father as for her employer."

"Is Takama a loyal servant and friend, or a traitor to yourself and Portugal? asked Luke.

"Or is this an attempt by family members and other employees to undermine my confidence in Takama?"

"I will question her again."

"She will be here at nine in the morning."

"Don't forewarn her about the ring. Her initial reaction could be critical."

Luke gave Takama ten minutes before he joined them in Catarina's accommodation. Takama commented, "Catarina tells me you have advanced considerably in your probing of Mario's death. Did Mario take a lover?"

"I doubt it, but I want to ask you a few questions regarding the emerald Islamic ring—the one you took south to the Sultan."

Takama looked at Catarina for guidance, but the latter fixed her gaze on her own her own shoes. Takama experienced a moment of apprehension. "My only role was to act as courier for Catarina and take the ring she and the Sultan's representative had obtained and hand it over to his Grand Vizier who came to Casablanca to receive it."

"Did you make a drawing of the striations on that ring in any effort to prove its authenticity?"

"No, but clearly the ring had such striations. It was fluorite, and not emerald as were Gabriela's fakes."

"You definitely handed over a fluorite ring to the Grand Vizier of Morocco?"

"Yes."

"You did not substitute a fake for the real ring, you believed you had?"

Takama was affronted. "Why these absurd questions?

"If the real ring is in Morocco, how do you account for this?"

Luke withdrew the jewel case from one of his deep pockets, and confronted Takama with the ring. Takama was taken aback. Her heart began to race, and her breathing was coming in short breaths. "My God, how did it find its way back here? And more concerning, why?"

Catarina spoke, "Just calm yourself, and peruse the ring carefully. It may not be the ring you took south on my behalf. Let us take it to the roof where full sunlight may highlight its features you can examine it in detail."

Catarina and Luke drank light red wine while Takama, with the aid of Thomas's lens, analysed the ring. Eventually Luke asked," Is this the ring that you took to Casablanca?"

"No."

"Why not?"

"The darker striations are darker, and the lighter striations are lighter on this ring than the one I carried. I just do not recall noting such a difference on my ring. And looking at this one in full sunlight such differences should have been less visible here. However, my memory of the original ring may be faulty, but the silver mounting is also different. On the ring I took south there was a tiny pinprick of an indentation on the mount where a minute amount had been drilled out to be tested for authenticity. This ring has no such indentation."

"An excellent observation! This ring is not the one you took to the Sultan. This creates a major problem. Who brought this ring to Tangiers and why?"

Takama asked, "Where was it found?"

"It was left by an unknown person in the reception hall of the Pimentos. Micaela suspects that it could have been left there by Mario."

"Any other suspects?"

"Only the other guests at that dinner party, of which you were one. What sort of mood was Mario in? Did he behave in any way that appeared unusual?"

"The major difference was that the quiet Micaela tried to live up to her new position with the most lavish dinner and a much more outgoing approach to her guests. She even got Mario to outline his plans for the future, much of which I am sure, Catarina was unaware.

"Being what? she asked.

"After successfully completing a number of enterprises in Tangiers over the last few months he was in a position to start a new life probably back in Portugal, although when Carlos hinted that maybe the government had offered him a position similar to the one he held here in another part of the Empire, he appeared disconcerted."

"A typical pack of lies to enhance his standing. He was in no position to complete any sort of mission—commercial or military," commented Catarina acidly.

"Any other observations of that dinner party?" Luke asked Takama.

"It may be nothing, but Major Coval seemed to spend the night flirting with the young guest of honor, Andrea Pimento. It was so over the top that Carlos after each particular course had us change seats. This separated Andrea and the major.

"Did you get the impression that Andrea and the major had met before?"

"Yes."

Later that day Luke called on the Pimentos and asked to speak to Andrea. Micaela insisted on being present. Mother and daughter could have passed as sisters and their darker coloring suggested Moorish blood in their distant ancestry.

"Why do you wish to speak to Andrea. She has just arrived in Tangiers and can have nothing to contribute to your enquiry into the death of Mario de Silva?"

"Perhaps not to his death, but she may have seen something on the night of the dinner party when the ring mysteriously appeared. Andrea, did you see any of the guests that night lingering in the vicinity of the niche at the entrance to the reception hall."

"Only two people, the tall Berber lady and Leo."

"Together or on two separate occasions?"

"On separate occasions."

"I hear that you and Major Leo Coval enjoyed each other's company."

"Too much so!" interjected Micaela. "We had to separate them."

"You are a sensible young girl who would not be swept of your feet by a much older man in the presence of your parents and their friends. You had met the Major before?"

"Yes, his was the only face I knew, in what was becoming a boring dinner party."

"How did you meet Leo?"

"That was our doing," admitted Micaela. "When we heard that Andrea's convent had been destroyed, Carlos asked Leo to arrange for the Portuguese military to organize her trip to Tangiers."

"And just before I left Portugal, I was given a package by an officer in the Queen's bodyguard to deliver to Major Coval."

"Was this a large package?"

"No, it was very small, but quite heavy."

Luke's mind began to race. Could the ring that suddenly appeared in the Pimento's niche been sent by the Portuguese government? But to what end?

"You handed the package to the major?"

"Yes, and he asked if I could do him a favor. Could I persuade my father to give him promotion and a commission in his regiment before they took up their new position on the Portuguese-Spanish frontier."

"Why would a senior intelligence officer want to take a position with a defensive cavalry unit on the front line of current hostilities with Spain? And why would he ask a young girl to further his case?"

"I can answer that. Leo has talked with Carlos on this matter earlier. Leo feels that he is too close to current regime and when the King takes over from his mother, he will not have a job," commented Micaela.

"And how has Carlos reacted to this request?"

"You must ask him. The topic is not one to be canvassed in the presence of a teenage girl," said Micaela putting an abrupt end to the questioning.

Luke checked out the girl's account with Leo. It tallied. Luke probed further. "What was in the package Andrea delivered to you?"

"The Governor had requested from the Queen some sort of authority for him to sign off on the various details of the transfer of Crown assets in Tangiers to England. The package contained a royal seal."

"Why use a teenage civilian to deliver it?"

"Who would suspect that a daughter joining her parents for their last few weeks in Tangiers would be carrying anything related to national security. I discussed it with Carlos before using his daughter. It was not a last-minute decision."

"I can see why you are trying to make provisions for your future. The current temporary re-organization has turned you from an intelligence officer into a transport and logistics official. I miss your help on my current investigations. With both you and Serano in new positions, any criminal investigations have been left to me to me."

"And what do these currently involve?"

"The murder of Mario, the attack on Catarina and the re-emergence of the ring dominate, but there are a number of minor issues I would like to clear up such as the role of the Fez fanatics in any of these events."

"I can help you regarding the ring. The ring that lay in the Dominican chapel for years was transferred with the agreement of the Dominicans and the government to Catarina to give to the Sultan on gaining his support for the expansion of Portuguese bases along the African coast. However, when this was made known to the court an elderly courtier informed the government that there was a similar ring in the archives of the Braganza family which had been there for over a century."

"Placing the government in a very embarrassing position and on the edge of major diplomatic catastrophe. What did they do?"

"They sent the ring to me. It was contained in the parcel containing the royal seal that Andrea brought with her."

"Why leave it at the Pimentos?"

"My government did not want to admit in any way that it had been misled for centuries. I was to hide it among the Tangiers elite where it would be easily found and the local authorities would take the blame for the confusion of rings and Catarina would sort out any problems with the Sultan."

"So it was not the enemies of Portugal but the central government itself that threw this bomb into delicate negotiations with the Sultan. How is you new job progressing?" Luke asked.

"Fraught with problems from an uncooperative clientele. I fear the disbanded infantry may do more than be uncooperative. I have warned Serano and Pimento and have sent a message to your office to expect trouble. They expect to be relocated, found jobs and receive some sort of payment—everything paid for by the state. My brief is simply to find transport out of Tangiers for them, nothing more except for an opportunity to re-enlist in one of regiments within Portugal."

"I cannot see what they would have to gain by causing trouble. My men with the help of your cavalry could put them aboard the ships and simply dump them anywhere in the Mediterranean. If they want to get home to Portugal, they must accept your good offices. They have no bargaining power."

29

The following day Luke was informed that the Governor's house was besieged by armed men and that he had asked Serano, Pimento and himself to visit the scene immediately.

Gil Serano and Carlos Pimento arrived at Luke's barracks just after the messenger had left. Luke asked, "Is the governor in danger?"

"No, although the mob outside is villa is armed, the Governor has with him an able bodyguard of veteran troops. They could withstand any attack. The possible assailants claim they only want to present a petition to him outlining their grievances. The governor wants us to be present when he receives their leaders and their petition, but to have our troops ready to disperse the mob should the situation deteriorate. My cavalry is ready to move in and disperse the mob," advised Pimento.

"Do you want English infantry troops to support you?"

"A company of your men could move immediately to the area but as observers," said Gil.

"What about your reliable police force?" asked Luke. "Do they not have the situation in hand?"

"A growing worry Luke! Since I was elevated to my current position many of my men have realized that soon they will have similar problems to confront as the disbanded infantry. Immediately you take over, they will all leave Tangiers. My police are no longer trustworthy and several may join the mob surrounding the governor. That is why our cavalry, and your infantry as a reserve are needed at the site," confessed Gil.

The three officers arrived at the Governor's villa and made their way through the assembled throng. The initial jeers changed rapidly to silent antagonism as their leaders appeared to have been silenced by a senior officer—Major Dimas Vento.

On entering the Governor's chamber Gil asked, "Is Dimas leading this upheaval?"

"No! As soon as the group gathered, I sent for Dimas and asked him to talk to his former comrades and ascertain what exactly their grievances were and to accompany them when they presented their petition to me. GIven your arrival, which I asked them to await, that should be them requesting entry now."

"If Dimas is simply a go-between, who is their leader?" asked Luke.

"One of your kidnappers, and a special aide to both Colonel Lopez and General de Silva—Sergeant Bruno Costa."

Costa with two comrades entered the room followed by Dimas.

Costa bowed towards the governor and presented the petition, "Your excellency, we ask that you grant us the requests made in this document. It is small recompence for the service we have given to the Portuguese state."

"And what exactly are these demands?" asked Pimento.

"That the large number of our former comrades who are imprisoned in the Tower be pardoned and released to join the rest of us in our relocation.

That Major Coval be ordered to provide us with free transportation to three ports in Portugal, one along the Atlantic coast and one in Brazil.

That we receive automatic re-enlistment in the Portuguese army should it be sought.

That we receive the equivalent of a month's salary that we previously received to assist in establishing a new life the Portuguese government has forced on us," answered Bruno, reading from the document.

Dimas intervened, "The first two requests are in your domain to grant immediately, the third needs further funding from Portugal."

The governor consulted no one and responded immediately. "The first request to free prisoners is denied. I will not have Tangiers invaded by thirty or forty more unruly ex-soldiers. However, they will be deported along with the rest of the troops and granted a pardon on leaving the city. Secondly as time is of the essence, Coval will put your men on any ship that is available and sailing to a mainland Portuguese port. I cannot guarantee reenlistment but seeing that our war with Spain continues the demand for military manpower will continue. There should be no problem in re-enlisting. I have no funds to accede to the third request."

Costa showed his first signs of aggression. "Not true, your excellency. You have been selling Crown assets at a great rate. There is nothing left of value for you English, Colonel Tremayne. Some of this newly acquired capital would easily cover our demands."

"Major Vento, you and your former comrades may leave. In summary, I will grant a pardon to the prisoners as they leave the island, you take your chance on the site of your relocation in Portugal, re-enlistment is probable, and no funds are available to be given to individuals."

"You have not heard the last of us," declaimed Bruno as he left.

"I think we have," replied Pimento. "You are lucky to be treated as well as you have been. You have no bargaining power at all. You could all be dumped on some foreign shore, or the prisoners sold as slaves to our Moslem neighbors. If you have not dispersed by the time I come outside, my men will ride you down."

"We are not without allies," called out Costa's companion.

"At this very moment they may be at the gates of the city."

After further discussion with the Governor on routine matters the three officers left. The gathered throng had completely disappeared, and an eerie silence dominated the area. Carlos commented, "I will send a small patrol around the town to locate any troublemakers. The rest of our troops should be returned to barracks, but be in readiness for whatever may eventuate."

Luke and Gil agreed.

Next morning Luke received a visit from Admiral Lawson. "What brings our sea lord ashore?" quipped Luke.

"With so many locals leaving and a multitude of empty houses becoming available I and my senior officers will live ashore in Tangiers, until our garrison arrives."

"I am sure that your living arrangements are no concern of mine. Why are you really here?"

"A serious security problem has arisen. Lookouts on two of our ships noticed several small boats laden with men and without lights, escaping the harbor during the early hours of this morning. One of our captains involved ordered a long boat to follow the flotilla of small boats at a distance. They landed the men, probably between forty and fifty on the shore two inlets to the east. The men assembled in military fashion and marched inland, the boats returned to the harbor."

"Were the men appeared armed?"

"They probably had their personal weapons, but no muskets were visible as they marched off."

"I will inform Carlos. These are a group of rebellious demobilized infantry who may attempt to attack the city with the aid of Spanish or Moroccan forces. They threatened us with such activity yesterday."

"I will delay my house hunting. I will move our ships into positions where they direct the few cannons that remain on board on the harbor and most of the lower town. If the attackers break through your defenses withdraw to the harbor under the protection of those guns."

"It may be more strategic, sir, to send a couple of armed ships into the next bay. From there our cannons could decimate any armies approaching from the east before they reach the city gate," suggested Luke. Lawson thought for a while and agreed.

A few minutes later Luke was explaining the situation to Carlos when one of his officers entered the room. "Sir, our patrol has just returned and reports that an army of Ghailan's men have descended from the mountains and are heading in this direction."

"It all fits. Our disgruntled infantry with the aid of Ghailan will try to take the town." commented Luke.

"I have sent a man to warn the Berber villages to the west. Ghailan might be after them as well as the city," added the officer.

"Does the patrol have anything else to report?"

"One of men claims that amongst the group leading these troops was a European officer. His helmet covered his face, so he was not recognized."

"Probably Dimas!" said Luke.

"No, Dimas is here with me," answered Carlos. "And there are none of my officers missing. He is probably Spanish."

Moving to the gate tower, Carlos and Luke could see several miles back along the eastern road a small army that had stopped advancing.

"They are probably waiting for reinforcements," said Luke.

"And if you look to the north, out to sea, your admiral has made a smart strategic move."

"Which I suggested," boasted Luke.

He noted with satisfaction, that three English man-of-war had moved into the next bay, and had anchored parallel to shore, from where they could direct cannon fire into the advancing army before it reached the city.

Luke asked, "Carlos, will you attack Ghailan's army before it settles?"

"No way! We are outnumbered. Our best defense against Ghailan has always be to close the gates, and direct constant fire into the attacking army from the safety of our walls. They cannot breach our defenses."

From the gate tower the English and Portuguese officers observed the growing army begin to move slowly down the road towards the southern gate. Carlos Pimento was relaxed. "This is the fourth so called attack on the city instigated by Ghailan since I have been here. They can achieve nothing militarily. You can only enter Tangiers by force if your breach the walls. Ghailan has little artillery, and what he has so little power that the cannon balls will bounce off the walls, causing little damage. The constant and covering fire from the walls and tower prevent his troops attacking the gate itself."

"Then what is the point?" asked Luke.

"In the past it was an attempt to gain concessions from us. Normally he would claim to besiege the city until we agreed to one of his minor demands. His sieges were never too damaging as he had no ships, and the port remained open to resupply us. The situation is even better for us now with your powerful English fleet."

"He will bring the engagement to a speedy end, because his people need to trade with us as much as we used to need to trade with them," added Gil who had joined the other officials.

"That is not as relevant now. Our population has decreased dramatically. Trade with our citizens has almost stopped, and the English do not buy the goods they need from Ghailan's people," countered Carlos.

Jack Moon took charge of the array of cannons and delayed any attempts to fire at the advancing throng. Luke supervised the infantry who well concealed behind the parapets and within the tower, from where they could fire at will and not be in any great danger from returning fire.

To Carlos's surprise the tower and walls were subjected to a barrage of mortar fire. Ghailan must have bought the weapons from agents of the Ottoman or from his Spanish allies. Equally Ghailan must have been surprised by what happened next. A sudden cannonade erupted from the three English warships which found their mark in the middle of his advancing army. Redeployment of the troops held in reserve that were subject to this English fire took time as they were marched out of the firing line, but further away from the city walls.

Just as the final advance to the city walls seemed imminent, all parties were astounded by another unexpected development. Riding from the west to confront the advancing army was a very large contingent of cavalry, comprising a mixture of the Sultan's men under Colonel Zammit and his lowland Berber allies led by Majid Khirri.

They ignored the city and began an offensive charge at Ghailan's advancing men.

Ghailan and his European companion wasted no time. Trumpet calls across the battlefield signaled, not immediate withdrawal, but dispersal. Within minutes the advancing army had virtually disappeared, and its high command was last seen moving towards the mountain passes from which it had come.

Zammit did not waste his resources trying to mow down isolated units as they scattered in all direction. Carlos now led a detachment of Portuguese cavalry through the gate to greet Zammit as he returned. Luke wondered when Zammit would be leading an attack against the English occupation. He must impress on the King that Tangiers will be more trouble than it's worth.

Next day Luke received an unexpected visitor. It was Bruno Costa.

"I did not think I would see you again, sergeant. I assumed you were in the group of deserters who joined Ghailan' s attack on the city."

"You misjudge me, colonel. Those men were desperate. They had either escaped from prison or wanted to stay in the area. The former did not trust the promise of a pardon, and the latter could see a future as mercenaries for Ghailan. Many have Berber wives."

"Then why are you here?"

"I need your help?"

"How can I possibly assist you?"

"Either by persuading the Portuguese authorities to help us, or if not to undertake the solution yourself."

"Sergeant, I was present when the Governor gave a very clear answer to all your requests. I am not here to solve Portuguese problems."

"I have a new solution to our basic problem of re-employment, which I have not yet put to the authorities."

"Which is?"

"Re-instate most of the infantry and move them to Casablanca."

"Where did that idea originate?"

"Portugal is moving its North African base from Tangiers to Casablanca. With renewed hostilities against Spain at home, our government will have trouble raising a regiment to create a garrison in Casablanca. My men have experience and would rather continue our service in the empire than at home. Most of them could transfer their civilian activities from Tangiers more readily to Casablanca, than mainland Portugal. Dona Catarina says there is an immediate need for such a force."

"You have spoken to her on this matter?"

30

"Yes, the idea came from her in the first place. At the moment she claimed her alliance with the Sultan provided some protection, but it would be foolish if a Portuguese city did not have its own defense should that alliance break down."

"It appears a plausible solution to your problem."

"Not to the local high command. They insist that they have clear orders from the Governor that we must be shipped back to Portugal and nowhere else."

"Surely Dona Catarina has influence. She should be talking to the authorities here and in Portugal. The government's move to Casablanca very much depends on Catarina and her alliance with the Sultan. I will talk to her and if she agrees, we will both see the Governor to put the proposition to him."

Two days after Luke and Catarina had briefed the Governor on their Casablanca proposal for at least part of the disbanded infantry, they received news that he would reject their suggestion due to the united opposition of Gil and Carlos.

Luke and Catarina met Bruno and three of his supporters and explained that their request was not likely to be agreed to. Bruno and his men received the news with growing anger, and increasingly more serious threats.

Luke intervened. "Bruno, all is not lost. Dona Catarina has a solution. You are no longer enlisted soldiers. You are legally civilians.

Dona Catarina owns a vast commercial network. She can temporarily employ many of you as private mercenaries until she manages to gain government support for your recognition as the government garrison. She has a ship ready to sail within the week."

"There may be a hitch to this plan. As I will need support from the Portuguese government in Casablanca, I cannot alienate their representatives here. Therefore, I will need the Governor to agree to this revised plan. It removes a problem from Tangiers and solves a problem confronting Casablanca. And it costs the local and central administration nothing. It in fact saves them the cost of transporting dozens of demobilized soldiers to Portugal," she explained.

"I will discuss your plan with the rest of my men," replied an enthusiastic Bruno.

"Any of your men wishing to take advantage of my offer should visit my villa before noon on Sunday and sign up. The ship leaves on Tuesday."

Next day an angry Catarina informed Luke that the Governor had refused to allow Bruno and his group to leave Tangiers.

"Why has he done this?" asked an equally dismayed Luke.

"Some rubbish about not wishing to influence developments in our new hub for African trade without specific authorization from Lisbon, but I understand he was brow beaten by Pimento and Gil who were strongly supported by Coval."

"I will talk to Carlos. It is England's interest to have marauding former soldiers removed from the scene as soon as possible."

Luke's discussion with the military commandant, Colonel Carlos Pimento did not maintain its original cordiality.

"I am surprised Luke that you have taken up the cause of these renegades. You know as well as I do that, they were a disgrace to the Portuguese military, embarking on many activities that were both illegal, immoral and against the interests of the Portuguese state. They even kidnapped you. I would not inflict such lawlessness on our growing settlement at Casablanca. Surely Catarina realizes that their behavior could destroy her close relationship with the Sultan. Both Father

Antonio and Leo Coval indicated that they believe that my approach would be that of the Portuguese government."

"As these men are now civilians surely you could not stop them boarding ships in the harbor, and being transported anywhere, even Casablanca."

"We anticipated that Catarina or her would-be-mercenaries might ignore the Governor's decision. They will not sail for Casablanca because by now they should all be behind bars in the tower. A troop of my cavalry have taken over the administration of the tower and are filling its dungeons with these malignants. I have asked Coval to speed up their repatriation to Portugal."

While Carlos dealt with the recalcitrant former infantry, his wife Micaela was confronted by a domestic crisis. Their daughter Andrea was increasingly unhappy with the visit to her parents. Life in the Pimento villa was boring and uneventful. Her social activities were limited to visits to her mother's friends. After yet another confrontation between daughter and mother, Micaela agreed to allow Andrea to visit the markets where the girl was interested in surveying the exotic goods, the baby animals and the general atmosphere of a public rendezvous. She would be accompanied by a female servant and one of Carlos's bodyguards.

The atmosphere of the souk lifted Andrea's spirits and she gained increasing confidence in dealing with stall holders. Soon the female servant was laden with purchases of exotic fruits and colorful fabrics. Eventually the trio reached the animal market where Andrea was captivated by an array of young animals.

Soon the children of the stallholders and unattached street urchins recognized Andrea as a soft touch. They began to plague her with requests for money or her purchase of unwanted goods. Her bodyguard became almost totally engaged in forcing these troublemakers away from his charge.

He finally convinced Andrea that it was wise to leave the scene. The female servant had already left for their villa, laden down with the purchased goods. Andrea agreed but insisted that she return to the baby animals. She would purchase a young lamb. When the seller asked whether Andrea wanted its throat cut and its body dismembered into edible portions, she appeared shocked. She gathered up the animal and strode off leaving the bodyguard to pay the seller. There was a haggle over the price and once settled the bodyguard took off after Andrea.

But she was nowhere to be seen.

He assumed she may have run home clutching her newfound pet.

He reported the details of their expedition to Micaela who informed him that Andrea had not yet returned. He, with five servants immediately returned along the route they had expected Andrea to follow. An hour's searching proved fruitless, and both the police and her father were informed. Gil himself took over the investigation and quickly elicited that Andrea had been followed through the bazaar by chanting children demanding she buy from them. A stallholder said that the girl appeared frightened, especially as some of the children grabbed at the lamb. This stallholder thought that a couple of men further along the souk came to her rescue and were seen escorting her away from the chanting mob.

Next day with no sign of Andrea, Luke allocated several units of his infantry to assist in the search. Her failure to appear, left the authorities with two equally unpalatable possibilities—she had been murdered or abducted. The abduction of young European girls to become slaves within the Islamic world was not uncommon. She was probably miles away from Tangiers heading for a slave market in Algiers or Timbuktu.

Next morning Luke was summoned to a meeting by the new deputy Governor Gil Serano. Also present were the military commander Carlos Pimento and Majors Leo Coval and Dimas Vento. Gil revealed the latest developments regarding Andrea Pimento's abduction.

"Last night a child delivered a letter to Carlos. It claimed that if all of the former infantry that wished to move to Casablanca were aboard Dona Catarina's ship on Tuesday morning, Andrea would be released as soon as that ship left port."

"This proves that friends of the imprisoned infantry have kidnapped the young girl to achieve their move to Casablanca," announced Leo.

"I thought all these men had been rounded up and imprisoned in the tower until their departure for Portugal," commented Luke.

"All but one or two are in the tower. My men could not find their leader Bruno Costa. He is obviously behind the abduction. He and I have had several confrontations. He used his friendship with General de Silva and Colonel Lopez to ignore many of my instructions in the past. Costa has my daughter," claimed an almost tearful Carlos.

Gil and Leo nodded in agreement.

"I do not agree," declaimed Dimas. "I have been close to these men and especially to Costa. He is not a fool. To kidnap the daughter of the military commandant to achieve this end makes no sense. We would not reward such an act. The Portuguese authorities would seek the men out in Casablanca, and summarily execute them. By indulging in this caper, they are destroying their future. It is suicidal."

Luke agreed with Dimas. "This behavior, given their alleged aim is senseless and entirely counter-productive."

"If it is not Costa and his men, who is it? What is gained by any group pretending to be them? There is no logic in assuming it is not Costa," countered Carlos.

"It could be a personal enemy of yours Carlos, out to shift blame," said Dimas.

"There is another possibility," suggested Luke. "The one interpretation that makes sense is that it is designed to discredit Costa and his men, and possibly their potential employer, Dona Catarina."

"Well gentlemen, what is our next step?" asked Gil.

After a long discussion the group agreed to two initiatives—the prisoners would not be released to sail to Casablanca as demanded, but the kidnappers would be offered a large sum for the immediate return of the girl.

Later that afternoon Thomas Smith, Luke's valet and silversmith extraordinaire received a surprised visit—his friend from the souk, Miriam Barros. Tom was initially embarrassed, "You should not have openly come here. Your husband may have had you followed."

As she stroked his hand and gave him a peck on the cheek she commented,

"Thomas, you are confused. I am here to see your Colonel, not you."

Tom led the woman into Luke's office where she made it clear that Tom should leave. She followed him to the door and firmly shut it making sure that there would be no eavesdroppers.

"What is so important that even your friend has to be excluded?"

"The rescue of the kidnapped girl!"

"What do you know about it?"

"Absolutely nothing. I have been asked that you come alone to my house behind our stall in the bazaar after dark tonight. Then both of us will be enlightened."

Without allowing time for Luke to comment, she strode from the room.

That night Luke left the barracks and disappeared into the darkened streets of the city. He took no taper to light his way, relying on the intermittent moonlight to navigate his clandestine trip to the area of the souk.

On arriving at Miriam's house behind her stall, he knocked gently. The door was opened only enough for Luke to sidle in. One room was partially lit by a single tallow candle. As Luke's eyes adjusted to the dim light, he recognized the man that rose from the bench against the wall. It was Bruno Costa.

Luke spoke, "Have you come to hand yourself in and return Andrea to her parents?"

"I had nothing to do with the girl's abduction, but the attempt of a third party to blame us will destroy our future."

"Yes, neither Major Vento nor I believe it was your work. It undermines everything you are working towards. If you are innocent, why this meeting?"

"For you to help me rescue the girl."

"If you know where the girl is, why can't you rescue her yourself?"

"There is a price on my head. I am sure Pimento's men will shoot me on sight. You are my only guarantee that our joint mission will not end in my unfortunate death, which I believe is the aim of more than one person in authority."

"If you did not abduct the girl, how do you know where she is?"

"When her disappearance was blamed on us with the arrival of that blackmail note, I sent a general request to our friends throughout the city for any information regarding her kidnapping."

"With good results?"

"Yes! Acting on a mass of information I ascertained that the girl had been taken by two men whom I discovered were seamen. They had taken the girl aboard a ship which I also discovered was heading for the slave market of Algiers. It already has several kidnapped African women aboard."

"Are these kidnappings the work of a couple of rogue sailors, or is the captain and most of crew involved?"

"I don't know, but my guess is that as this is a full-blown slaver which has gathered its victims in darkest Africa it took an opportunity that presented itself to add one or more European girls from Tangiers. You will be of especial help as the ship is Bristol based. It is an English merchantman, *The Maid of the West.*"

"We have traders along the African coast engaged in the slave trade, but I assumed they concentrated on African slaves for our sugar and tobacco plantations in the Americas."

"The North African slave trade for the Islamic world is just as profitable. We must act now. The prohibition against ships leaving port following the Pimento girl's disappearance will be lifted at full tide tomorrow morning. Let's move to the docks!" demanded Bruno.

"No sergeant! We have the upper hand. Any action by the two of us alone, will not only endanger our lives, but that of the girl."

"Then what do you suggest?"

"I will return to the barracks and have a company of men descend on the docks at first light. I will also inform our fleet, and one of our ships will prevent *The Maid of the West* getting too far, if it should leave port. You will stay here until morning. I will collect you then. For your own safety do not venture abroad. I will not inform Pimento because he may act unilaterally. The English will rescue the girl, and you Bruno Costa will be giving the credit."

31

Luke had a midnight meeting with a suddenly awakened admiral. Together they discussed the interception of *The Maid of the West.* Just after dawn three longboats from the fleet put ashore in the harbor. They were soon filled with troops from Luke's barracks. When *The Maid* prepared to sale, two of the longboats moved in behind the ship to ensure that nothing was dispatched overboard, and the third with Luke in command boarded the vessel after it had been informed by the nearest English man-of-war that it was about be searched for stolen goods. Several English warships ensured that it reduced sail as required.

The plan had worked perfectly despite The *Maid's* late departure due to the need to find crewmen to replace those that had deserted in Tangiers. Luke was angry that Bruno had disappeared. He was not waiting for Luke at Miriam's souk location.

Once aboard the ship Luke was confronted by its captain who was in no mood to co-operate. "This is an outrage. We are an English merchantman taking African slaves and assorted goods to Islamic ports along the North African coast. There is no reason to detain us. It is a disgrace that we should be boarded by our own people."

"There may be true, but we have information that in the interests of maintaining good relations with Portugal must be investigated."

"What information?"

"That you kidnapped the daughter of the military commandant of Tangiers, and that she is aboard this ship destined for the slave markets of Algiers."

"Rubbish, I have thirty dark African girls from Senegal and ten Berber women from Agadir—no Portuguese. There is nothing illegal in my activities. In fact, the King's brother, the Duke of York is a patron, if not investor in the company that owns this ship."

While Luke questioned the captain, Jack Moon disarmed the recalcitrant sailors before commencing a thorough search of the ship. To everybody's surprise the search proved unnecessary. Just as Luke was about to lead the captain out of his cabin to join the search, Bruno Costa confronted them, leading Andrea Pimento by the hand.

Luke turned on the captain. "So, this is the Portuguese girl you did not have. How do explain her presence on board?"

"I have never seen her before. Nor have I ever seen this man who has brought her here. She probably came aboard with you. This is an act of piracy."

"Let us hear what this man has to say. What are you doing aboard this ship and where did you find the girl?"

"This morning I discovered that the ship was short of crew. I volunteered my services. I was given the task of cleaning the lower decks where the slaves are held. This gave me a chance to inspect the area. Most of the women were lying on the floor, or in hammocks at two levels above the deck. One hammock was so high above the others that its occupant could not be seen from the lower levels. At this time, I noticed the longboats pulling alongside the ship. I suggested to my shipmates that we may be under attack, and we should rally on deck. After they left the area, I brought down the hammock and freed the girl—it was Andrea."

"How did you get the girl from the lower deck to the captain's cabin?"

"Your men were in progress of disarming most of the sailors and to those that were still free I simply announced that the captain wanted this girl in his cabin."

Luke turned to Andrea. "We will soon have you back home with your parents. and I will question you at length then. For now, do you know if you were kidnapped on orders of the captain here or one or more of his rogue crew?"

"I have no idea. Two men offered to carry the goods I had purchased and in conversation I commented how I envied the people sailing around the harbor on such a perfect day. That told me they were sailors and could take me for a sail. This they did but instead of returning to shore they forced me up a rope ladder and aboard this ship. They gagged me, tied me up very tightly, placed me in a hammock and then pulled it up very high. In effect I could not move or make my presence felt."

"Would you recognize these men?"

"Not for certain."

Luke was silent for a while. He then announced. "Captain, I have no evidence that you were behind this abduction, and my sole mission is to rescue this girl, not to interfere in your commercial activities. To isolate the men responsible may be impossible. We will leave your ship without further ado. Proceed on your voyage!"

"You might wish to change your mind, colonel. As well as Andrea I freed seven or eight female urchins taken from the souk. The captain may not be aware of one illegal victim but how could he not know of his men's raid on the souk. Andrea was simply an unexpected bonus of a carefully planned raid to gather European slaves."

Luke thought for a while and declared to the captain, "I am arresting you and seizing your ship for your unannounced act of war against an English ally—the raiding of Portuguese territory and the abduction of Portuguese citizens. I leave further action to Admiral Lawson."

Luke, Bruno and Andrea made their way to the Pimento villa. Carlos have received word that he was wanted immediately at home as there was news of Andrea. Luke waited until Carlos and Micaela were together and joined them with Bruno.

Carlos was incandescent with rage. "Why have you brought this renegade here? At least you have captured him. Where is Andrea?"

Luke said, "Calm down Carlos! Do not abuse Bruno! He rescued Andrea. I will call her in."

Luke and Bruno withdrew into the far corners of the room while parents and daughter embraced, and the women wept. Carlos then asked, "Did you have second thoughts and returned my daughter in the hope that I will allow your departure for Casablanca?"

Luke answered, "Andrea was abducted by English slave traders. It had nothing to do with the former Portuguese infantry."

"Then how do you explain the note suggesting she would be released once the soldiers had sailed to Casablanca?"

"A separate mystery. Someone took advantage of the situation to blacken the name of Bruno and his men."

"Who would gain by such an action?" asked Carlos.

"Someone who may not want the Casablanca enterprise to succeed. It could be commercial rivals of Dona Catarina or enemies of the Sultan. Bruno and his men were innocent pawns in this complex game," Luke explained.

Decisions were quickly but quietly reversed—at all levels. Catarina's ship left on Tuesday with most of the men who would be her mercenaries—and provide a temporary garrison for Casablanca. Neither Catarina nor Bruno Costa were aboard.

Dona Takama would act for Catarina and carried with her the emerald ring that appeared at the Pimentos. It would be given to the Sultan as an act of good faith. The Governor gave Major Vento leave from his Tangier's post as he was to lead Catarina's mercenary garrison at Casablanca. The rumor that Catia Lopez would leave with him proved to be false. Bruno decided to remain in Tangiers until the last of his men were relocated.

Luke's hopeful assumption that the few weeks remaining until the English takeover would now be quiet was immediately shattered. A few days after the ship left for Tangiers, Gil Serano without warning arrived at Luke's office. "Am I welcoming the deputy governor or the chief of police—or is this a social visit?" Luke asked.

Gil gave a wry smile. "I come to inform you of a dramatic turn of events which may have repercussions for the incoming English, rather than the outgoing Portuguese."

"Which is?"

"General Mario de Silva is probably still alive—or at least the body that we assumed was his, is not."

"How do you know this?"

"The de Silva family decided that Mario, despite his illegitimate birth, would be buried in a family crypt on one of their estates. They sent an embalmer here to prepare the body who had been given details from some of Mario's childhood acquaintances that would help verify his identity. He immediately concluded that the body he was about to embalm was not Mario de Silva."

"How could he? The head was so macerated by a combination of the wagon wheels and horses' hooves that no one could recognize the body."

"Apparently Mario had a minor accident as a child and lost most of the little toe on his left foot. The macerated corpse that you speak of, had two perfect little toes. It could not be Mario."

"That creates a few problems. What is the family going to do?"

"They wish the revelation to remain a secret. The body of the unknown man has already been buried."

"Secondly this affects you personally. I heard that you and Mario's widow were to marry after a reasonable time of mourning."

"That will not change, except Lidia must now proceed with her case for annulment."

"The third problem is to discover what has happened to Mario. He may still be dead. Or he may have been the European officer who rode with Ghailan towards Tangiers."

"I want you to take the lead in the investigation of this last matter," commented Gil. "Leo has almost completed his relocation mission, so I have asked the Governor to assign him to your investigation."

Luke briefed Leo the next day. "You must be pleased that the bureaucratic relocation work is almost finished?"

"It was a nightmare. More difficult than I expected as half of the demobilized troops refused to go along with my brief. On the other hand, it meant that I only had to relocate this group. The other half either went to Casablanca, joined Ghailan, decided to stay here or simply disappeared in about equal numbers."

"Frankly I do not know where to start in finding Mario, but I suggest we add to our team someone who was a loyal servant of his commanding officers, Miguel Lopez and Mario de Silva, and who was privy to many of their secret operations—Sergeant Bruno Costa."

Luke and Leo found Bruno in his house at the end of the souk that had been partially destroyed by Colonel Lopez but was now largely renovated. They explained their proposal. Leo surprised Luke with an added incentive. "Sergeant, if this enquiry is successful, I will suggest to the Governor that he commission you as a captain before you depart for Casablanca. You will become Dimas Vento's deputy."

"How can I be of help?" asked Bruno.

"You acted for both Colonel Lopez and General de Silva in clandestine matters that suggest you were, despite your rank, a close confidante of those disgraced officers," Luke replied

"Yes, I did act in many a clandestine mission for both those officers but my loyalty and that of others was rewarded by treachery and death. We know that Lopez killed three of my closest comrades and now it emerges from what I hear that Mario may have had six of his own men killed—the three pretend kidnappers and the three men trampled by the horses and wagons. To be honest gentlemen you may want justice, I want revenge."

"To the outsider, there wasn't much of a link between those two officers," commented Leo.

"But there was. Much more than that simply between the military commandant and the commander of the infantry."

"Tell us more?" probed Luke.

"Initially they did not trust each other. De Silva believed that Lopez supported Gabriela and was trying to persuade Dona Catarina to transfer the inheritance due to De Silva's wife to her younger sister

This seemed to change after the attempt to blow up Catarina's ship with Gabriela aboard. It was under Lopez's instructions that we allowed that group to transfer what we thought were arms. The murder of the agents involved was on orders from further up the chain of command. It had to be De Silva. After Lopez tried to kill us, and was detained, who was his most frequent visitor? Mario de Silva."

"Do you know why?" Leo asked

"No, but my guess is that they had developed a common enemy and were unsure of their future."

"Who was this mutual enemy?" asked Luke.

32

"**D**ona Catarina and her offsider, the Berber woman Takama."

"Do you know why Mario would fake his own death?" asked Luke.

"Maybe he feared apprehension for either treason or murder. Did you gentlemen have anything against him?" asked Bruno.

"As regards treason, Mario's loyalties were obtuse. At one time he seemed too friendly with Ghailan, at others with the latter's enemies, the local Berbers. He could have been linked with the Sufi brotherhood over the bombing of Catarina's boat, and the sudden execution of the Sufi agents. Mario covered his tracks. More recently he took part in signing of the agreement between the local Berbers and the Sultan. And now there is possibility that the European officer with Ghailan on his last attempt to besiege the city was Mario," was Leo's surprisingly lengthy reply.

"Leo, while you and Bruno question the locals, I will visit Ghailan. If the officer that rode beside him on the recent attack on the city was Mario, then half our problem is solved. We will know that Mario is alive and possibly where he is."

"Will Ghailan see you?" asked Leo.

"I will present him with the outlines of a treaty for him to consider once we English are in control. My reference to any European officer will be incidental."

A week later Luke accompanied only by Thomas waited in antechamber of the cold stone mountain retreat that Ghailan considered his palace.

"This is a surprise visit. Are you really here for some long-term negotiations, or for a brief spying visit to assess whether a preemptive English attack is feasible?" asked the astute warlord.

"Your Excellency is no fool. Everything I see will be useful for any future attack our new garrison is forced to make. That is why our escort since we entered your territory has kept us away from any significant military installations, which I am sure you are in the process of upgrading. You do not fear our occupation of Tangiers as much as the growing power of the Sultan who after he deals with the Sufi brotherhood at Fez will attack this mountain stronghold. His field artillery will destroy your defenses at one attempt. We English only have a few low caliber ships' cannons to put against your solid stone defenses. Consequently, you need to reach an agreement with us, before the Sultan expands his control in the area."

"What do you want and what are you offering me?" asked Ghailan.

"Very simply that you continue to supply the city with the resources in food, fuel and clothing that it needs and that you refrain from your periodical raids against the city."

"And what do I get in return?"

"Unlike the Portuguese our troops will not sally forth and attack your crops, cattle and women. Your traders will be able to enter the city in person on designated days."

"Above all I need military assistance. You must guarantee that you will not attack my territory, that you will come to my aid if I am attacked by a third party, and finally that you will provide a regular and cheap supply of arms and ammunition."

"I can implement what I suggested immediately. The military aspects of your demands need approval from London and would be part of a formal agreement between you and our new Governor when he arrives. I will certainly pass your requests on to my superiors."

"I don't trust you Tremayne. You have not come all this way to discuss a nebulous treaty, the first half of which is currently operating, and the second half over which you have no final authority. Why are you here? Have some of those men who joined me and then had second thoughts, run back to Tangiers with their tail between their legs, advancing some complicated conspiracy that you need to investigate?"

"I have not spoken to such men, although I know a handful have returned."

"If you had, you would have learnt that I am now in receipt of massive Spanish aid and advice. A Spanish officer accompanied me on my recent attempt on Tangiers, in fact he is still here— and knows you very well."

Ghailan ordered a servant to bring the Spanish officer to the antechamber.

It was Luke's old acquaintance, adversary and one time ally, the English born but Spanish aristocrat, Nicholas, Count of Varga and Verganza, the one- time Governor of the Spanish enclave of Oran.

Nicholas was effusive but critical. "Well Luke, I never expected with the death of Cromwell and the collapse of the English Republic that I would ever see you occupying a high position in the administration of the once hated Stuart monarchy."

"No, but the King is equally rewarded his enemies and his friends. He is reconciling the nation."

"Enough of old times gentlemen! Let us eat and drink. The Colonel will have to return to Tangiers as soon as possible," commented Ghailan, making it clear that he had nothing further to discuss.

As Luke made his way down from the mountain he commented to Thomas, "At least I got an answer to the main task of this visit without even asking the question."

A day later Luke, Leo and Bruno met to compare their investigations. Luke's report was simple. "The officer accompanying Ghailan was not Mario."

"Bruno and I have uncovered further mystery and intrigue," said Leo with enthusiasm

"In what sense?" asked a very interested Luke.

"Mario acted completely out of normal, leading up to his supposed death. He did not leave on that supposedly fatal journey to the barracks from his home, nor was he accompanied by his own men," commented Bruno.

"I want you to hear what happened from our source, the former head of Mario's bodyguard, Ensign Arturo Magellan who has come with us," responded Leo who went to the door and admitted the junior officer. "Tell the Colonel what you told us regarding the evening before, and the day of the general's alleged death."

"Our gubernatorial guard consists of ten cavalry. The night before his supposed death, we escorted the governor from the barracks to his home. On reaching his villa, he refused to dismount. He ordered seven of my men to stay at the villa and protect his wife. He told me to bring two other men and escort him to a secret destination. When I asked him why, he said he feared for his life, and he felt safer away from his villa, hidden in a location that his enemies would never suspect."

"And where was that?" asked Luke.

"Within Dona Catarina's large complex. As most of her people had already moved to Casablanca, there were plenty of empty rooms."

"The story becomes even more interesting," emphasized Bruno.

Arturo continued. "Next morning at dawn the general ordered us to go to the docks and abduct three drunken seamen and bring them back to Catarina's complex. After they had sobered up the general explained to them that they would be well paid as they were only required to impersonate us soldiers for a short trip to the barracks. He then ordered my men and I to leave for the barracks. He suggested that if anyone was after him, they would attack us. I was to wear his cape to confuse any attacker into thinking it was the general. He would follow sometime later with his newly recruited pretend soldiers."

"As we know Arturo's trio were not attacked, but that which was supposed to include the general was. All three of that group were killed, and the man dressed as the general was badly mutilated. Note only three bodies were found. The fourth man the real general was never among them," commented Leo.

"And a minor detail fits into place. Only one of the three men was riding. Two of them were leading their horses—a strange maneuver for a cavalry bodyguard. It was my fault. When we abducted the seamen, I did not ascertain whether they could ride or not. Two of them could not," added Arturo.

"This suggests that the general carefully planned his own disappearance," observed Leo.

"Yes, and orchestrated the killing of three innocent men," answered Luke.

"At least he showed some decency. He did not kill any of us, his loyal bodyguard," muttered Arturo.

After Arturo departed the three investigators visited Dona Catarina's complex. Luke decided to question Aristotle de Gama, before raising the issue with Catarina herself, who was still sheltering in the English barracks.

Aristotle greeted Luke with the remark," I was just about to visit you after I had seen Catarina."

"And why would that be?"

"Our ship that left for Casablanca last Tuesday removed most of assets and most of our staff. I now run a largely deserted complex with masses of empty space. My mistress is offering villas to English officers at very reduced prices. You should snap up one yourself, before a host of your naval officers do."

"Thank you for the offer, but my mission ends here very shortly. Our complete Atlantic Mediterranean fleet will return in October to take away any remaining Portuguese citizens who wish to leave. Our garrison will be in place by mid-January. More men from the returning fleet will occupy the city, expanding on the force I currently control. I will execute authority on behalf of the English sovereign until governor and garrison arrive subject to the commander of the fleet."

"Why are you here?" asked Aristotle.

"Mario de Silva!" replied Bruno.

"Yes, despite official attempts to keep it quiet, I heard that it was not his body run down by a couple of wagons. You know he was here the night before this fake death occurred?"

"Yes, that is why we are here. Why did he come here?"

"He told me he had irritated a number of people and felt for his safety. He believed he would be safer here, because his enemies would not know that this was where he was located."

"And you readily accommodated him?"

"Of course! He was not only the deputy governor and military commandant, but he was also my employer's nephew who already had rooms here."

"You had no inkling of what he was planning?"

"No, but in hindsight I inadvertently saved the life of three of our servants. He asked if I could spare three of my men for an hour the following morning to impersonate his bodyguard and reduce the chances of an attack on him. I refused and suggested he find some lowlife around the docks."

"Did you see he or his men leave here on that fateful morning?" asked Leo.

"I saw his real bodyguard set out some time before I heard that Mario and his pretend guard had left the villa, but I did not see them."

"Would any of your servants have witnessed that departure?"

"Possibly, but the majority of them are now on the high seas bound for Casablanca."

"Could you summon everybody still here to the reception hall so that we can question them?" requested Luke.

Seven servants turned up—five men and two women.

Only one, a groom had any relevant information. "Yes, I saw the four just before they left. I was alerted by a shouting match between the general and the three men. He was taken aback that two of them could not ride, and asked me to help the one that could, to mount his horse. He then gave the mounted replacement his own ornate plumed head dress and placed the sash of some order around the man. From a distance he would be mistaken for the general."

"Anything else you noticed?"

"The general had produced a flask earlier in the morning and continued to ply these men, persuading all three to take continuous deep swigs."

"He kept them intoxicated. No wonder they took a no action to escape the rampaging horses and wagons," commented Leo.

"Did you see the general himself leave?" asked Bruno.

"No."

"Do you know anything about the horses and wagons used in the attack?" Luke asked.

"Yes, everything! Those two wagons had been used by the carriers who took Dona Catarina's possessions to her ship. The carriers left them here, as there were further goods to be taken around Tangiers. The horses and wagons only had to be led a few yards outside our main gate to reach the start of the incline down which they were later directed."

"Could one man have done that?" continued Luke.

"Yes, one man could lead both sets of horses."

"But could one man set them off down the hill?"

"Yes, if he did what the perpetrator apparently did. Unharness the horses! The beasts broke away from the wagons which careened uncontrolled down the slope. The horses had to keep going to avoid being hit by the wagons. That is why most of the horses were located at the bottom of the incline and a few escaped uninjured. The wagons were completely wrecked."

Luke thanked the groom. He turned to his fellow investigators and concluded, "We have an accurate picture of what Mario did, and how he accomplished it. Our task now is to find him."

"And how do we do that?" asked Leo.

"Hard work and a lot of luck," was Luke reply. "Have our men station themselves outside Dona Catarina's complex and ask everybody who passes that way regularly what they saw during the two hours during which we know Mario must have left. It is a long shot, but it is a start."

"We might be luckier than you think. Mario was a well-known figure. Someone must have seen him," said Bruno.

"Not if he was in disguise," retorted Leo.

"If you two organize our mass street-interrogation, I will see Lidia. She may know more about the lead up to Mario's disappearance than she has told us."

33

Luke's initial attempt to see Lidia failed. He was turned back by a mature female servant who said her mistress had been ill for a few days. When he returned a few days later he was warmly received "Since I was told that Mario was not one of the bodies mown down in the street, I have been expecting a visit."

"I am sorry to hear you have been unwell. I hope you have recovered."

A tear rolled down Lidia's cheeks. "I was in little physical danger, but it has been heartbreaking. I had a miscarriage. You were one of the few people who knew I was pregnant."

Luke expressed his sympathy and asked if Lidia was up to answering a few questions.

She nodded her willingness.

"We have established what Mario did in the lead-up to what amounts to his murder of three innocent men, but we are unclear as to his motives and are totally ignorant of his current whereabouts. Did Mario give you any clues as why he had to disappear?"

"Not really, we were not close, especially over the last few months. Mario has been obsessed with creating a viable future for himself from the moment the transfer of Tangiers from Portugal to England was announced. Initially he believed that could be achieved by increasing the inheritance I was to obtain from my aunt. He may have acted against my sister in order to achieve this. Then talk that my aunt had changed her will clearly disturbed him and he became furious with her."

"To the point of organizing her death?"

"I doubt it. If he was involved in such an enterprise, it would have been in collaboration with others whose motives may have been different."

"Such as a short-lived association with the Sufi Brotherhood?"

"I know nothing of that. On the day before he disappeared, he explained that he would not stay the night at our villa, as he feared that his enemies might try to kill him. He did not name them. Mario was an incompetent whose half-hearted and failed enterprises upset a host of people—the Portuguese government, his own military officers and their families, Ghalain, the supporters of the Sultan, the Sufi brotherhood, and Catarina and her range of associates. Everybody engaged in the replication and sale of the Islamic emerald ring would have found Mario's changing role in that fiasco reprehensible."

"Clearly Mario feared for his life, but for what exact reason remains unclear. Where would he disappear to?"

"In the past, when he wanted to escape, he either went into the mountains and fraternized with Ghailan, or with that warlord's enemies, the lowland Berbers. He was very close to Dona Takama's family. On occasion, he found a retreat in the Dominican friary, which is now closed."

"I am beginning to feel sympathy for Mario. It is possible that he has been blamed for a host of incidents for which he is not responsible. Even more unfortunate, he may have been deliberately made the scapegoat for a number of these by his enemies," commented Luke.

"This will be last time we talk, Colonel. Gil believes that giving the probable chaos of the next few months here, I would be better off back in Portugal from where I can more readily forward my case for annulment."

Luke had no sooner returned to his barracks when Father Roberto arrived in a high state of concern. "What is it Father?"

"Miguel Lopez, he has disappeared again."

"I thought you had him restrained. What happened?"

"When he was first sent to us, he was restrained by being strapped to the bed with his arms and feet tied together as he was prone to violent outbursts. Over the weeks of his confinement as his behavior improved these restraints were removed. For the last week he was totally unrestrained, but never left alone. One of the brothers has been always in the room with him. I thought he was close to having fully recovered from his mental breakdown."

"But you were wrong! How did he get away?"

"He chose a time when all the friary, except the brother in his room, were at prayer. He attacked the brother, tied his hands together with his own girdle, and then gagged him. It was a halfhearted attempt and the brother soon freed himself and alerted me just as prayers were concluding. I came straight here to alert the deputy governor, the military commandant and yourself."

"There may be no need for alarm. He may have indeed recovered, and simply returned home. Have you checked that he is not at his villa?"

"The first thing I did. No! I am afraid his absconding is indeed very serious and potentially fatal. He told the brother he assaulted that he was driven to do God's work and avenge those who destroyed his relationship with Gabriela."

"Did he name his victims?"

"No, but in his disturbed state it could include most of Tangier's elite. You must increase your protection of Dona Catarina. She would be an obvious target of his disturbed mind."

"You seem to have been surprised by his recent regression. Did something happen in the last few days that could have triggered this bad reaction?"

"Apart from the occasional visitor, nothing really ever happened during our care of him."

"And who were his visitors?"

"Regular, except for the last few weeks were his sister Catia, and one of those soldiers that he tried to kill—Sergeant Costa."

"Costa was a regular?"

"Yes, and he was the only one that seemed to improve Miguel's spirits but a few days ago he had a surprise visitor—Aristotle da Gama."

"Did your attendant brother hear what they discussed?"

"No, we try to give the visitors and the patient as much privacy as possible. The brother would stand just inside the door from where it would be difficult to hear any whispered conversation."

"So, it could be something that Aristotle said that provoked this latest escapade?"

"Possibly."

"From my understanding of the issue, the four persons who did most to prevent Miguel and Gabriela from coming together were all women—Catarina, Lidia, Catia and Gabriela herself. We could be in crisis with two former senior army officers loose in the city both possibly with murderous intent. We must find both men before they kill someone else."

"You must warn the three women who are still in the city, and I will now inform the deputy governor and the military commandant who were not in their offices when I called there a few minutes ago," advised Roberto.

Luke doubled the guard around Catarina's residence and explained the reasons for it.

"I should be safe from either. After all I supported Mario for years and am in no way responsible for the failure of his marriage to Lidia, and while I initially opposed Gabriela's relationship with Miguel, I felt in the end his offer of marriage was a reasonable solution to the difficulties she had created for herself."

"You cannot take any risks. Mario resents your failure to help him adapt to post-Tangiers while Miguel is not thinking rationally and may only remember your initial opposition to his courtship. Would you feel safer if we transferred you back onto one of our ships?"

"No, I found life on board too confining, and the constant movement of the vessel made me feel unwell."

By the time Luke reached Lidia's house she had already been taken by Gil to his own villa and provided with part of the deputy governor's guard. Luke talked to Gil regarding the Lopez disappearance and to co-ordinate their search for him.

"Not so long ago, you and Miguel were close friends—the city's most debonair bachelors. Was there anywhere within the city or beyond that a distraught Miguel might go to?" asked Luke.

"Nowhere in particular!"

"So, there is nothing in your knowledge of Miguel's past that would suggest any special place where he might hide while planning his revenge?"

"Miguel was a very astute planner, who spent ages in his preparation for any enterprise. The Miguel I know would have stayed in the priory until he is ready to strike. That is why I took Lidia away from her villa as soon as Roberto told me of Miguel's plans. He won't be hiding away planning. He is ready to strike now—and he will."

"In that case I must get to Catia immediately," said a concerned Luke.

Luke arrived at Catia's villa with a half a dozen troops. The ever-aggressive Catia responded, "Come to arrest me?"

"On the contrary my lady, we have come to protect you."

"From what?"

"There are two potential murderers loose in the city. You have annoyed both and we fear you could become a victim."

"You can't be serious. I know that there is an alert out for old Mario. That old codger is harmless, and I never crossed him. In fact, I think he saw me as ally in denigrating his sister-in-law Gabriela, which he believed would enhance the prospects of wife Lidia receiving more of Catarina's wealth."

"That may be so, but the second potential murderer may be more dangerous."

"Who is that?"

"Your brother, Miguel."

"Ridiculous! What led you to such a silly idea? Isn't Miguel protected and safely confined in the Friary of St Francis. I visit him there regularly."

Luke explained the recent developments concerning Miguel and concluded, "He is out to get his revenge against those whom he thinks contributed to the failure of his relationship with Gabriela. You took the lead in the campaign. Your hatred of Gabriela was the talk of the town."

"I have explained to Miguel the reasons for my actions dozens of times, and I have tried to convince him that events proved me right. The only person responsible for the failure of Miguel's courtship with Gabriela was Gabriela herself."

"None of us can be sure what Miguel in his troubled mind really believes. It is wise to take precautions. Is there any special place where Miguel might go to hide?"

"Yes, but it is miles away and he would have been seen attempting to reach it."

"Where would it be?"

"Caves on the Atlantic coast. Miguel learnt to swim in Brazil and became fascinated with underground caves. When we first came to Tangiers we were told of these Atlantic caves. We explored them together quite often, until he became obsessed with Gabriela. She had no interest in such activities. Are you sure Miguel left the friary with murder in his heart? Could it not have been suicide? He is very troubled soul."

"Not according to the friar he assaulted to make his getaway," answered Luke.

"If he does not surface locally within the next few days, visit those caves! I will come with you."

"I will take up your offer if nothing eventuates over the next day or so. Were you ever present with your brother when Sergeant Costa was there?"

"Yes, and it was I who persuaded Bruno to visit."

"That must have been difficult. After all Miguel killed Bruno's comrades and had tried to kill him."

"I suggested that that killing spree had been a result of a mental aberration and that Miguel probably needed to be reminded of earlier days when Bruno and his men were Miguel's trusted elite. All of the times that our visits coincided Bruno talked to Miguel about the good old days, which clearly improved his demeanour."

Over the next few days Luke and Leo become more and more frustrated. Leo complained that their investigation of the people who regularly frequented the area of Catarina's complex regarding what they had seen on the morning of Mario's disappearance had slowed, as Bruno had disappeared for a couple of days, claiming he had matters involving some of his former comrades to address. Neither Mario nor Miguel had struck—or even been seen.

Eventually Luke sought the assistance of a troop of Carlos's cavalry and with Catia left the city for the Atlantic coast. Enquiries along the way were inconclusive. People in the Berber villages confirmed that numerous groups and individuals had passed along the coast road, but nobody recognised either Miguel or Mario.

On reaching the coast any searching of the caves was delayed several hours as they could only be entered at low tide, unless one wished to dive and swim through the submerged entrance. The tide finally receded, and Luke's party entered the first cave. Catia pointed out that Miguel's favourite haunt was deeper into the complex which was nevertheless still lit by sunlight that penetrated through a fissure in the roof. "There is a flat altar like rock there on which Miguel and I used to eat the provisions we brought with us," explained Catia.

In her eagerness to find her brother Catia pushed ahead as Luke who was not as sure footed slipped repeatedly on the wet rocks. She suddenly cried out, "My God, he is here, asleep on that low rock!"

This elation was suddenly followed by a scream and hysterical sobbing as her shaking of Miguel's partially submerged body failed to waken him. On reaching the scene Luke comforted the distraught Catia. One of the troops led Catia away from her brother's body while Luke tried to ascertain whether Miguel had committed suicide, or had been murdered.

For over half an hour Luke and one of the troopers carefully examined the body. There appeared to no wounds. Miguel had simply drowned but was it by his own volition or with the aid of others.

On their way back to Tangiers, Catia asked Luke, "Was Miguel murdered?"

"Not likely, but it can't be ruled out. Your earlier comment may have been more accurate. I think he committed suicide."

On reporting to Leo and Bruno on his mission to the caves he received further good news. "In your absence we interviewed many people. The only sighting that was not a regular morning event is that one person saw a friar leave Catarina's complex at the relevant time," explained Leo.

"How is that unusual? The city is full of friars."

"But no longer any Dominicans. All Dominicans left the city weeks ago. This friar was wearing the habit of the Dominicans, and we know that Mario had close associations with them before they left. I suggest we surround their vacated premised. Mario may be hiding there," advised Bruno.

34

When advised of Luke's plan to surround and search the vacated Dominican priory, Gil acted. He vetoed the participation of English protestant troops. "Popular opinion is very anti-Protestant. I do not want to increase popular discontent during our last weeks here. The search of the priory will be conducted by the remnants of my local police, aided by the Portuguese cavalry. I will lead the enterprise in person."

"May I participate as one of your officers?" asked Luke.

"Only if you do not reveal that you are English. Accompany Major Coval and Sergeant Costa as observers. As soon as we complete the search, you can resume control of your investigation into Mario's activities."

Gil initially questioned the current nominal head of the church remaining in Tangiers, the secular priest Monsignor Blanco. "Since the Dominicans left have you used their friary for any ecclesiastical purposes?"

"Their chapel, which was also part of our church has been used by our congregation but the friary building itself has been locked and unused since Father Cisneros departed."

"Do you inspect the premises on a regular basis?"

"No, we leave ourselves within the month. The English can do what they like with the buildings."

"You have not had any reports of people using it as a temporary home?"

"Yes, the city's homeless have taken over parts of it."

Gil was given the key to the main door and accompanied by Leo, Bruno and Luke he entered the building.

The smell was overwhelming. It was clearly being used by numerous vagrants who had left food rotting all over the place and had defecated in inappropriate places. There were dozens of signs of habitation. A few sleeping stragglers were disturbed by the troops. Mario could have been there, but it would be impossible to prove. It would also have been an ideal place for Mario dressed as a friar to change garb, with any of the other inhabitants and disappear again as an inconspicuous vagrant.

Unexpectedly the investigation was disrupted. Without any advice to the English a Portuguese galleon appeared outside the harbor. It towered over the sleeker English warships and was too large to enter the inner harbor. It had been sent to collect the remaining Portuguese officials and those Tangerine citizens wishing to leave before the English took over. Those officials required to leave on this vessel on orders of the Queen herself included the Governor, Father Antonio, Major Coval, all Catholic clergy other than the Franciscans, and most of Gil's police.

A skeleton Portuguese administration in the persons of the deputy governor, Gil Serano, the military commandant Carlos Pimento and Father Roberto remained. The Portuguese cavalry and the English mixed force of soldiers and sailors were now solely responsible for law and order, and the defense of the city.

The situation for Luke worsened when one of Catarina's maid servants informed him that afternoon that her mistress had left English protection and made her way to the Portuguese galleon. Had she received a similar royal directive?

"Did her ladyship explain why this sudden change of plan?" Luke asked.

"Yes, the Portuguese galleon had brought an order from the Queen herself that the mistress should return to Portugal immediately to defend herself in court against a claimant who argued that all her possessions belonged to him—that he was the rightful heir to her father's estates. As the Crown had placed its short-term survival in Casablanca in her hands, it wanted the matter clarified as quickly as possible."

"Why have you told me this? I might try to stop your mistress leaving?"

"I am not betraying her. We went to join her about an hour after she had left. She had not arrived. We waited for an hour or two, and I decided to come back here and inform you."

"Was she going to go anywhere else on her way to the ship?"

"Yes, she was going to her villa to collect various papers that she needed for the court case."

"What was she wearing?"

"She couldn't have been missed. She had an emerald, green skirt and bodice but these were concealed by her long iridescent white cape."

"Did she appear anxious before she left?"

"Yes, but only over trivia. Her favorite gold and sapphire bracelet had lost a gem and she was worried that more might fall out before she had a chance to have them reset. I suggested that all she needed to do to contain any wayward gems was to wear long gloves. She gave me a kiss on the cheek and put on long white gloves to match her iridescent cape."

Luke with a platoon of his infantry, and accompanied by Thomas to translate, traced Catarina's path from the barracks to her villa. Luke was amazed that an area which only days before had been a hub for local commerce was deserted. The main gate to this complex of villas was firmly locked. One of Luke's men rang the bell to alert anybody left in the villas that they had visitors. No one appeared, and Luke was considering forcing his way in when a small man appeared at the far end of the largest courtyard, and slowly made his way towards the gate.

"Sorry sir, I was at the far end of the complex, and only heard the bell when I was halfway back in this direction. There is nobody here except me. The household left for Casablanca with Dona Takama a few days ago. The mistress is under the protection of the English, and Da Gama and his three personal servants left early this morning."

"Your mistress did not see Da Gama before he left?"

"Not that I am aware of."

"Could you open the gate and accompany me while my men search every inch of these numerous villas. You mistress has disappeared and could have come here for what would probably be her last look at what was her home for decades," asked Luke.

Thomas who had fallen behind the troops, questioning many of the locals informed Luke, "Colonel, a lady in a glistening white cape was seen in the street leading to Catarina's villa by several inhabitants of that street. She was certainly almost here."

Luke and Thomas personally searched the villas of Catarina and Aristotle while his men would go through the other villas. Aristotle's villa was devoid of all personal material. These had either been sent ahead to Casablanca, or Aristotle had taken them with him that morning.

Catarina's villa was the opposite. She had clearly not removed all her personal assets.

Luke searched it thoroughly, but no evidence of her recent attendance was visible. The files of papers in her library showed no sign of being disturbed.

A disappointed and frustrated Luke returned to the barracks and spent the evening drinking with some of his men. Late in the evening a very intoxicated Thomas remarked to the assembled throng "We may have failed to find the lady, but I found a fortune."

"Tell us another!" remarked one of the soldiers.

Thomas stumbled towards a bench and removed a handkerchief from his pocket. He lay it on the table revealing three very large blue gemstones.

"Colored glass," observed the same soldier.

Luke turned on the interjector, "Maybe not, Tom is a silversmith who knows real gems from glass. Are they real, Tommy?"

"Colonel, I have never seen such large brilliant blue sapphires as these."

Luke could hardly contain himself. "Where exactly in Catarina's villa did you find them?"

"In the smaller reception hall near the large chest of drawers on the southern wall. In fact, I saw one of them and felt under the chest and located the other two."

"Thomas, you have provided the proof that Dona Catarina entered her own villa." He explained to the group that Catarina had a bracelet with large loose sapphires of which only one was missing when she left their barracks. "I am returning to the villa now. Catarina may still be there—dead or alive. I will awake some of our sober comrades to help me conduct a second search. You can continue drinking."

It was about midnight when Luke with a small group of sober soldiers arrived at the villa. Luke rang the bell, but no one came to the gate. Luke convinced himself that Catarina might still be alive, trapped in her own house. He ordered his men to smash the gate. They entered her villa equipped with lighted tapers and made their way to the small reception hall.

They were ordered to pull the chest of drawers away from the wall. Luke was astonished and delighted to find that it had concealed a small door in the wall which was clearly locked from the outside. Another two sapphires were found under the drawers. The door was opened and revealed steps leading down to what was either a cellar or some type of escape tunnel. As Luke descended the steps, he called out Catarina's name several times.

After a few minutes he suddenly hushed his men who were noisily following him. "I thought I heard something" As the soldiers stood motionless and silent, a muffled murmur was heard. Luke ran deep into the chamber in the direction of the noise. The light of the increasing number of tapers now revealed in the distance, tied to a fitting of what had been a wine cellar, a body.

Luke reached the figure. The feet were tied together as were the hands. The mouth had been taped. There was nasty gash on the back of the head. It was Catarina.

"Is she still alive?" asked one of men.

Luke placed his head against hers, and then listened carefully with his head against her breast. Finally, he placed the shiny blade of his dagger against her mouth.

"She is still alive, but only just. I cannot hear any breathing, but the blade of my dagger revealed traces of her breath. Find a portable bed in one of rooms and we will take her to the friary! I will send Greg Pickering there to assist."

Two hours later both Roberto and Greg agreed that Catarina was in a deep coma, brought about by a massive blow or blows to the back of head. "When will she come out of it?" asked Luke.

"In an hour, a day, a month, never—we cannot tell!" replied Greg.

Four days later well after the Portuguese galleon had departed for Lisbon, Luke received a friar who informed him that Catarina had stirred, and Father Roberto thought he may wish to question her. Catarina was indeed awake and rather chatty, perhaps due to the herbal medicine that the friars had been giving her. "My favorite English Colonel! Father Roberto tells me that I have you to thank for saving my life."

"Not me! You should thank your bracelet. If one of your maids had not mentioned the loose sapphires and my valet had not found some in your reception hall, we would not have found you."

"That is the last thing I remember. I was hit from behind and as I fell, I put out my arm to save myself and felt the bracelet take the weight of fall. I had removed my gloves to sort through some papers. I blacked out at the same time as my bracelet shattered."

"Do you remember anything leading up to the hit on the head?"

"I dropped into my home of over a decade to collect papers from the library that I thought I might need in the imminent court case. I was surprised that I could not find them, and was heading to Aristotle's, who as my lawyer had access to them. He might have already isolated them for my use. I must ask him."

"That may be difficult. Aristotle boarded the Portuguese galleon which unfortunately you have missed. Did this court case come out of the blue, or have you been expecting it?"

"My succession to father's estate was originally fraught with legal obstacles but I overcame them. The problem involved the claims of a very distant male heir above that of a daughter. My father declared that there were no male claimants close enough to inherit, and his daughter was his sole heir. The court accepted this. Now apparently someone is trying to resurrect these old claims. I must get to Portugal as soon as possible."

"Is Aristotle aware of these claims?"

"Yes."

"Was he aware that you were going to Portugal on the galleon?"

"No, I told no one but my maids."

"Could Aristotle have received a letter similar to the one you received suggesting that to defend your position he must be in Portugal for the court case?"

"It is possible, but he would have consulted me."

"Maybe he tried, but you were a missing person from the time of your attack until the galleon left."

35

Luke was unhappy. He would not worry Catarina with his concerns at this stage of her recovery. Was Aristotle the loyal lawyer simply carrying out what his mistress would have expected of him or was he in some way involved in the attempt to deprive her of her inheritance. Even more worrying was that he may have been behind the assault and attempted murder of his mistress. It was imperative to discover all he could about Aristotle da Gama.

Luke returned to the Sarmento complex alone where he was greeted by the caretaker who was repairing the gate that Luke's men had smashed. Luke gave a half apology "Sorry about the gate!" The man responded, "I hear it was necessary to save the mistress. The gate or her life didn't give you much of the choice. Why have you returned?"

Luke lied. "Your mistress asked me to look for some papers that Mr. da Gama may have in his files." As he had discovered on his earlier visit, Aristotle's library was now bereft of most books, and the cupboards once full of files, were empty. After several hours of fruitless searching Luke left despondently. The caretaker noted his mood.

"No luck sir?"

"No, it appears that Da Gama has already sent all of his papers and files to Casablanca."

"Not all sir! The last trunks and boxes to go are on a wagon in the stables waiting to be taken to the next Sarmento ship going to Casablanca." Luke gave the man a hug and almost ran to the stables.

The wagon had two large trunks and several smaller boxes. Luke opened one of the large trunks. It was full of papers. He hitched up one of the stronger horses to the wagon and carefully drove it back to his barracks. A glance through the papers suggested that more than one reader would be necessary.

All the following day Luke, Jack, Greg and Thomas made their way progressively through the boxes. The aim was simple. Did the files tell Luke anything about Aristotle's past? By the end of the day Luke realized that this multiple reading was probably a waste of time. With four readers, the possible links between what appeared as a piece of trivia in one document, and an illuminating reference in another, would be missed.

He would have to read all the documents. After a week Luke had put together a most revealing set of possibilities. Aristotle was an illegitimate twin born to a woman in Fez. A girl twin Miriam was brought up in that city as a slave, but eventually was bought, freed and married to a Tangerine. Aristotle was brought by his father to Tangiers as a baby where he was adopted and brought up by the Da Gama family.

Aristotle had a privileged upbringing as his real father contributed heavily to his upkeep and education. He was educated in law from within a Portuguese community of converso migrants in Paris, and on his return to Tangiers was immediately appointed as lawyer to the Sarmento enterprise.

After the death of his real father, he was still receiving regular funds from a trust and it appears that when Miriam came to Tangiers, Aristotle regularly helped his sister with large cash gifts.

Luke then came across a document which in an aside named his real father. Luke was astounded. The father was Abram Falcone, Catarina's father. Aristotle was half-brother to his mistress. And perhaps Catarina's half-sister Miriam, was the fruit seller and property owner of the souk.

Luke had already come to a likely scenario. Aristotle was about to claim Catarina's inheritance as the closest male descendent of Abram Falcone. His illegitimacy would lose him the case immediately, but if he had a letter from his father legitimizing him, and he simply wished the court to register this fact, Catarina could lose everything.

Luke spent a restless night. How should he confront Miriam?

In the end he would try one of his favorite approaches. Give the person you are questioning the impression that you know it all already. Next morning, he went to the souk and approached Miriam who was placing various fruits onto trays in the front of her stall. "And what does the English Colonel, wish to buy?"

"I will spend up big in a moment. For the present I wish to ask you about your brother Aristotle?"

The unfazed Miriam asked, "Did he tell you of our relationship?"

Luke did not answer directly, remarking, "I know that you and he are twin siblings born to a Fez woman and Abram Falcone, Dona Catarina's father. And now he is a suspect in yet another attempt to kill your half-sister."

"No way! Aristotle is devoted to Catarina."

"He is a suspect because he has embarked urgently to Portugal to make a claim to the Sarmento enterprises."

"Rubbish! Aristotle has gone to Portugal to protect Catarina from a usurping outsider. He has no need to deprive Catarina of her empire. He will inherit half of it and in the not-too-distant future."

"How can that be? Catarina could live for many, many decades."

"I hope she does, but in discussing her new will she told Dona Takama and Aristotle the joint equal beneficiaries that she intended to retire, and that they would enjoy her bequests for years before her death."

"She has left everything to Aristotle and Takama? Nothing for her two nieces?"

"That is what Aristotle told me."

"Does Catarina know that you and Aristotle are her half siblings?"

"She has never been told. Aristotle wants it that way, and I hope you do not have to tell her."

"Could she have guessed? She must be aware that her father contributed greatly to Aristotle's upbringing. She must have wondered why?"

"You would have to ask her."

Luke thanked Miriam and bought as much fruit as he could wheel back to the barracks in a barrow that he borrowed from her. He now tended to favor Miriam's view of her brother as the devoted servant, and he discarded his original assumption that he was a murderous pretender.

Luke dropped into the friary for further talks with the recovering Catarina. Would he be able to pursue his questioning without revealing the existence of her twin half siblings? He would try, but the need to uncover the truth had to prevail.

"And what have you discovered since we last spoke? Have you found who locked me in the cellar to die?" she said.

"No, but I have confirmed in my own mind who it was not."

"Who was this prime suspect that you now feel you have cleared?"

"Your steward, Aristotle da Gama."

"And why did you suspect him?"

"Dashing off to Portugal! I thought he may be the claimant to your inheritance putting a case to the court."

Catarina gave Luke a fetching smile," You know, don't you?"

"Know what my lady?"

"That Aristotle would have a very strong claim as he is my half-brother."

"You know this? I had the impression that neither of you knew of the relationship."

"I am sure that we both have known since our schooldays, but father made me promise never to raise the matter with Aristotle, and he probably made Aristotle make the same promise."

"Why did your father tell both of you. It would have been an issue he could have best kept secret?"

"Young love! Aristotle and I were brought up in neighboring houses, and he was often at my villa, and I at his. We became very fond of each other. Suddenly Aristotle disappeared, and I was told he had gone to

France to train as a lawyer. I was distraught. Father in consoling me, revealed that we were half siblings. I expect he told Aristotle the truth in explaining why he was suddenly being sent to Paris. Half siblings could not be lovers."

"If I am to discard Aristotle as your attempted murderer, have you any further thoughts as to who it might be?"

"I have thought about this for weeks and can add nothing to what I told you previously. I have made many enemies but to the point of killing me now, when I am about to leave the city for good, it can only be a person who has a deep and personal hatred of me."

"I agree. Someone whom you have dealt with harshly and which you saw as simply effective business may have taken such action to heart, and over the years this resentment has festered into outright hatred. You must be destroyed before you escape to Casablanca."

"Put in those terms you have an impossible task. Over the years I have acted harshly against most of the elite and authorities in this city including governors and military officials, as well as members of my own family."

"Well, for the moment I am going to combine the two issues currently confronting me—the search for Mario, and for your killer. I am going to assume that for purposes of giving my investigation a clear direction, that Mario is your attempted killer."

"A waste of time! Mario may hate me, but he lacks the ability to organize the decapitation of a chicken let alone my murder."

"Over the years with him as your nephew- in- law you must have some idea where he might hide in within the city."

"He is not the brightest of men. He would gravitate to the obvious. Lidia has left their villa, so it is theoretically vacant. He may have returned there. Knowing you have already searched the old Dominican friary; he may go back there."

"The same could apply to the apartment you allotted to Mario and Lidia in your complex."

"That would be a good choice. It contains the entrance to a series of underground tunnels that lead to the seashore or into the countryside.

They were built a hundred years ago as escape tunnels should the city be invaded. I had the entrances blocked up once I took over the property. I do not know if Mario knew about them."

"Now I have three locations to search."

Luke began his search. Mario and Lidia's villa was not vacant. Although Mario had disappeared, and Lidia moved in with Gil, the house was still functioning with a host of servants. While Lidia had dropped in several times since her move, to collect possessions, no one had sighted Mario.

A second search of the Dominican friary simply indicated that it had had several visitors since the first investigation, but it provided no evidence that one of them had been Mario.

The search of Mario and Lidia's apartment in the Sarmento complex proved more promising. Luke immediately noted that the door of an antechamber next to the small reception hall was locked. He was sure that he had left it unlocked on his last visit. Its key was not in the lock.

It was a thick oak door with the hinges on the inside.

It would need an effective battering ram that he knew some English warships possessed. While he awaited the arrival of such an implement his search of the rest of the villa revealed nothing.

Eventually four burly seamen arrived and began their assault on the door.

Eventually a disintegrating door smashed to the ground.

Luke entered the room.

There was a body lying on a desktop.

It was Mario.

The nauseous aroma suggested he had been dead some time.

He had been stabbed several times, but a closer examination suggested he had been garroted first. As the marks around his neck indicated that this had been done by a knotted rope it immediately suggested to Luke that the perpetrators were agents of the Fez based Sufi brotherhood. The lack of blood around the multiple stab wounds indicated that the stabbings had occurred after death. He had been murdered but why the postmortem stabbings? One dagger to the heart or a knife across the throat would have been enough to make sure that Mario was dead. Thomas had a simple explanation. "This is a ritualistic killing of an infidel who had in the past created Islamic martyrs."

Luke agreed and soon found evidence pointing in that direction. He found nothing in Mario's pockets but his backpack that lay on the floor beside the desk was enlightening. Luke was elated but his men were non-plussed. It contained a few oranges and other fruit that they did not recognize. "What does this tell you colonel? asked one of them.

"That just before Mario came to hide in this villa, he visited a woman with whom he had dealings in the past, and who might have assisted his murderers—Miriam Barros the queen of the souk and probably an agent in the city of the Sufi brotherhood."

After arranging for the body to be taken to the Franciscan friary, Luke went alone to the souk to question Miriam. A warm response greeted him. "More questions about my brother?"

"No, something more serious! What do you know about the murder of the former deputy governor, Mario de Silva?"

'Why would I know anything about de Silva? I never moved in his exalted circles."

"That is not exactly true. You were a go-between for the Fez fanatics who were supposed to be buying arms, and who ultimately tried to blow up Catarina's ship, and Mario who probably provided the ammunition and who certainly facilitated its transport to the ship. I suspect that when Mario discovered that this attempt on Catarina had failed, and he had had links with the Fez fanatics he panicked and had the Fez agents murdered. His death by garroting is probably their revenge."

"Come Luke, I am not going to incriminate myself in a murder, but I understood Fez agents were determined to exact revenge on a man who they believed had betrayed them. Mario did visit me and obtain supplies which he said would keep him going until he had settled his debts. I knew both the local and Fez authorities were searching for him, so that when he left, I had one of the boys who frequent the souk follow him."

"And what did the boy report?"

"That he was hiding in a deserted apartment in the Sarmento complex."

"Information that you imparted to your Fez allies?"

"Information that I was also about to impart to you," was Miriam's smart response.

36

Luke aware that Catarina had been attacked in the complex, asked Miriam for details of the surveillance of Mario by her boys. "The boys took it turns. They saw Dona Catarina arrive and enter her villa an hour after they saw Aristotle leave. Mario did not leave his apartment. He could not have attacked my half-sister. The next day the boys reported that four men had entered Mario's apartment, but left in a hurry narrowly avoiding a company of English soldiers who had begun to search of the premises"

"Why do you act for the Sufi Brotherhood?" Luke suddenly asked.

"I don't act for the Sufi Brotherhood, but much of the trade that we do in fruit and vegetables comes from within territory controlled by them. It is a wise business decision to keep on side with those local authorities."

"And is your husband aware of what you have been engaged in?"

"Of course not! He is currently out of town accompanying four Fez residents back to their homes. He has been promised two wagon loads of goods at much reduced prices," answered Miriam with a big smile, and mischievous wink.

"Who carried out Mario's orders to kill the original Fez agents?"

"Ask your new associate, Costa!"

Luke didn't have to. Bruno revealed all in response to Luke's information that the body of Mario had been found.

"Damnation, I wanted to kill the treacherous two-timing renegade myself."

"He was killed by agents of the Sufi Brotherhood. Did Mario use your group to kill the original four agents?"

"He would have, but most of my group were dead and I was in a coma."

"Then who did he use?"

"He used his own bodyguard."

"Arturo Magellan is a strait-laced cavalry officer. He would not have strangled them and then made it appear that they were garroted."

"Very astute Colonel—but they had help. Ask Arturo for the details?"

Within an hour Arturo had answered Luke's request to visit him and Bruno.

"What can I do for you Colonel?"

"The general's body has been found. He was garroted by Fez fanatics. As you and your men actually committed the four murders for which Mario has been killed, you may be their next victim."

"Colonel we took no part in their murder. The general said there were four enemy spies in the city who had blown up a boat owned by Dona Catarina with the loss of many Portuguese lives. We tracked them down and arrested them. My men made them kneel, but we did not kill them."

"The who did?"

"A giant of an infantry sergeant which Mario brought with him. The general claimed that given the enemy spies had been captured within Portuguese territory it was within the rules of war for them to summarily tried and executed. I protested that my men were not a common firing squad, and the general did not in himself constitute a court martial. While I argued with the general the killer broke the necks of all four prisoners with a sudden twist of their heads. The killer suggested to the general that it would be a further advantage if we could place the blame for the killings on the Fez authorities themselves. He then garroted the bodies with a piece of wire."

Bruno then added, "I received a hint of Mario's role when I visited the recovering Colonel Lopez. He suspected that Mario was trying to hide his role in the incident by killing his partners in crime. My anger increased when I heard that Mario blamed the killing on so-called rogue elements in Colonel Lopez's regiment."

"Well, the Fez authorities have their revenge."

Luke still had some doubts. Miriam was Costa's friend. What if Bruno had murdered Mario, and with Miriam putting the blame on the Fez group. However, it was prudent to close the book on this murder. It was of no great security concern whether Mario had been executed by Portuguese soldiers or the Sufi religious. Luke now had one simple issue left to solve. Who tried to kill Catarina on more than one occasion? It would have been tidier to finish his investigations by putting all these attempts down to Mario.

Despite the evidence of the boys, it could still have been him. Perhaps in the network of tunnels emanating from Mario's apartment there may have been one leading into Catarina's. The street boys could not have seen this. Luke returned to the Sarmento complex with a body of troops to explore all the tunnels. After a full morning's search, the soldiers reported to Luke. They had traced all the tunnels leading from Mario's hub. None of them led into Catarina's villa. Mario could not have been the person who gagged and bound Catarina and left her to die.

The soldiers were surprised that Luke did express disappointment nor frustration. Instead, he appeared highly elated.

"What did you discover sir, that overrides any disappointment with our finds?" asked one of the men.

"I searched again the tunnel where we found Catarina. For most of its length the dustless slate floor revealed no footprints. However, as I approached its exit, the floor became covered with dust. On it I found two sets of footprints. One was that of a very heavy male and the other of a petite woman. Her print revealed that she was wearing a strange shoe with little heel imprint, but a ridge running lengthways along the foot. I have drawn an outline of it and will ask a few women if they can identify it."

He asked Catarina. She recognized it immediately. "This is a half shoe that is not enclosed in its back half. To maintain the integrity of shoe an additional ridge is added to make up for the lack of covering around the heel. It is used by aristocratic women in very hot weather."

"This changes my perspective. If the person out to kill you is a well-to- do woman, then the possibilities become more limited. Of those you have associated with recently Gabriela is in England, and Takama in Casablanca. Maybe the culprit is Lidia, Catia or Micaela?"

"That shoe could have been that of a child, or partner of the male who should remain your prime suspect," suggested Catarina.

"I must first clear the three women I have named. Does your niece Lidia know she is to receive no inheritance? If she does then this provides ample motive."

"Not for certain, but I did suggest that when she wed Gil, after her marriage to Mario was annulled, I would no longer support her. She seemed happy with that."

"I fear for your safety my lady. We are in a worse position than before. Previously we had assumed that your would-be murderer was General de Silva or Colonel Lopez, now it is possibly an unknown woman. You must leave Tangiers as soon as possible."

"I am ahead of you Colonel. I have consulted your Admiral and he has approved passage on your relief frigate which leaves tomorrow, and which will take me to Lisbon. As neither I nor Aristotle will return to Tangiers, I have given my villa complex to my half- sister Miriam. She made an excellent job of controlling the souk and increasing her ownership of most of land on which it operated. She is one of the few people who intends to stay here when you take over. She will make a fortune selling my villas to the English navy and officers of your incoming garrison."

"Then it appears that I have only one task left—to get you safely from here to the frigate. I have a few suggestions."

Next morning Catarina wearing her famous white cape and with a gigantic hat, that concealed her face, and three servants were escorted in a coach to the dockside, put aboard a ship's boat with soldiers forming a close protective ring around them.

Luke ordered his men to row towards the English fleet.

Suddenly a shot was heard. To Luke's amazement and distress Catarina slumped forward—the victim of an excellent marksman.

The boat continued towards the frigate where the captain immediately asked about the shot that was heard. He was appalled as the sailors carried the body of Catarina aboard.

Once aboard Luke examined the body and announced with relief, "Great news, the double chain mail deflected the shot. Tommy Smith is fine. You can get up now Tom!"

One of three maids reclaimed her white cape. It was the real Catarina.

Catarina thanked Tommy for risking his life in impersonating her and suggested that if he tired of life as an English soldier, she would give him a position in Casablanca as her silversmith.

"This incident proves that your enemy has the services of a brilliant marksman. There would be very few left in the city and my military acquaintances must be able to name them. I am sure your would-be is a petite woman who has the services of a marksman with exceptional talent.

Catarina gave Luke a final hug and invited him to visit her in Casablanca when his mission in Tangiers ended. She suggested that England should appoint an envoy there if it wished to continue trade along the African coast.

A sad and depressed Luke was rowed ashore. He would miss Catarina Sarmento. There were not many women he had met who had her personality, character and determination to succeed as she did.

Tangiers was now a ghost town. As he made his way back to the barracks Luke heard more English spoken than Portuguese, Arabic or Berber. The only place where a remnant of the old Tangiers remained was in the souk, despite the desertion of half the stall holders.

Most of the Portuguese inhabitants, officials and soldiers had gone. All Luke was required to do with the support of the English fleet was to hold the city until the English Governor and garrison arrived at which point the last of the Portuguese army, its cavalry would also depart.

Jack Moon was happy to spend the time training the new Berber auxiliaries from Takama Khirri's village, but Luke remained troubled that the person or persons who tried to murder Catarina were still at large. In discussion with his officers, he announced that he would continue his investigation. "If successful I will be able to tell Dona Catarina that she did not import her would-be murderer with her to Casablanca."

"But where do you start?" asked Greg.

"We have nothing to go on regarding the poisoning attempt and the subsequent failed shooting. All I have are the two sets of shoeprints in the tunnel, that of a heavily built man and of a petite woman or child."

"According to Catarina most upper and middle-class Portuguese women and girls in Tangiers would have a pair of shoes similar to those that left the print."

"Then the only clue you really have is the murderer is a heavily built male," said Jack.

"Not quite, we are all forgetting the most recent clue. Our murderer is an excellent marksman. Bruno is still in town. He might know of possible suspects."

"He has already told you of one. His long-term deputy, Sergeant Rios the notorious Gigante, is a renowned marksman—and he is heavily built," suggested Jack.

"Very true. Gigante might be the instrument, but for whom does he perform?" announced Luke.

"It's a start. I will ask around regarding his movements and associates of the last month or two."

Luke's first hopeful source was Father Roberto.

"When Bruno Costa visited Colonel Lopez was he accompanied by any other soldiers?"

Roberto thought for some time and finally replied, "No, Bruno always came alone."

"So, no soldiers have been to the friary in the last month?"

"There was one. You could not miss him. It was that tall and solid man that the locals call Gigante."

"Who did he see, and who did he come with?"

"He saw nobody. He simply waited outside our reception hall."

"Who did he come with?"

"I have no idea."

"Perhaps one of the brothers might know?"

"It is possible. They would certainly have recognized Gigante. Come back in three hours. We will have just finished prayers and all of them will be gathered in the chapel. You can question them then."

Luke quickly regretted his decision to seek the help of the Franciscan friars. They had too much information most of which confused the issue. One brother said Gigante was a regular visitor who never entered the premises. He brought homeless boys which he had disciplined in the souk to find a meal and a bed with the friars. Another said in the past Gigante often accompanied the deputy governor Mario to the friary."

"Brothers, can any of you verify that the Gigante ever came here as a companion or bodyguard to any women?"

There was a long silence until one brother said, "I cannot say whether he came with a woman, but he was here once at the same time as Colonel Lopez's sister."

An elated Luke thanked the friars and bounded back to the barracks.

He announced to his officers, "There may be a link between Catia Lopez and Gigante. My questioning of Bruno might confirm it."

Bruno who was living in the largely rebuilt house that had been partially demolished by Lopez's attack surprised by Luke's visit. "I thought your investigative work had concluded with the deaths of De Silva and Lopez, and the attempted departure of Dona Catarina which I hear ended tragically in her death. I leave for Casablanca in two days as a captain to take up duty as Major Dimas's deputy."

Luke was in two minds whether to alert Bruno to the survival of Catarina or let him discover it for himself when he arrived in Casablanca. For the moment he decided not to enlighten the newly promoted soldier who asked, "Why the visit?"

"I don't like loose ends, so I have continued the investigation into the attempts on the life of Dona Catarina. A name that has arisen as a possible suspect is your long-term deputy Cornelio Rios. What do you know of his movements and whereabouts during the last few weeks?"

37

"Hardly anything! Since Lopez's attack on this house, I have rarely seen him. He never returned to duty after that incident. I half suspected that he was in league with Lopez in attacking his former comrades, but I have no proof, and cannot think of a motive."

"Why did he desert the army?"

"We were about to be disbanded in any case, but he told me on the one meeting we have had that he had an excellent offer to complete his time in Tangiers on three times the salary he received as a sergeant. I imagined he was employed by a wealthy citizen as a servant, probably in these unruly times as a bodyguard."

"Do you have any idea who that might be?"

"No, but there are very few wealthy citizens left who it could be?"

"Catia Lopez, Lidia de Silva, or anyone else that comes to mind?"

"Interesting that you mentioned Catia Lopez. Some years ago, when Gabriela Sarmento and Catia Lopez were wild young things satisfying their sexual appetite, I remember Catia may have had a fling with Cornelio."

"More than a little below her class," mused a status-oriented Luke.

"That was the young Catia. While Gabriela seduced and blackmailed married men of the middle and upper classes, Catia preferred to experiment with the common man. Gigante would have been a magnificent catch," concluded Bruno with a chuckle.

"Has Catia been seen with Cornelio of late?"

"Not to my certain knowledge but I heard she had appointed a personal bodyguard some weeks ago. It could have been Gigante. Why do you suspect him?"

"On two occasions the attempt on Catarina involved an excellent marksman. I need to establish a link between Gigante and an employer, whether it is Catia or not."

Luke left Bruno and decided to amble up the souk. He was quickly besieged by a group of urchins who remembered him as a soft touch. One of them shouted, "I can tell you more about the day that the wealthy lady was almost murdered."

"All I want to know and all I will pay for are the names of anybody you saw within the villa's ground on the morning of that day," replied Luke, not expecting any real information.

A group of boys went into a huddle and eventually one of them emerged and announced, "There were several people who we did not recognize, but one that we did, was the horrible monster Gigante."

"Were there any well-dressed woman?"

"Quite a few, but we don't know their names. They were all very mean. Gave us nothing!"

Luke paid out and decided to visit Miriam Barros in her new abode. He explained that he was still looking into the murder attempts on of her half-sister and that suspicion had fallen on Cornelio Rios and his unknown master or mistress."

"Your urchin boys have just told me he was in these ground on the morning of Catarina's imprisonment."

"Do not believe a word they say about Gigante. Long ago he appointed himself the representative of law and order in the souk and constantly grabbed the boys in their acts of theft and gave them a good beating. He is hated by them, yet I know he had a soft side and often took the neediest to the friary for a meal and decent bed."

"Yes, the friars confirmed that. Was Gigante inclined to have affairs with women of the superior classes?"

Miriam blushed and giggled, "Gigante was in demand by women of all classes. By report he was a big man in every respect."

"Was Catia Lopez one of his lovers?"

"Years ago, but I have no evidence of any recent contact."

Luke decided to recruit Miriam to assist in his investigation.

"I firmly believe that Catia Lopez employed Gigante to kill your sister on three occasions. All the evidence is circumstantial so I must catch them in another attempt."

"Well, that is impossible. Everybody in Tangiers believes that my sister was killed trying to leave the city—including the murderers, and in truth she has left the city for good."

"I want you to spread the story that Dona Catarina was not killed, but badly wounded. She has been recovering aboard an English ship and is about to return to what are now the English barracks, before she finally leaves for Casablanca."

"Well, that is easy enough, but you have no Catarina for the villains to attack."

"Leave that to me."

Luke dropped in on Bruno and told him of Catarina's survival. He asked Bruno to spread the word as far as possible, especially that she was returning to the English barracks.

Back at the barracks Luke outlined his plan. "But we have no Catarina to act as bait for your trap Luke," said Jack.

"But we have. Tommy will impersonate the lady a second time. The double chain mail shirt will protect you again."

"All we have to do is to buy you a brilliant white cape," said Jack half-jokingly.

"What are the details of your plan?" asked Greg.

Tommy who had remained silent following Luke statement finally replied," Yes, colonel, I will impersonate Dona Catarina on condition that you discharge me from your service and that of the English army at the end of this month. I wish to stay in Tangiers working for Miriam, before I decide whether to join her sister in Casablanca."

Luke outlined his trap. "We will avoid Tangiers's harbour and escort Catarina in a coach through the friendly Berber villages to the Atlantic coast where one of her ships would be waiting to collect her. I am assuming that a marksman will deliver his blow from a concealed high point. Once out of the city we will with the help of the Berbers clear a path which would prevent any marksmen getting close enough to shoot. This fact must also get through to the would-be murderer. We must force him into shooting from somewhere on the southern wall."

"So, he will have a free shot at the victim before we can identify him?" asked an alarmed Jack.

"Yes, but our own Berber marksmen will man each tower to monitor the complete length of the wall. They should be able to locate the source of that initial shot."

"Do they shoot him or try to effect a capture?" asked Greg.

"Neither! I want him to lead us to his master or mistress."

"This is fanciful Luke. If we are dealing with Gigante he, as an experienced soldier will become aware of anybody following him and would equally become suspicious if nobody was. He will avoid contact with his paymaster unless he is certain that he has given any pursuers the slip."

"I have thought about that. I have employed at almost no cost a team that will shadow the shooter who will have no clue that he is being followed."

"And where did your recruit such an expert team of phantom pursuers?" joked Greg.

"From the souk! There will be two urchin boys in each tower ready to follow the shooter as soon as he has revealed himself."

Luke made sure that the journey to the coast and the precautions taken once out of city were widely known in the barracks, but the employment of the urchins was kept a tight secret. Luke deliberately boasted that his security was so tight that there was no need to hide the day and hour of his departure with Dona Catarina.

The day arrived. Everything was in place. The coach with its escort left the barracks and was awaiting at the southern gate for it to be opened.

Then the unexpected happened. Suddenly from somewhere in the gate tower a host of grenades were lobbed onto the stationary coach. It was totally destroyed. Everybody aboard would have been killed instantly. Several of the mounted escort were injured by flying debris.

Luke approached the devasting scene completely shattered.

He had planned for an attack of one skilled marksman, not for one or more grenade throwers.

He desperately tried to locate the throwers. Dozens of troops invaded the tower. Finally one of his men found a small alcove that rested above the roadway in line with the gate. Several grenades still rested on the windowsill. The Berber lookouts had been watching the length of the wall, not what was happening in a small cubicle within a small room in one of the towers. Men had been seen coming and going from the area, but none had acted suspiciously to arouse attention. The grenadier had completed his task and escaped.

But had he.

Sometime after a despondent Luke left the tower, one of the urchins ran across the barrack square and grabbed him by the hand. "Come quickly, my friend Mateo and I followed the big man after he left the small room upstairs. We followed him to the complex of Dona Catarina which we know well. He met a woman there, but they seemed surprised that it was now occupied by our friend, Mistress Miriam. They then moved to a wine stall in the souk. Mateo is still there watching them."

Luke with a platoon of soldiers entered the souk. He signalled for one of his men to take Mateo and his friend to any of the stalls that took their fancy as a reward for their services.

Their quarry was sitting at a table at the darkened far end of the stall. Gigante faced the street but the woman, obviously Catia, had her back to the approaching Luke.

Some of his men were sent to the rear of the stall in case an attempt to escape was made. The rest of the troops quietly surrounded the drinking couple. The woman handed over to Gigante a calico bag which Luke assumed contained payment for the job he had just completed.

Luke appeared from nowhere, grabbed the bag, and simply announced, "Cornelio Rios I arrest you for the many attempts to murder Dona Catarina Sarmento and for the murder of four Fez agents."

He then turned to the woman who was heavily veiled.

He was shocked.

It was not Catia Lopez.

He quickly adjusted. "Lidia de Silva, I arrest you for conspiracy to kill you aunt."

Luke was surprised that there was no denial. Instead, he faced an explosion of vitriol.

"At least this time the bitch is dead. Cornelio said no one in the coach could survive the number of grenades he threw at it," said an apparently buoyant Lidia.

"Why my lady? I thought you had a good future planned with Gil."

"After the loss of our baby my relationship with Gil cooled."

"How does killing Catarina change the situation?"

"You must be stupid Colonel to ask such a question. It was bad enough that I was originally to share my rightful inheritance with my tramp of a sister. It became intolerable when I heard that it was all going to a Berber convert and a half Berber lawyer. What a disgrace and humiliation! Her death activates this heinous will which I have already taken steps to have put aside. It is justice—not revenge. The claims of a pure-blooded Portuguese niece must take precedence over those of foreign blood."

"Even if you succeed you will not be able to enjoy your inheritance from within a prison."

Cornelio who had been disarmed by the soldiers and his hands tied together commented, "Surely I will now be executed for my successful killing of that woman?"

"Perhaps not. Unfortunately, Cornelio you failed again, and your killing of the Fez agents might be excused as a legitimate military action."

"No one could have survived that onslaught of grenades."

"True, but there was nobody in the coach to be killed. There were only three straw figures dressed appropriately to confuse you. Originally, I planned to use some of my men as decoys, but your prowess as a marksman convinced me against putting my comrades at risk. Thank God I did. Otherwise, my elation at your capture would have been destroyed by the death of three of my men."

"Then where is my aunt?" asked a devastated Lidia.

"She left for Lisbon the day on which your attempt to shoot her in the long boat failed. She took an English frigate to Lisbon, but now she would be on her way to Casablanca. I am aware of your attempts, Cornelio, to use your skill as a marksman to attack Catarina, but how did you manage to poison her carafes and imprison her in the cellar to die?"

It was Lidia who answered. "I thought both those attempts might have led you to us. To me someone living on the premises had a greater chance than an outsider to achieve such ends. Cornelio hid in my apartment in the complex. When the area was clear he went to the cellar to poison my aunt's special carafes."

"I had intended to poison both the white and red wine, but I heard a servant coming down the stairs. I hid, followed him back up into the house and knocked him out so as I could escape."

"How were you in a position to take a shot at her just a little later?"

"That was pure luck. After I had poisoned the carafe and knocked out one of the servants I left for a villa two doors up, where the owner had asked me to shoot wild birds that were being troublesome. While on the roof engaged in this task I looked back at the gate of Catarina's villa and was amazed to see her headed towards the exit. I took a shot at her, but I was probably too far away for it to have been accurate."

"And the attempt to let her die in the cellar tunnel?"

"The attempt to lock Catarina in the tunnel to die was very easy. Lidia waited until her aunt arrived. I hid behind a door and knocked her out as she left a room. I carried her well into that escape tunnel where I gagged and bound her. Catia and I left through the far door that led into the grounds."

"Leaving incriminating footprints that were your undoing."

Luke's men led Lidia and Cornelio away.

Luke immediately visited Gil and explained the situation. He was shattered. His anguish turned to anger as he stamped the floor. "Those Sarmento sisters are evil. Gabriela destroyed Miguel and now Lidia had done the same to me."

EPILOGUE

Gil Serano immediately resigned as acting governor and passed the mantle to Carlos Pimento who would see out Portuguese sovereignty of Tangiers as acting governor and military commandant.

Carlos's first act was to try Cornelio Rios on five counts of attempted murder. He was convicted and sent to a penal colony in Brazil. Lidia was sent back to Portugal.

Luke learnt later from Miriam Barros that given her outright denial of any complicity in the deeds of Gigante and as the witnesses were dispersed, or foreigners, Lidia was sent to convent, not as a nun but as a menial servant. The convent was asked to ensure that she never rose above that status, or it would not receive the huge annual gift from a relative of Lidia's living in Casablanca.

Luke smiled on hearing this; Dona Catarina was ruthless to the end.

Luke left Tangiers a few weeks later. His sage advice to sell Tangiers was ignored.

# HISTORICAL EPILOGUE

An English governor and garrison were in place by the beginning of 1662. England immediately spent a fortune in rebuilding the harbor. The English troops, ill-disciplined and drunken, were also no better than the Portuguese in the treatment of their Moroccan neighbors. One governor remarked that more soldiers in Tangiers were killed by brandy than by the Moor. The cost of maintaining the garrison escalated over the years and in 1684 the English parliament refused to provide the funds needed. After destroying most of the improvements they had made, the English withdrew and allowed the Sultan of Morocco, Ismael ben Sharif, the successor to Moulay Al Rashid, to take over the city. His family continues to rule Morocco, and its important port of Tangiers to this day.